The Creation

Part One: Axis Mundi

Also by The Behrg

Stillborn
Housebroken

The Creation

Part One: Axis Mundi

A Novel

by The Behrg

Cover by Elder Lemon Design

ISBN-13: 9780692500651
ISBN-10: 0692500650

Dedication

To the driver in the Gran Sabana, who miraculously kept our jeep from flipping when the back wheel of the vehicle suddenly dislodged and flew forty feet into the air, and to my companion on that trip: my then soon-to-be wife, though she didn't know it at the time … (I certainly did). Thank you for believing in me.

(My wife, not the driver)

"It comforts me to think that if we are created beings the thing that created us would have to be greater than us, so much greater, in fact, that we would not be able to understand it.

"It would have to be greater than the facts of our reality and so it would seem to us, looking out from within our reality, that it would contradict reason.

"But reason itself would suggest it would have to be greater than reality or it would not be reasonable."

--Donald Miller, *Blue Like Jazz: Nonreligious Thoughts on Christian Spirituality*

"In the beginning God created the heaven and the earth."
Genesis 1:1

IN THE BEGINNING

Chapter One

Verse I.

Contributed by USGS National Earthquake Information Center

A 5.1 magnitude earthquake struck South Eastern Venezuela late Saturday evening in the region known as the Gran Sabana. The moderate quake hit 28 kilometers west of the southern Brazil border, its epicenter 12 kilometers from the former mining town turned logging community of Santa Elena de Uairen.

Saturday's quake occurred at 7:33 local time (UTC) at a depth of 68 kilometers along the geologically complex southern boundary of the Caribbean Plate, a mostly oceanic tectonic plate underlying Central America and the Caribbean Sea off the northern coast.

Government officials have thus far received no estimates of casualties. Several indigenous tribes also populate the southern Amazonian area, though there has been no word as to their status.

This boundary is a rich area of seismic activity with the collision of the Caribbean and South American plates. The Venezuelan petroleum fields are believed to be a result of this complex plate interaction.

This is the first time in noted history that an earthquake has occurred at such a southern point along the Caribbean plate within the country.

Verse II.

"Don't you want the lights on?"

Frantz ignored the interruption, sitting behind his BIFMA level-three-certified desk. He didn't bother glancing at the time on the upper right corner of the laptop he was working at, he knew the hour was ungodly.

"Ruin those pretty eyes, with nothing but the glow of a computer screen. They say it's like staring at an eclipse."

It wasn't, but he saved his breath.

Light sprang from the florescent bulbs overhead, causing Frantz to blink through the sudden change. He was surprised to find what his mémé had always called the sandman's boogers at the corners of his eyes.

He stifled a yawn on the back of one hand, dimly aware of how bare his office looked when lit. Small round black table of reclaimed wood, three Hiyashi stools in the far corner, synthetic poly-wood bookcase still waiting to be filled, and not a painting or poster on the walls. From the look of it, he could have moved in yesterday. Perhaps there were reasons he preferred working in the dark.

"It's late. You should be home," he said, his French accent thicker than normal.

Faye Moanna moved to the window overlooking Bryant Park. She twisted the hanging cylindrical stick, the slats of the blinds opening like a hundred synchronized eyes. She wore one of her business suits, a black powerful Ellecante that only served to accentuate her small figure and contrasting golden auburn hair.

She was striking; the kind of woman every man noticed though few were brave enough to approach.

Or that insane.

She stared down at the garden, mushroomed tops of trees entrenched on all sides by monolithic skyscrapers. Not an inch of room to grow or expand. Frantz had often stood there himself. Respectfully, he gave her time.

Moving their headquarters into the Bank of America Tower last year had been beyond controversial despite the building being considered the greenest skyscraper in all of Manhattan. But to affect change you had to stand out – do things differently.

The next few days would certainly accomplish that.

Faye finally spoke, though she remained at the window. "You heard about Venezuela."

Frantz noticed it wasn't a question. "Did President Maduro pen an apology to the U.S.?"

"I want to go."

Her bangs hung over her right eye keeping most of her face hidden. From this angle she could have passed for an average attorney or up-and-coming politician's aide.

No, Frantz thought, *average was not a word to describe Faye Moanna.*

She turned from the blinds, walking towards him with her purposeful stride. Seeing the other half of her profile always gave Frantz pause.

The left side of her head was shaved, a tattooed arm with claw-like talons reaching from below her collar up behind her ear and over the side of her left temple, visible even through the few days growth of fuzz. Her face carried more sharp lines than curves, her nose ring, a diamond stud, twinkling both coyly and menacingly at the same time. The smart business woman had been replaced with a hardened street junkie who had just robbed a fashion store.

Frantz wondered, not for the first time, which side more accurately represented the real Faye Moanna.

"We have to go," she said, pushing his laptop aside and sitting at the corner of his desk. "You know what an opportunity this is."

"We looked at their operation and it —"

"When? This is the first I've heard of any lumber mill in southern Venezuela."

Frantz adjusted the small wire frames on the bridge of his nose. This was an argument he had hoped successfully avoided.

That damn earthquake.

"It wasn't right for what we're trying to accomplish," he finished.

Her green eyes glinted, acknowledging his lie. She knew he had kept that location off their reports for other reasons, reasons they both pretended he didn't know.

"I need you in Guatemala. It's too late to be making changes —"

"Don't bullshit me, Frantz." She accentuated his name with a poor imitation of his accent. She scooted further onto his desk, her skirt sliding up. It had been short to begin with. "We change our strategy; go in bringing aid to an area even the local government's ignoring. You know Red Cross won't touch this; maybe you'll get some Mormons down there, but in Venezuela even that's iffy. This is headline news."

"It's too dangerous."

"It's advantageous! Almost ... meant to be."

"You know there weren't any reported deaths," Frantz continued. "You did read the article."

"We can't let personal —" He stopped, not wanting to say the wrong thing. His fingers thrummed against an invisible keyboard as they always did when he was searching for the right way to phrase something in English. Unfortunately all his mental keyboard came up with was "*asdf;lkj.*"

"It is personal. For every one of us." She stood, flipping her hair as she moved back towards the door.

"I won't allow it," Frantz said, standing. He somehow felt smaller than he had when seated in his chair.

Faye paused at the doorway, the tattooed hand scraping against the side of her head seeming to sway back and forth. Waving goodbye or beckoning him onward? Or maybe it was the calculated rise of claws just before the first strike.

"It's late, Frantz. You should go home."

The lights went out.

Frantz fell back into his Cobi chair and immediately picked up his phone, dialing the first of many numbers he would need to call. His night's work apparently had just begun.

Verse III.

James Dugan brushed back a branch, letting it snap back behind him as he joined the small group gathered before the sheer face of solid earth. Up close, these plateaus felt unnatural.

Tepuis, they were called, table-top mountains, like floating islands in the sky. They dotted the savannahs of this part of the Amazon rainforest, jutting from the jungle floor upwards of a thousand meters. Their natural evolutionary state created some of the most isolated fauna and flora known to man. The locals however knew them by another name.

Temples of the Gods.

And Dugan had ascended every one.

"What's the problem?" he asked.

"She's afraid of heights." Rojo, his thick red beard rising to meet a complete absence of hair on top, spit a glob of brown juice onto the ground. His chest was almost as wide as he was tall; dressed in dark khakis and a flannel shirt, he could have passed for a lumberjack – except that all the leñadores around here were Venezuelan.

The source of their delay recoiled at Rojo's words. "I am not!"

Dugan removed his shades. The Venezuelan girl before him was the fourth student the University of Maturin had sent in the past six weeks, the third whose name escaped him.

He hoped it remained that way.

"Then what's the problem, Negra?" He loved how calling someone by their skin color or stereotype wasn't seen as offensive in this country.

"He is telling me we have to climb up, that the helicopter won't take us." Her accent was thick, despite her grasp of the English language.

"Did you ever consid-ugh –" Dugan's words were lost as his throat tightened. A familiar wheezing rasp soon became the gasps of a dying muffler, heavy and wet.

He was forced low to the ground, eyes watering, covering his mouth with one fist while he unslung his shoulder pack and began rifling through it.

A thick native in cargo pants and a leather jerkin pushed past the girl, raising Dugan back up. His long black hair, thick as a horse's mane, covered most of his sagging cheeks and pock-marked face. In his hands he held a cigarette.

Dugan dropped the pack, taking the cig in a shaky hand. He brought it to his lips, fighting the cough leaping out, as the native lit it for him. He inhaled, holding the breath in. Not until his lungs felt at the point of bursting did he let the smoke curl out from his nostrils.

"Thank you, Oso," he said, his voice throaty and sore.

The native tilted his head in acknowledgement and stepped back behind the girl without a word.

The girl's face suddenly lit up. "Is that why you're doing this? To find a cure?" She pronounced the word *coor*. "You're like the guy on *Metastasis* ... the, uh, the Walter White. *Breaking Bad?* With, uh, Jesse? Y las drogas?"

Rojo avoided looking at Dugan. Of his entire team Dugan was the only one to not take a nickname. Not that they hadn't tried.

"My grandmother had cancer," the girl continued. "She died. Do you think we will find something up there today? Something to help cure the cancer?"

"Negra," Dugan said, his breathing still raspy. "We're not Indiana Jones. We don't go into a temple and walk out with a holy relic. We take samples; endemic plants or flowers, the root of a heliamphora, stem of a bromeliad, and we send these to labs, far from here. The results of those tests may not even come back in our lifetime. It can take that long just to figure out what we're testing for, much longer if it proves of any worth. That, my dear, is phytopharmacology – we don't look for cures, we pick lotto tickets whose numbers won't be pulled 'til we're long dead."

The girl's brow furrowed, a line forming at the corner of her mouth. "You won't talk me out of going."

"Good, then grab the rope."

Rojo swung it toward her, the knotted cord dangling from the abyss above.

"You're joking," she said.

Dugan exhaled another plume of smoke then flicked the cigarette into a nearby brush. At the girl's sudden panic, he added, "We're in the rainforest, Negra, nothing dry enough to light."

Trust me, we've tried, he thought.

"Now strap in or we leave. Your choice."

"But the helicopter ..."

"Does not land on a tepui," Dugan said. "Ever."

Rojo held up a harness, spitting more brown juice onto the unsuspecting plant life around them. "We tie you in. It's not even dangerous."

"Why can't we land on top?"

"Ground's ... unstable," Dugan said.

Temple of the Gods.

Rojo glanced at him, recognizing the lie, or half lie. Still it was better than the truth. Sharing with her the fate of their last student who had fallen through a sinkhole, the weight of the helicopter causing the shifting sandstone to break loose and drop out from beneath them, certainly wouldn't improve her chances of climbing to the top. Tepuis channeled the unknown, each harboring their own distinct evolutionary tract. But one thing Dugan did know, despite the endemic species of plants and animal life found atop each one, what he was searching for was hidden somewhere else.

The young girl's head tilted back, continuing until the muscles on her neck were strained.

"Twenty two hundred meters high," Rojo said.

In the end Dugan had to hand it to her, at least she tried. Harnessed in she hadn't gone up fifty feet before she was screaming to be brought back down. Rojo took his time lowering her, his childlike grin never leaving his face.

Dugan however hadn't been smiling. Half a day wasted all to keep up pretenses they most likely no longer needed. He sent the girl back to town in the helicopter accompanied with promises he had no intention of keeping.

Now they could go back to their real task, not searching for a *what*, but a *who*.

Verse IV.

Zachary Morley sang the guitar solo to Led Zeppelin's "Good Times, Bad Times" as he rolled his chair across the seamless white tile floor. The hard crunch of electric guitars and Robert Plant's wailing shrieks overpowered the blips of hospital equipment – computers, monitors and electrical devices unable to keep tempo with the song.

At the chair's arrival, with one too many forced foot thrusts to counteract the sheer mass Morley had become, he pulled himself up into a standing position.

Set on a roll-in table was a large glass sphere held in place by a metallic pedestal. It was filled with a viscous liquid, a two foot almost alien-like mass of grey tissue, suspended at its center like a deflated basketball. Thick tubes connected to the sphere from above, entering the controlled environment with smaller tubes hanging down, connected to the growth.

"Think this little guy knows what it means to be alone?" Morley asked.

A heavy set Venezuelan woman in white, germ mask strapped over her face, did not reply. Not that Morley had expected her to. They never sent him help that could speak English.

As if they couldn't afford the additional cost.

"After we finish here how 'bout we head on over to my place?" He laughed, his entire body shaking from the effort. Remaining sane could be a task in this country, he had discovered, and Morley had never been one for multi-tasking.

The assistant's eyes darted from him to the large glass sphere. At least this one had some meat on her, he thought.

"Quieres el pollo?" the assistant asked, Morley catching only the final word.

"Yes, pollo. Pollo, pollo, pollo. Let's do the pollo again," he sang to the tune of the Time Warp, motioning for her to get on with it.

She approached the sterile aluminum counters against the back wall of the room, fiddling with the latch to the crate set on top. Out came a chicken, its feathers pressed flush against its body. The assistant closed the crate, deftly placing the bird against the metal counter, one hand wrapped around its body.

With the other, she lifted a heavy butcher's blade.

Morley turned his head. He hated this part of the job.

The metallic thwank of metal against metal was as harsh as a hand lifting the needle from a record player.

"Over here," he said, keeping his sight away from the limp and headless body dangling from the assistant's rubber gloved hand.

She finished feeding the pollo through the Blender, a small chamber with precision blades that ground the chicken – meat, bones, feathers and all – into a pasty mulch.

At the glass sphere, Morley hummed along to the next track on the album, a song he never remembered the name to. The warm paste remains of what had moments ago been a live chicken moved through the tubes and began its descent within the sphere.

"Open wide," he said, unable to control his laughter.

The assistant pulled down her mask. Several thick black hairs lifted from her upper lip like a spider's legs.

Morley thought he might throw up.

"Que es esta brujeria?" she asked.

Though Morley spoke no Spanish, he understood what she was asking. At least in principle. He decided for the easy answer. After all, she'd have no one to tell. Not after today.

There was a reason he was assigned a new assistant every day.

"It's a stomach. A human stomach. And we're feeding it."

Verse V.

Faye's condo was what New Yorker's considered a flat — a studio apartment with one room, kitchenette and bed separated only by a half wall. The only door, beyond the entrance, lead to the shower and bath. Totaling just under five-hundred square feet, and at twelve-hundred dollars a square foot, it was an atrociously expensive way to guarantee a place to rest her head. Especially considering how little she was there.

Her job required more travel than most commercial pilots saw in a year, and when it wasn't work, it was Donavon, who lived almost three-thousand miles away in the smog-ensconced hills of glittering Hollywood.

In December she had actually taken the time to add up the number of days she had been in town last year, dividing it by her monthly mortgage, to determine how much her place truly cost. She could have had her pick of the most luxurious hotels in the area and still saved a quiet fortune. But, she argued to herself, no hotel maid service — no matter how prestigious — would give the kind of love Georgie and Penelope required.

"You know, every time you bring me back here, I start to question our relationship," Donavon said from the bathroom.

Faye set down her watering pitcher and rubbed Penelope's stems. "Did I forget to hide the used rubber in the bathroom again?"

Donavon laughed, a sound that always began like a bark that could no longer be contained. "Well I wonder whether you come out to see me or if it's just to sleep in a room with enough space to sneeze."

The water from the sink shut off and Donavon stepped out, running his hands through his thick black hair. "You know we can afford a bigger place."

"I like a small place and besides, I'm not sure I'm the one needing to make a change. I mean the garage for your servants is three times as palatial as my humble abode."

"I don't have servants," he said, moving toward her.

"Oh, I forget, you Hollywood type refer to them as 'personal assistants.'"

He grimaced. "That's not fair."

Faye reached up and kissed him, her pierced tongue pressing briefly against his. She always felt tiny next to him, his barrel chest and linebacker physique so much more intimidating in person than on screen.

"You're amazing," she said, "and the fact you changed your plans to do this? Well it makes up for at least half the emissions of your army of yesmen."

He laughed, relaxing, his whitened teeth showing the chip in front that only made him more perfect by revealing him flawed. "Only half?"

"And that's generous. Make the bed?" Faye said, twisting out of his arms. "Or is that a skill you've forgotten?"

"If I wanted this much abuse I'd visit my mother," he said, though he picked up one of the pillows that had been thrown to the floor.

"You weren't complaining when you flung them off the bed."

She returned her attention to Penelope. The tips of her smooth leaves had curled inward like a dog wagging its tail at its master's touch. A Mimosa pudica, Faye had groomed this particular strain for the past four years. Its blooming lavender and violet-tinged flowers, like dandelions gone to seed, were the largest she had ever seen on such a plant.

Georgie, on the other hand, was a shingle plant of the apocynaceae family. His flesh-colored leaves shone with an interior gloss when cared for. Little clusters of cream blooms hung from the pot dangling by the window.

Donavon called Georgie the White Rastafarian.

After saying goodbye she cracked the window before turning to leave. Donavon stood at the mirrored dresser next to the bed, the lumps beneath the bedspread something she was willing to ignore. She wondered what trinket had captured his fascination this time – the petrified wood specimen from Bali or maybe the carved fertility statue that, when picked up, revealed a large wooden dong that stuck straight out.

As she joined him she felt the temperature in the room drop though she knew it was her imagination. He wasn't looking at her collection but the postcards hanging from the top of her mirror.

Borneo Island.

Mount Cameroon.

Angel Falls.

"You never told me you'd been there," Donavon said. "Venezuela?"

Faye ran one hand against the side of her shaved head, the tiny bristled hairs massaging her fingertips. "I haven't."

"Well, nothing like a redeye," Donavan said with a chuckle, lightening the mood.

Faye pressed her body against his back, hugging him from behind. Of all Donavan's traits she was most grateful for his uncanny sense to know when not to press, to let her open up as she was ready. There had been a lot of opening up in the sixteen months they had been together and still they were barely at the surface. Did he have any idea how deep her scars ran?

Her hands moved down from his pectorals, following the ridges of his tight abdomen beneath his shirt, then slid between the gap of flesh and jeans, continuing lower. Maybe there were other traits she appreciated more, she thought with a smile.

"I just made the bed," he said.

"Yeah but I can do it better."

A few seconds later the pillows were back on the floor.

Verse VI.

Fingertips cradled over the lip of the large armoire like blind larvae; searching, searching, finally alighting upon a small brass key. A thick carpet of unmolested dust covered the top of the dresser except for the few inches of wood in front of the key where prints frequently tread. Like a worn path where snow hadn't time to settle.

Remmy Shumway walked the narrow room in his thick heavy robes. His right eye twitched with the spasm of a dying dog's last kick. The tile of the floor was cool against his bare feet, at such odds with the dampness at his neck and pits, and crawling up his lower back.

He was old – at seventy three he should have been long retired, living in some form of luxury. Even a nursing home, at times, seemed preferable to his circumstance. Instead he bore the weight of each day like the mule he had become, trudging in an endless circle of scenery that never changed.

His eye twitched.

At the end of the long room he knelt before an old chest. Its unlacquered wood and rusted bronze straps allowed it to pass without remark. Like a well-worn disguise. Often Remmy found himself looking in the mirror, wondering when the wrinkles would peel back from his skin, his white hair returning to its natural dark roots, staunch flesh regaining its once smooth texture.

Some masks, when worn too long, could no longer be pulled away.

The thick heavy sleeves of his robes hung down as he pressed the key into the lock at the chest's center. This was the moment he always feared and yet secretly longed for – that small key bending at the weight of the gears within. One day it would snap and he would pull out a handle that would no longer open a passage to the past, the only escape he could afford, and that barely. But today was not that day.

Above him, a crucified Savior looked away with mournful eyes.

Remmy lifted the heavy lid, its hinges groaning. He stared down at the contents of the chest.

Prayers were useless now.

A knock sounded at the door, startling him.

"Quien es?" he asked, his voice anything but calm.

"Father?" a young man's voice asked from the other side of the door, heavily accented. "There are more people. Refugios."

The knock came again.

"Father?"

Remmy looked longingly at the artifacts in his chest, his left eye twittering, reminding him of his want – his need. A few minutes and he could be back on his knees, praying to the only God who had ever answered his cries.

He almost laughed. Instead he blinked back heavy tears.

"Father?" the voice came again from outside.

The heavy lid fell back, brass key disappearing into an inner pocket of his robe. Remmy dabbed his forehead against the arm of one sleeve, then opened the door.

Josue stood in the outer room, a look of concern flashing across his face like sunlight breaking through clouds, gone almost before there was time to notice. At fourteen he was a scrawny kid, malnourishment accounting only partly for his childlike frame. He had a black birthmark the size of an open fist just beneath his left eye that looked like a mole had exploded outward, spreading like a fungus. The deformation had been so prominent at birth that his parents had left the child at the doors of the church, the previous pastor not finding the crying baby until the following morning.

In a town the size of Santa Elena one would think it easy to uncover the culprits of such a crime. But small towns, Remmy had learned, held to their secrets tighter than their riches.

He reached one hand out, resting it atop Josue's head. "Thank you, my son."

He only spoke English to Josue, one of the few semi-bilinguals in the community. A good thing, considering Remmy's Spanish was as crude as a newborn's. "I thought we had reached everyone in need?"

Josue answered as they walked down the narrow hallway. "They were in the campos when the terramoto hit."

"Earthquake."

Josue continued as if Remmy hadn't interrupted. "They just returned to discover their homes perished. I know we are full but I remember the mother Mary and the men who said there was no room."

"Innkeepers."

"Innkeepers," Josue repeated. "They could have made some room, somewhere, no?"

Remmy's heart was still hammering in his chest, like being worked up almost to the point of orgasm only to have your partner walk away – that excitement still took a moment to fetter down, yet he knew what the boy was hinting at. Damn him, he knew the boy was right.

It was a problem a few days ago they could never have hoped for, the average weekly attendance less than fifteen, and those comprised of several women and their many children. Even at Christmas or el Domingo de Pascua they were lucky to have half of the church pews filled.

The building itself was small, an open assembly hall with two rows of six wooden benches that had all been stacked and pushed to the side to make room for the displaced families. The earthquake hadn't been that strong but these homes, many made of sheet metal and slats of aluminum or tin, required barely a huff and a puff to be blown in.

Sheets were strung up in the assembly hall, sectioning off areas of the room for some semblance of privacy, while the families waited. For what, Remmy wasn't sure.

God?

Their government?

Both had been equally silent.

Of the four adjoining rooms to the small building – a kitchenette, small classroom they used for a nursery, Josue and Lucas's room, and Remmy's own quarters – his was the only domicile occupied by one.

Unless you counted their storage room, but Remmy had no intention of changing that.

"I can sleep outside. On the dirt," Josue said. "I have done it before."

"Let us see what God will provide."

They walked into the main assembly, Remmy ducking beneath a rope, to greet the two families standing near the entrance. Seven, no eight children. A baby's wail reverberated in the hollow room.

"Bienvenidos," Remmy said.

The cold eyes and hardened faces that met him didn't soften in the slightest. Even when you have nothing, seeing it ripped away could be devastating.

Before he could tell them there was food, a large voice carried from the church's entrance into the hall. It felt like a gust of wind vanquishing every lit candle at once.

"El pastor de las ovejas!"

Every muscle in Remmy's fragile body went taut.

A bull of a man stepped in from the entrance dressed in dark grey army fatigues, a fedora gripping tightly to his massive head. General Marco Gutiérrez, the alcalde or mayor of Santa Elena de Uairen. Also their chief of police. He was one of the most corrupt men Remmy had ever known, which said a lot.

The General was mustached, his face moist, covered in a constant sheen of sweat he seemed unaware of. "Por que no veo un carnero aqui," he shouted in his booming voice. Laughter followed, both from the man and his cohorts around him, thinner and younger soldiers with equally cruel eyes.

"If you're going to insult me at least do it in English," Remmy said. "You brought these people?"

"Dey are gifts, Pastor! More souls for jou to save."

More laughter followed from just outside the church. The General never went anywhere alone.

"And where do you expect me to put them? Look around!"

"Maybe jour God will tell you," Gutierrez answered.

"Close the tavern for a few days. You can put a roof over these people's heads while homes are repaired or rebuilt."

"The tavern is a private business. I cannot dictate what does or does not happen dere."

"A private business you yourself own!"

"Ahhh," Gutierrez spread his hands wide as if caught. "Is it a sin to be, uh, investing?"

"If you and your men spent half the time you do in that alehouse whoring about we'd have whole homes rebuilt already. These people need leadership! Someone who can help them pick up their lives and start over."

Gutierrez snorted then spit onto the church floor. It splatted near Josue's feet. "What do you know of da needs of a Venezolano? A woman, a beer. Dose are our needs. Not jour God or jour hope."

"Get out!" Remmy shouted. He could feel his cheeks flush, his frame quivering.

The General's face darkened. "Careful, Pastor. Or perhaps it will be a new spiritual leader the people demand."

He left without another word, lugging his heavy frame through the open door. His lackeys followed him out.

Remmy was shaking, the confrontation taking more from him than he had to give, at least at the moment. Than most moments, he admitted to himself. Josue closed the entry door.

What he had said was true; these people needed someone to lead them. But the General was just as correct – Remmy was not that man. He felt the pull toward the locked chest in his quarters and knew at least he could forget for a time.

How often will I fail them? he wondered, his eyes looking upward. For once he was grateful God had no answer.

Verse VII.

The Gran Sabana was an interesting playing field, some parts spread open in great rolling savannahs, other areas as dense as the thickest jungles. Add the hundreds of cenotes and waterfalls, tepui mountains, above and underground rivers, and it was no wonder Dugan's work had brought him back here.

The Amazon rainforest was home to over a third of the world's population of animal species; over two thirds of all plant species. It was believed a third of the fauna and flora had yet to even be identified. With a quarter of all medicine used today having some form of their origins in the rainforests, and with almost every plant known to have anti-cancer properties coming from the Amazon itself, there was enough work here to last lifetimes.

But Dugan didn't have lifetimes. His own clock was running perilously close to its slow-winding end. An end he might be able to prevent.

He bent down inspecting the leaf of a Puya raimondii. It was the largest species of bromeliad, a family that included the pineapple, and was typically found in higher elevations like the Andes. Its stickered flower spike, like an elongated pine cone, rose a good eighteen feet into the air. The plant was useless; Dugan had no intention of carrying a sample back, but the bent tips of its pointed leaves near its base were of concern.

Dugan turned, stepping back the way he had come, his boot catching the end of the leaves to see how it would crease with his weight.

Someone had been here, and recently.

Beneath the cover of towering trees and brush that prevented any sunlight from reaching the ground, Dugan had tread into an area the vehicles were incapable of entering. Fallen logs and stones the size of Venezuelan houses littered the grounds, undisturbed for who knew how many millennia. His team had followed orders, taking the Humvees and leaving him behind.

A silver beam of sunlight shot through a solitary crack in the branches above. It looked like the trail of a bullet passing in slow motion. The amount of particles and mites floating in those snatches of light always made Dugan question his need to breathe.

He paused, casting his eyes about.

Something wasn't right.

The air was as thick as ever, a humidity that hung on you. The many toned calls of native birds and insects, animals and snakes rustling leaves and plants; all continued as if Dugan weren't present. And yet he sensed something ... off. Something he couldn't explain.

Two tiger-herons sprung from the trees above not from a sudden noise but perhaps the lack thereof. They leapt from tree to tree, gliding on their short wings before disappearing with a crackle of leaves.

A mining frog, its red bulbous eyes unblinking, crouched at an intersecting branch a foot away. Dugan had had great hopes with that one; the poison secreted from its glands long used by natives on the tips of arrows. But that had been before he had come in contact with the Makuxi.

Everything had changed since then.

Despite the quickening palpitations of his heart, he decided to press on. With his first step, he stopped – the guaco, twining vines that spread, covering the jungle floor like a series of veins, had scaled the base of trees here, creating a net-like appearance. And within its latticed network of interconnected tubular branches, a face peered back at him.

A human face.

Dugan exhaled slowly, wishing he had lit a cigarette.

The longer he looked at the face more details emerged, a Polaroid slowly fading to life. A man, brown-skinned and bare, black tattooed circles around his unblinking eyes. A thick reed threaded in and out of the skin beneath his bottom lip. His face was hard, all sharp lines and prodding jaw.

The eyes blinked.

"Makuxi," Dugan said.

The native stepped forward through the guaco which clung to him like a spider's web.

"Inktomi," he said, voice soft yet firm, the voice of someone used to being obeyed. His chest was covered in intricate tribal tattoos, their circular pattern spreading from his center like ripples of a pond. In his hands he held a blackened wooden spear.

Dugan ran.

His worn military boots slid on the undergrowth beneath him as he abandoned the path he had taken, moving instead through denser jungle. Vines and strangling branches whipped at him, snagging at clothing and the pack bouncing against his back.

A flesh-colored borer beetle the size of a swallow buzzed up near his head and he swatted it away. He leapt down a small gulley, following the wisp of a path created by some furrowing animal. His breathing, growing haggard.

The path disappeared into scraggly brush too thick to traverse. The gulley had turned into a ravine on his right, loose dirt and rock climbing at an unscaleable angle. To his left, dense prickly-ash rose in a canopy as thick as woven tarps. Dugan's weary-lined face contorted in pain – or the anticipation of pain.

Then the coughing ensued.

He slid out of the backpack just as he was wrenched forward, the heaves not simply coming from his chest but his entire body. He looked like a man possessed, unable to control his limbs as the coughing burrowed further, chunks of blood and pink tissue sputtering from his mouth. With one hand he struggled with the zipper to the backpack now lying atop weed-like grass, the back of his other hand pressed to his mouth as if trying to keep his innards from spilling out.

A rustling of motion from the trees behind him. Too large to be an animal.

The native broke through, eyes darting, seeking, finding. Dugan saw now that he wore a crudely lashed cloth around his waist, his thick and muscled legs likewise covered in symbols down to his bare and leather-hardened feet. His earlobes hung almost to his shoulders, a thick spike of wood sticking from them as if recently impaled.

Another retching cough burst from Dugan's lungs. He turned back to the pack on the ground in a desperate search, hands plunging into its depths.

A howl ripped through the air as the native whirled his spear overhead and began his charge. With the pain of the coughs ripping apart his insides, Dugan found it easy to suppress a smile.

Just as the native closed the last feet of distance, Dugan dropped the pack, turning to face the man with his finding.

The native drew up, expecting a gun.

Instead Dugan tapped a cigarette from a wrinkled and bent pack.

A two inch flame shot from the lighter he had been searching for, the tip of the cigarette turning a smoldering red. He brought it to his lips and took a heavy drag. Speckles of black formed in his vision before he let the smoke spill from his nostrils.

This close to the native Dugan realized the tattoos covering his body like scales weren't ink at all – they were scars.

That's new.

The native lumbered back a step, sensing a trap but far too late.

Seeming to materialize from air, Dugan's men appeared from the jungle growth, some leaping from the rise above, others slithering out from between branches and brush. All in camouflaged gear, they surrounded the native, each carrying enough artillery equipment to start and end their own personal war.

These were men who sweat violence.

The native's spear dropped to the jungle floor.

Dugan blew out another long stream of smoke into the native's face. This time his smile was unsuppressed.

"Sorry, friend. I'm the one doing the hunting."

Rojo bent down to retrieve the native's spear, handing it to Zephyr, the larger of the two black men Dugan employed. Zephyr's arms were as thick as Dugan's calves, veins pulsing on his barrel neck.

"And I'm the one doing the hurting," Zephyr said in his deep voice before swiveling the blunt end of the spear upward, catching the native in the skull.

Of the many predators that roamed the countless miles of Amazonian jungle – tigers, jaguars, pumas, and anacondas – none were as skilled or vicious as the men Dugan had surrounded himself with.

He didn't need a lifetime. They would find what they needed – *who* they needed – and then lifetimes would be a thing of the past.

Verse VIII.

Newark to Florida, Florida to Caracas.

Over thirteen hours in cramped planes and insipid airports toting rolling cases that would have exceeded an airline's weight guidelines, had Grey been willing to check them.

Uncomfortable padded seats traded for cramped airplane chairs. With a four hour wait in Caracas, another five and a half hours on what passed for a "luxury" bus in a third-world country, and Grey was not only exhausted, he felt dirty. That oily skin, clogged pore, sweaty to the point it wasn't even attractive kind of dirty.

They had gotten through customs with only minor hiccups, Faye's boyfriend having to autograph paper, travel brochures, even an iPhone before they were finally through. Donavon Hughes wasn't the biggest name in Hollywood, but for a celebrity he was a pretty decent human being. Grey had yet to spot the ego that clung to most celebs like a gorilla riding their backs. Hopefully the lack of luxuries down here wouldn't change that.

Grey watched the footage he had shot so far today, already uploaded to his MacBook Air.

Faye descending the stairs from the plane in Caracas. Her reaction to the humidity that hit them like a brick wall. The uniformed security guards toting machine guns.

Streets full of filth, graffiti the new form of advertising. Taxi drivers that turned road rage into a career. Pornographic billboards and dilapidated housing and on every corner a handful of drunken men and empty bottles.

Diseased and stray dogs so thin their ribs almost pressed through their skin. Children that should have been in school throwing rocks at a window.

Donavon's smile – that infectious grin that played so well on camera – as two Venezuelan children climbed on and over him while on the bus. Their filthy blackened feet leaving print marks on his Hugo Boss shirt.

A close-up of the oblivious mother across from Faye and Donavan; hot little thing. The mother lifting her shirt to expose a swollen breast, taking her time to bring her infant up to feed. Looking back at the camera with a secretive smile.

There was no doubt he'd have to edit that shot out, though he might forward it to a few of his film school buddies back in la-la land. He fast-forwarded through the remaining bus ride then hit play. This next part he would have to find a way to work in.

At the bus depot in Puerto Ordaz, a strike had been going on. But this was no American protest. Rather than holding signs out front these protestors waved assault rifles and pistols in the air, the occasional shot ringing through the town square.

Panicked yells and curses from men so drunk they started fights with light poles and stray dogs.

Shots of men lying in the street face down, though Grey suspected they were drunk not dead. Still, juxtaposition could be powerful.

Because of the strike they had been forced to contract helicopters to get to their destination. Faye had been more than upset, not because of the price but because of their "carbon footprint." Grey suspected it had more to do with what others might perceive of them than the actual flights themselves. It wasn't like they had walked to Venezuela in the first place. Considering their objective however, she was probably right to be concerned.

Grey looked up from the laptop shaking on his lap, glancing out the window at the surrounding landscape. He had never seen so much greenery in all his life. A sea of treetops stretched as far into the horizon as he could see, like looking from a plane window down at a blanket of clouds.

If clouds were green, that was.

He chewed off the end of a yawn, his jaw clicking. For about the hundredth time he wished the cafés here had coffees larger than the size of a thimble. No forty-four ounce beverages either, to give him the caffeine fix he so desperately needed.

Over the gyrating thrum of the engine that rattled from his teeth all the way down through his boots, Faye leaned toward him, yelling into his ear. "This is why we're here! Amazing, isn't it?"

She hadn't taken her eyes off the landscape since they had risen into the air. Donavon, strapped in beside her, was out cold – mouth open, head back. Grey half expected to see a line of drool spilling over that enormous chin. Somehow celebrities were immune to such trivialities.

"We need this footage," Grey said, raising his voice to be heard. "Show the forest through the trees."

Faye's smile was almost flirtatious. "It's the other way around. And no shots of *or from* the chopper."

Grey nodded acquiescently. What Faye didn't know was that one of his crew members in the other helicopter had been ordered to film the entire flight from the moment their birds lifted into the air. Faye would thank him when it was all said and done.

The pilot's voice cackled through their headphones. Grey was sure the heavy-set Venezuelan spoke English but insisted on speaking to them in Spanish. Once his indecipherable bark cut off Faye bent forward again, leaning in close. How the hell she could smell so good after almost two days of travel was beyond him.

"Over there," she said pointing.

Grey squinted, following her hand.

"You see them? The plateaus?"

In the distance he caught sight of a group of large rotund mountains, sheer cliffs on all sides. They jutted from the trees like the towering ruins of ancient castles.

"What are they?"

"Pilot called them tepuis. The highest waterfall in the world is atop one. Angel Falls. He says it's not too far out of our way."

"But let me guess, you don't want video of it," Grey said.

The coy smile on her face was enough of an answer.

"Welcome to the Amazon," she said.

Verse IX.

A rough gulley in the unpaved road caused the left side of the Humvee to bounce hard, Dugan biting his cigarette almost in two. He lowered the window, tossing it out, then lit another from the center console.

"You get his name?" he asked, another jostle in the road rocking the vehicle.

The long-haired native, Oso, glanced across at him from behind the wheel, nodding sullenly. He was always sullen. Despite his almost hairless face, arms and chest, the native had been given the nickname the Bear in Spanish. At his almost three hundred pounds of muscle, he was certainly large enough to earn it.

Oso pulled a black marker from behind his ear, jotting something on the pad of yellow Sticky's mounted to the dash. He did so without once glancing away from the road, or what passed for a road in this cancerous jungle.

He tore the sheet from the pad and handed it to Dugan, replacing the marker behind his ear. Dugan read the name Oso had written.

Guayanata.

Dugan pulled a soft leather book from the inside pocket sewn into his blazer, its faded cover no longer showing any sign of inscription. He untied the leather strip winding around its back.

"Get a look at his chest? The scars?"

This time Oso only nodded. If he had anything to add, he would have. The distinct smell of marijuana wafted up from the rear of the vehicle.

Cy, a Vietnamese-American former U.S. army lieutenant, sat between Kendall and Chupa, shaking his head. He no longer wore the patch he had when he first joined them, the grey mucinous mass in his sunken right eye like an open wound that would never heal. The nickname however, short for Cyclops, had remained.

The man was a brilliant tactician, had trained as a medical officer and was now here for the same reasons Dugan was. He was the only one of their group who had Dugan beat in age.

"That shit shrinks your balls," Cy said.

"Good cause your mom couldn't keep 'em in her mouth last night, they're so big," Kendall said.

Chupa, short for Chupacabra, sat opposite Kendall on the other side of Cy. He was a wiry black man originally from Somali, with dreadlocks wound tightly across his scalp, forming a bun in the back. In Spanish, the verb *chupar* meant "to suck." Every one of them knew it was a double entendre, the men taking every chance to call him by name when in public. Fortunately, Chupa was one of the few with a sense of humor in the group.

Chupa reached over Cy, handing the joint off to Kendall. The white prom king soldier had gotten his nickname for looking like the Mattel match to the blonde plastic beauty – Ken doll.

At least that was the version he told.

"Whas'up, Doogon?" Chupa asked, his sunken eyes and hollowed cheeks always reminding Dugan of a skull.

"This isn't the glass house. Keep that crap in the other vehicle."

"So it's okay for you to smoke but not for us?" Kendall asked.

"Yeah," Dugan said. "Exactly."

He ignored Kendall's eye roll, turning back to his leather notebook. He fanned his finger across the pages almost reverently. "How's our guest?"

"Comfortable," Kendall said.

"Yeah, he is real comfor-tabul," Chupa said with a laugh, glancing behind at the gagged and bound native.

Guayanata.

Dugan wondered if the man had any premonitions when he woke that morning that by day's end he would be only a name and a number. Just an entry in a logbook.

He barely registered Kendall tossing the joint from the window. The leather notebook fell open on his lap, the natural crease falling to two pages filled with names. Halfway down on the right, one name had been inscribed over so many times it had worn several holes through the page. No other names were written below it, though they continued on the next page.

And so many after that.

Two twin trails of smoke shot from Dugan's nostrils as he quickly turned to the first open line in the bound book. He wondered if the remaining blank pages would be enough.

In shaky lettering he added Guayanata's name.

Verse X.

Mammoth eight-wheelers with long mechanical cranes crawled over a half-moon shaped area covered in fallen branches. The vehicles looked like monstrous scorpions, their cranes tails swinging to strike.

The harvester's heads, hanging from the crane's end, attached to the trunks of thin pines, ripping them out with a single thrust. Thirty to forty foot trees fell, caught in the arms of the surrounding branches beside them. But the harvesters were far from finished. The trunks slid through the heads claw, a blade like a chainsaw slipping from its end and sawing the trunk into sections as its branches were simultaneously stripped. They fell to the earth like the bodies of fallen soldiers.

Quick and efficient.

Beyond the scorpions and their tank-like tracks, heavy loaders called Rhinos roamed behind, snatching the fallen logs and lifting them onto their backs. More Venezuelan loggers scouted the area, moving about on foot with rudimentary gas-powered chainsaws; ants squirming atop a hill. Many of them not old enough to shave.

Zephyr steered the lead Humvee onto the dirt road connecting from the rough trail they had been on. He watched the desecration before them with equal parts approbation and indifference. In less than a minute an entire row of trees was uprooted and prepared for loading.

Given the right circumstance he was confident he could do better. At least with the amount of destruction in sixty seconds.

He ignored the dialogue taking place behind and around him – he wasn't here to make friends. Besides, the new Kid was a white supremacist, not that former allegiances meant much down here.

In his past life, as they all liked to call it, the Kid had been a professional cage fighter, running underground circuits. He had the blunt face and notched nose to prove it. When he had first arrived he had gone shirtless almost every day, his bony chest and thin muscled arms like a chicken leg whose skin had been pulled off. Now he kept the swastika tattoo on his chest covered, ever since Chupa had offered to skin it off for him.

Zephyr probably would have joined in.

They had yet to give the Kid a real name; it was something he would have to earn.

Zephyr had a unique ability to push all surroundings into his peripheral, the Kid included, in order to hone in on a single target. It was how he had been recruited from the Navy Seals to the UIFL, Ultimate Indoor Football League, in early two-thousand four. How he had been able to lead the Stings to their first national championship. It was also how he permanently disabled four players from opposing teams within a single season, not counting the two from his own.

But he didn't regret giving up the game. Not that he had much of a choice. Still, his skills were far better served where he was now.

Besides, Dugan paid better.

Over the drone of conversation, he heard something he shouldn't have. Without warning, he slammed on the brakes. They were almost rear-ended, the Bear pulling the second Humvee behind them at an angle, just in time.

"Woah, what the hell man?" The Kid barely caught himself from slamming into Zephyr's headrest. "Why we stoppin'?"

"Shut up," Zephyr said.

On the far side of the road a line of trees came hurtling down, crashing branches hiding what Zephyr knew was coming.

And then the others heard it.

The distinct thrum of a helicopter.

Rojo was the first out, dropping to the ground, his short-barreled machine gun raised, scanning the treetops and glimpses of sky. Zephyr joined him, grabbing his own Vektor, a futuristic-looking assault rifle manufactured in South Africa. It fit into the crook of his arm like a football; where it belonged.

He attached the 40mm grenade launcher in a single motion as he climbed onto the roof of the vehicle. He lay prostrate, sighting at where he expected the copter to appear.

The men in the other Humvee popped out, Dugan opening his door and propping himself up. He looked calm compared to the men scrambling for purchase, beetles scattering at the first drop of rain. The Kid appeared next to Zephyr, sitting on the rear window with his open mouthed sneer. He disappeared briefly inside the Humvee then was back, raising a heavy barrel up onto his shoulder.

The Grom.

A heavy green cylinder with a shoulder harness and black bulb for a trigger, it was a single-use rocket launcher designed specifically for surface-to-air defense. There wasn't a surprise in the world their team couldn't handle.

The whirring of the copter grew into the thundering of a hurricane — wind whipped at the tree tops around them, leaves like flightless birds flapping to no avail. The Venezuelan laborers in the clearing paused, looking upward, mechanical beasts stalled just before the next lunge.

Through the gaps in branches Zephyr caught sight of the gravity-defying machine. A faded blue, it had three elongated side windows, typically a feature reserved for commercial purposes. He closed his eyes as the torrential wind cut through the branches overhead, the skin on his face jiggling while his camouflaged clothing flapped.

As the wind tunnel swept past, he opened his eyes catching a glimpse of the helicopter's side. Something EXCURSIONES. All he needed to see.

Still this little copter was far from the Falls.

It swung out above the clearing, unaware of the artillery tracking its progress from below. The laborers raised their hands, shielding their eyes as wood chips and split branches blasted back at them, the byproduct of their handiwork rising to avenge.

"Dugan," the Kid yelled. "It a problem?"

Anything out of the ordinary was a problem, they all knew it. There was a tension in the air caused by much more than the settling forestry.

"Dugan?" the Kid called out again.

Dugan held up a fist.

Wait.

Zephyr caught the curse under the Kid's breath.

A second copter suddenly joined the first, this one a darker shade of blue. Before Dugan could change his mind they both passed beyond the clearing, disappearing from sight.

Two helicopters. More than a problem.

The Kid's body turned, still following the trajectory the helicopters had taken.

"BANG!" he shouted, glancing back at Dugan with a foolish grin. And then the Humvee behind them rocked wildly, glass exploding out its back. Dugan caught himself on the door, barely keeping from a hard tumble.

Zephyr slid to the edge of the roof to get a better view. Watched as a body hit the ground.

The native.

Blood trailed down his arms, dripping onto the grass and brush as he rolled to his feet.

"You muku!" the Kid shouted. He aimed the rocket launcher at the now fleeing native.

Without thinking Zephyr launched himself at the Kid.

His shoulder struck the Kid's arm as the rocket released, a loud thwump of hot air compressing into itself. A trail of smoke zipped out as Zephyr and the Kid both fell to the jungle floor. They hit in a tumble of body parts and weaponry, Zephyr's assault rifle flipping out onto the ground, a knee colliding with his chest.

The explosion that followed was deafening – a plume of black smoke rose, bark and debris from the trees it had struck raining down in front of them as a wave of heat swept past. A burning palm tilted and fell, crashing mere feet from the Humvee, raising all matter of dust and pollen.

Applause and sharp whistles sounded from the loggers across the road. The once captive native, having paused at the explosion, now continued to flee.

"Stop him!" Dugan shouted.

The Kid ditched the now empty launcher, unclipping Zephyr's side-arm, an X-2 CO_2 pistol. He raised it while still on one knee and fired.

A dart sunk into the shoulder of the native.

"Got him!" the Kid shouted. "Ya baby, I got him!"

The native plucked the dart from his back and dropped it to the ground then continued toward the smoking trees unfazed.

Zephyr struck the Kid in the face with a right hook just as the honkie turned toward him. Felt the bones in the Kid's nose shatter behind the force of his swing.

As the Kid dropped, Zephyr grabbed his arm, raking the dart gun from the Kid's grasp. He flipped the barrel port, a second dart rotating into the empty steel sleeve with a click. Sighting, he only had a chance to get off one round, the distance between them too far for the pistol.

The dart struck the fleeing native in the back of one leg. Zephyr flipped the barrel port to the last dart, already knowing it was too late. The native disappeared into the trees.

"Agh, wahrt the fark," the Kid said, head between his knees, blood spouting from his nose. His bottom lip was split in two and oozing. He hawked a big glop of blood onto the ground. "Like ta sree you jru that when I'm ready forj it."

Zephyr stepped into a kick, his steel-toed boot connecting with the side of the Kid's head. He went sprawling against the back of the Humvee. Blood spurting against the high bumper.

"Weren't ready for that one either? You're the muku," Zephyr said. "It takes three darts to drop a Makuxi."

The Kid pulled himself up, blood plastered on his face like a poorly shaven goatee. A switchblade sprung into his hand, his eyes wild. He flipped the blade to point outward as he brought his fist up. "One djart will djrop an elephrajnt!"

Zephyr raised his pistol and fired, point blank.

The Kid's head whipped back, a dart protruding from his long neck. The switchblade slipped from his fingers. Without a word, the Kid collapsed.

"Next time it won't be a dart."

Rojo laughed, coming up beside Zephyr. "Muku. Kid doesn't even know what it means."

Cy leaned into the back of the second Humvee, breaking off stray pieces of glass. "There's blood everywhere, Dugan. He must have had something with him, on him. Cut the bonds. Sharp necklace or stone; something."

"And the blood?" Dugan asked.

"His own," Cy answered. "Sliced through his wrists and ankles while cutting the ties."

"Motivated bastard," Rojo said.

"You blame him?" Zephyr looked off in the direction the native had run. More leaves and a burning branch dropped from somewhere above.

Oso, his long black hair draping his face, tore off a sheet of paper from a small spiral notepad and handed it to Dugan. The ugly native ignored Zephyr's glare.

Zephyr understood why Dugan kept the animal around, he needed someone who could communicate with these primitives; what he didn't know was why Dugan trusted the mute. Anyone who had their tongue cut out was certain to be a traitor. At least in Zephyr's book.

"You want us to track him?" Kendall asked, slapping at a mosquito on the back of his hand.

Zephyr knew the answer before Dugan spoke.

"We'll follow the tracer, till it wears off."

"Could work out better," Kendall said. "Homeboy thinks he flew the coop; could lead us right to him."

Him. *The Shaman.*

Kendall's words were met with an awkward silence, no one willing to voice the concern they all shared.

All but Dugan.

And maybe the mute bear.

No one could deny the miraculous abilities of the tribe they were hunting, distant cousins to the Pemoni's, a larger clan out of Brazil.

Larger and stupider; the clan Oso had been banished from. But months of chasing rumors had led them nowhere as to the supposed being who had divided the two clans, a ghost who, despite two hundred years having passed, was supposedly still alive.

Dugan insisted if you followed a shadow long enough you eventually caught whatever was casting it.

Zephyr preferred real targets to shadows. They bled easier.

Dugan kicked lightly at the Kid's limp body as he lit a cigarette. "Toss him in the back. We'll pick up whatever trail remains in the morning."

Zephyr moved to obey, but not without adding a kick of his own. It wasn't nearly as light.

Verse XI.

By the time the helicopters touched down in a dirt field in the small village of Santa Elena de Uairen, twilight was approaching. Faye stretched her legs out in the field, a duffel bag in one hand, staring at the changing tapestry in the sky.

"I've never seen so many colors," she said.

Donavon paused, hefting a large suitcase, a computer bag hanging from his shoulder. "I'm colorblind; just looks like one big giant swirl to me."

"You are not," Faye said, hitting him.

"On my mother's grave," Donavon said, a wild grin on his face.

Faye's smile slipped like the colors of the sky fading to dark purple.

"That was supposed to be a joke," he said.

"I know."

"Not that I'm colorblind; I really am, but 'cause my mother's still alive ..."

"It gets funnier the more you explain it. Hey!"

A young Venezuelan boy, no older than eight, snatched Faye's duffel bag from her hand, dragging it behind him through the dirt. He had shaggy hair that fell to his chin, a tattered shirt and no shoes, unless the layers of dirt and grime on his feet offered some form of support.

Faye ran the few steps to catch him and yanked the bag back. The boy, not expecting resistance, toppled backward, rolling over onto his bottom. Several other young children laughed, calling out either encouragements or insults. Most likely the latter.

"What do you think you're doing?" Faye asked in Spanish. The bewildered boy looked up at her with wide eyes. "You think you can steal from us just because we're Americans?"

Donavon crouched down beside her, offering his hand to the fallen child. "Chamo," he said, the slang word something he had picked up from one of his admirers in the airport or bus. "Take this one."

He unslung his computer bag, handing it to the boy who stood to take it. Donavon slipped the kid a twenty dollar bill. If his eyes had been wide when looking at Faye they now looked like they might pop out of his head.

The other children ran back to the helicopters, helping Grey and the others unload equipment or bags and truck them across the field.

"My chamos!" Donavon yelled, the children all hooting and calling back. Several gave Donavon a high-five as he held his hand out for them.

Faye felt like a complete idiot.

"He was only trying to help," Grey said, walking past. He pushed a large dolly filled with crates of the supplies they had brought for the survivors.

They followed the children toward an unpaved road barely large enough for a single vehicle. Chickens skirted around them. In the distance Faye heard a bird's cry that sounded almost like a child's scream.

"Where are their parents?" Faye asked, catching up with Grey.

"Drunk on some street corner, who knows? Look I grew up in the Bronx; I know it wasn't like this, but some things never change no matter where you are. Places like this, as a kid? You learn to fend for yourself or you don't survive."

Faye let Grey continue past, waiting for Donavon. He adjusted his sunglasses as he approached, several of the children marching along at his side. On his face he wore that contagious smile that had probably landed him his first role however many years ago. Behind him the other two camera men hefted a heavy canvas bag between them, their disproportionate heights not making the task any easier.

"Figures," she said, as she joined Donavon. "If you don't bring an entourage you just contract a new one."

Donavon squinted into the setting sun, not responding to her cut. He blew on his glasses, wiping them on his shirt.

"I'm sorry, that wasn't fair. It's been a long two days, not that that's an excuse for my bitchiness."

"Hey I had two sisters, I get it. Not saying I understand it, but I get it." Donavon's confident and relaxed smile let her know everything was okay. Sometimes she wondered what he saw in her.

"Comes with the territory, that what you're saying?" she asked.

He shrugged. "I think everyone's doing pretty well considering what we've gone through to get here. Can't wait to see what fancy accommodations await us. If we're lucky they may even have running water."

As they turned down the dirt road, hardened tracks where vehicles had passed crusted into grooves, Faye tapped Donavon on the arm, pointing.

"Over there," she said.

Though the location she was referring to was hidden from their vantage point, its poison rising into the air was impossible to miss. Twin plumes of black smoke rose like a devil's prayer sinking into an ever obscuring night.

"My god," Donavon said. "Is that a fire?"

"I think that's the lumber mill," she said.

The harsh contrast from the colors dancing in the sky to the affront rising in the distance caused them both to fall silent. They weren't the only ones to have noticed – Grey and one of his helpers, Kenny, Faye thought he was called, were pulling out equipment and cameras.

This would make for an indelible shot.

"The equivalent of thirty-five football fields of forest destroyed every minute," Faye said softly. "People don't have a clue. What we're doing to ourselves. The future we're creating?"

Donavon found her hand, squeezed it tightly. "You can't blame people; it's the agri-corps and governments allowing this to happen."

"No. It's every ignorant person who believes the world will remain the same while we toss our trash into giant heaps and pollute our air with our vehicles and consume and consume with our insatiable appetites hoping the next generation will figure out a solution. We're the monsters; we just don't realize it."

A dog yipped at a passing child, a girl with ratted hair and pimples on her arms. Her too-thin frame suggested her nourishment was close to non-existent.

"I'm glad you're here with me," Faye said, squeezing Donavon's hand back. "I know it probably wasn't easy, to make it work, but it means a lot."

Donavon, who was staring intently at the distant smoke, didn't seem to hear.

Verse XII.

The only hotel in town, the hotel de Maracao, was completely booked. All five of its rooms.

The local police had requisitioned the building for families who had been displaced during the recent earthquake. To Grey it looked like they were trying to fit a village into each room – he had never seen so many shirtless children pour out of a single door.

Apparently the damage from the quake had been greater than they had imagined. Back home a five-point-oh earthquake might knock over a few portraits; here it collapsed walls. Then again when your homes were as sturdy as a child's fort built out of blankets and kitchen chairs, it shouldn't have come as much of a surprise.

The kids who had been so willing to help with their luggage and equipment vanished after Donavon had emptied his billfold leaving Grey's team with two truckloads of gear to transport amongst the three of them. Considering they had been wandering rather aimlessly over the past half hour, both Kenny and Malcolm were past complaints – they had shut off their cameras.

They decided to park the equipment while Faye and Donavon went in search of a place they could stay. Grey was more than happy to oblige. He sat on a step leading up to the city square, literally a square of concrete, with a bronze statue of some historical figure at its center. The statue's features were so worn it could have passed for anyone.

If this was the town park it was pretty pathetic; no shade, grass or trees. Not even a bench to sit on. The stickered weeds growing through cracks in the concrete were the only flora in the area. Maybe when you were surrounded by trees and forest you craved something concrete.

He smiled. He'd have to share that one with the guys.

Across from the square was a small church in great need of some paint. Homes made of brick and cement ran alongside the square to the left, all standing, unlike the thin metal huts they had seen collapsed near the field. Someone had music playing at an absurd decibel level, the heavy beat of house music only abetting his headache.

So this is Venezuela, he thought, waving off a drunk man whose eyes were pink instead of white. The man staggered down the remaining step and trailed away.

What the hell had they been thinking?

Kenny came back from a small bodega, a tiny store operating out of the front window of someone's house, with three ice cold beers. He was an ugly dude, six-foot-two with long curly brown hair that hung to his neck and a belly that would have looked seven months pregnant on a woman.

Grey was one of the few people who knew Kenny still lived at his mother's, though of course he chalked it up to "caring" for her. As if he was doing more than just living off her dime. In his grey-green plaid button up and aqua denim shorts, Grey wouldn't have been surprised if Kenny's mother still dressed him.

"You're a godsend," Malcolm said, grabbing a mud-colored glass bottle and pressing it against his forehead. "Seriously how can it be this hot at night?"

Malcolm was an intern, another Asian-American protégée that, by being brilliant, had become just like everyone else. A blurred face in a crowd. And so to be different he had rebelled, ditching his scholarship at Georgetown to pursue his dreams of being a filmmaker. What the kid had yet to figure out was that he had only traded one insecure crowd for another. His face was destined to remain blurred.

Grey grabbed the other open bottle from Kenny, taking half the beer down in a single swallow. "Oh, gawd, tastes like drain water from a carwash."

"They say it's an acquired taste," Kenny said.

"Who? Carwash attendants?"

Malcolm laughed in the middle of a swallow, beer fizzing and dripping from his nose. He squinted in pain. The stuff was bad enough going down, Grey couldn't imagine it coming back up.

Kenny set one foot on a crate containing some of the supplies they had brought for victims of the quake. "You should see, I went by where the grocery store's at, shelves are empty. These cervezas cost me ten bucks, way more than it should have."

"That's 'cause you're a gringo who doesn't speak a lick of Spanish," Grey said, finishing the rest of his beer. Dirty water or not, he needed the buzz.

"No, what I'm sayin' is what we brought? It won't make a dent," Kenny continued. "And these people'll rip us apart wanting more. They're savages. And they look at us like we're millionaires."

Comparatively speaking they probably were, Grey thought, even when you removed Donavon from the equation.

He stretched out, leaning against a large duffel bag, his feet extending out into the dirt. Despite the hard object pressing into the middle of his back, it felt great to lie down. "Good thing we're not really here to help them then," he said, unable to keep from yawning.

"What do you mean?" Kenny asked.

"I mean all this goodwill crap and care packages? It's just for show. The truth, I don't think Faye even cares about these people. If we don't find a place to stay? It's fine by me. Just ups the time-table, maybe gets us home sooner."

"Yeah, makes sense," Malcolm said.

Always the yes-man, Grey thought. "You catch where the pilot was staying?"

"I look like I speak Venezuelan?" Kenny asked, following his words with an obnoxious burp. "Hey Mal, if you got a ten I'll get us another round."

Grey must have dozed, though not long; Faye and Donavon's approaching steps enough to bring him back.

"Any luck?" he asked, eyes still shut.

The voice that answered was not the one he had been expecting.

"Oye, amigos, que tienes aqui?"

Grey quickly sat up. Three men in uniforms stood together, their faces in shadow. Light from a nearby porch glinted off the submachine guns hanging at their sides.

Shit.

"Whas in the bags, amigos? Drogas?"

Before Grey could open his mouth he heard Kenny begin to blubber. "We … we brought uh blankets and emergency packs for the uh, for the earthquake?"

"For de uh, uh, earthquake?" one of the soldiers said, mocking him. The others laughed.

"We're here to help," Grey interjected. "All this – it's food; blankets."

"Cervezas?" one of the faceless men in shadows asked.

"No, no, food. Supplies. Help." Grey wasn't sure how much they were understanding.

One of the soldiers said something in Spanish. Where the hell was Faye?

The soldier in the middle, much larger than his companions, stepped forward. He wore a dark fedora and seemed to be in charge. "We have enough peoples begging on the street," he said in a thick accent.

"No, no, we're not begging," Kenny said, "we're just here to help! We're friendlies!"

Grey wanted to slap his forehead with an open palm.

"Jour with Red Cross?" the large man asked.

"No," Grey replied, "but we're like Red Cross."

"Jou are with de others? De Americans?" the man asked.

"Yes! A woman and a man – have you seen them?"

"De, uh, woman, she is asking queshions about a man. Why she is looking for him?"

"What? No, she's just looking for a place for us to stay," Grey said.

The large man snorted and again said something in Spanish. The men on either side of him brought their weapons up.

"Jou need to come with us."

"Wait, no – the rest of our group, they won't know where we've gone!"

"Don't worry, we have a place for jou to stay," the man said. "But jou will come with us now."

Grey looked at Kenny and Malcolm, both staring back at him with uncertainty. How the hell had he become the leader here? "What about our stuff?"

"We will take care of jour tings," the man said. "Don't worry, everyting is going to be a-okay."

The large man's laugh sent a shiver through Grey's entire body. As the two younger soldiers stepped forward, herding them away from their gear, Grey realized, not for the first time, that he really hated this country.

Verse XIII.

Morley's footsteps reverberated through the underground warehouse that had been dubbed the Freezer by all who knew about it. The nickname came not from its temperature, which was abnormally cool compared to the rest of the Facility, but because of what was kept within its walls. Housed there, you might say.

No one was allowed into the Freezer without Morley present yet often times he would find himself here alone, sharing a meal amongst friends. Silent, incapacitated friends.

The best kind.

His stomach grumbled and he realized he hadn't stopped for dinner again. It was impossible to remember everything he was supposed to do. No matter, food could wait. Dugan had called in with reports of a new playmate. Morley had a bed to prepare.

His thin LED flashlight lit his path just to the point where his feet made contact with the tiled floor. It provided no comfort against the darkness enveloping him on all sides. His flesh broke out in goose bumps beneath his lab coat as his steps echoed back to him with a steady clop – clop. He reminded himself it was just the cold causing the arrector pili muscles to contract at the base of each hair on his arms, making them stand erect. A very natural reaction.

Aren't all erections, he thought with a smile.

Down each aisle the flooring curved slightly inward to a line of drains that ran across the Freezer's floor, a recent addition he had added to make clean-up easier.

He turned down Aisle E, humming along to an old patriotic song he hadn't heard since grade school. *This Land is Your Land.* He wasn't sure why the song had popped into his head but found it soothing and more than fitting.

"From the Amazon forests to the floating islands," he sang. Shadows on either side of him loomed like great sentient beings intent on his demise.

He arrived at E-Seventeen and pressed the remote clicker he had snagged from the entrance. A bright spotlight shone down on an empty hospital bed with stained rust-colored sheets. Shiny steel shelving was visible behind it, a rolling metal tray next to the bed with several instruments atop.

Morley moved to the shelves, sliding open the bottom one and pulling out a thick inflatable polyurethane bag which he hung on a rolling metal rack.

"From the sweeping grasslands to the empty chasms ..."

A sharp rattle sounded an aisle over, Morley's heart leaping to his throat. He listened intently, peering out just beyond the radius of light.

It came again – the sound of chains clinking against railing.

Morley's breathing slowly returned to normal. For a moment he had forgotten his place in the world, a lion frightened at the sudden and unexpected movement of a gazelle.

He moved past the empty bed, slipping between the faux walls separating one aisle from the next. Another bright light shot down from overhead with the click of a button, reflecting off the forehead of a middle-aged woman.

She lay in the bed, eyes open but unseeing. IV's slipped from her neck and wrists into the hanging bags of poison at her side, a concentrate of synthetic opioids, halothane, and ketamine. She was nude, her dark native skin and thick unwashed hair giving her the look of a witch rather than an Indian.

Morley hovered beside her, unable to take his eyes away. Her breasts sagged along with her belly but he liked the fact that her eyes were open.

"From Mount Roraima to the Cruz cenotes ..."

No upper lip hair. That was a plus.

The scraping sound came again, reminding Morley of his task. He brought up two fingers, kissing them, then pressed them against the dry and cracked lips of the bound native woman on the bed.

To be continued, he thought.

He moved on, following the sound of that lightly grating metal. His heart continued to pound but not from fright. The woman native had gotten him aroused. There would be plenty of time to make acquaintances.

Her eyes were open! he thought.

He clicked on the second button on the remote, the entire Freezer coming alight like the glow of dawn rising. This was a button Morley rarely used, preferring to keep his work in the dark, but his appointment with the open-eyed native had given him a sense of urgency.

Row upon row of hospital beds now had lights shining down on their occupants – naked native women and men; some dead, in various stages of decay, others unconscious yet alive, with missing limbs or gaping holes and hideous scars. Wires and tubes ran from bodies to machines like intersecting webs.

He located the culprit of the noise, a dangling arm caught on an IV line, the metal ring strapped to the native's arm wiggling ever so slightly with the tubing's pull.

No boogie monsters here.

Except for me, he thought.

In a loud tenor voice he belted to an unhearing audience, his voice echoing in the giant hall. "This land was made for you and me!"

Verse XIV.

Three young soldiers carried crates, boxes and luggage from the town square to a dark brown jeep that was running. Faye rushed toward them.

"Hey, those are our things!"

Donavon kept his sigh to himself, content to watch Faye attempt the impossible. He had no idea he'd be spending his time down here just trying to keep her from stepping on the wrong person's foot. Sometimes he wondered if she truly had a death wish.

She had been abrasive to most of the people they had met, seeking a place to stay. Donavon couldn't blame them for shutting their doors to the visiting gringos. How many Americans would open their homes to a host of strangers visiting from another country? He knew the answer wasn't many.

While Faye could put on the charm like few women Donavon had met, her composure broke down when she didn't get her way.

"What are you doing? ... Set those down!"

The soldiers moved around her like a small stream skimming past a newly lodged rock. The engine of the jeep revved.

"Faye," Donavon said but she ignored him, instead latching onto one of the soldier's arms. She spoke something to him in Spanish. He responded with a sneer. "Faye?"

"Are you just gonna let them take our things?" she asked, turning on him.

"They could be bringing it to wherever the film crew's at. Like the kids that helped with the luggage. You consider that?"

"And have you considered why the others aren't here?"

"Not everyone's out to get you, Faye. People are a lot better than you give them credit for."

She spun back, snatching a box away from a surprised soldier with a crew cut. The other two uniforms raised their weapons, pointing them right at her. Heavy automatic-looking rifles, similar to guns Donavon had used in a film or two.

Though these were probably not loaded with blanks.

"Hold on," he said, walking forward slowly, palms out. He knew his presence was intimidating; he had at least a foot and a half on the tallest of these guys. But if anyone was going to diffuse the situation, it would have to be him.

The soldier's gun in the rear gravitated toward him.

"We brought this stuff for you. It's okay!" he said. "Here, we'll help you load it."

Donavon picked up one of the wooden crates from the ground and moved to follow the soldier. The man in the back with high cheekbones and a forced squint, despite the cover of night, rattled off something quickly in Spanish.

"What'd he say?" Donavon asked.

Faye's jawbones set as she ground her teeth. "He asked if we would like to join our friends."

"See? I'm telling you, you get a lot more with honey than you do with a flyswatter."

"In prison," Faye said.

"What?"

"We can join our friends in prison."

With one of the men standing his ground, rifle pointed at both of them, they watched in silence as the rest of their gear was loaded. The soldiers even took the crate Donavon had been holding. Before they left, one of them demanded Faye's backpack and Donavon's laptop bag. He slipped a movie script from the bag, its pages curling upward, then waved off the bluish-grey exhaust spilling from the jeep as it jolted forward, leaving them in the dark.

Faye glared at him almost as if the entire charade with the soldiers had been his fault. Her skin was shiny from the sweat and dirt of their travels which made him wonder how bad he looked. Even at night his clothes stuck to him from the humidity, the air stifling.

"Okay, so that didn't quite go as planned."

"You think?"

"Why don't we try the church?"

"I'd rather sleep outside." Faye stepped off the square onto the dirt road and began walking. A rambler's walk; the tired shuffle of a person with nowhere to go.

"There's gotta be a consulate or whatever-you-call-it around where we can get help," Donavon said, joining her.

"In Venezuela? I doubt there's even one in Caracas let alone the middle of freaking nowhere. The United States is not their number one ally."

They walked in silence, the buzzing of insects louder than ungrounded electrical lines. A gate rattled shut, a stout woman in a light-colored mumu watching as they passed in front of her home. After a few more houses, Donavon gave up waving to the local residents.

He regretted not letting his agent book the trip for them though he was sure if he had brought it up, David Sedall would have told him no.

Not just no, but absolutely you've-got-to-be-shitting-me-for-even-asking no. Especially considering he was leaving the country.

"Do you want to look guilty?"

"I am guilty."

"No one's guilty in this country, especially not celebrities. You get a get-out-of-jail card every time you pass 'Go' my friend. In fact, you're overdue for something like this to happen, some shit storm to clog up the tabloid drains for a week."

And what a shit storm he had walked into.

Or driven into.

The conversation in his head continued as if he had simply paused a DVR recording and had now hit play.

"I had to get out, had to get away; the fact that one of my gf's was leaving the country seemed like the perfect opportunity."

"This is why you don't make decisions without consulting with me first. Like driving home from Lure at two a.m. with half a bottle of scotch and a quarter mile of marching dust in you? Those are the times you're supposed to call me first so I can talk you down, keep the mosquitos from biting. I'm not just your agent Donny, I'm your friend. Probably the only real one you have."

The fact that his only real friend was an imaginary version of his agent was not lost on Donavon. And considering that *friend* called him by the name he despised more than any other – Donny – really brought some questions into play.

"I killed them."

"You don't know that."

"I couldn't see through her windshield it was so splattered with blood."

"It was the cracks – the splinters in the glass that kept you from seeing in. And besides, she could have veered out of your way – she wasn't paying attention! Probably on her phone."

"They'll nail me to the wall with this, after last year's DUI."

"Only if you let them."

"But if I'm involved in a cause – the face of this global eco-revolution, it could change their opinions ... get them to see I'm doing good in the world. Make them love me. Make them forget."

"It's a stretch but ... it could work."

"They'll see my passion for saving humanity. The trees, forests; children. The future."

"It could change your entire public image. Push you to A-list status. Where people flock to theaters for you and you alone."

"That's why I left the country, not to hide but to shine, spotlights beaming down on—"

Donavon plowed into a man who had stepped into the road from a shadowed alley, sending the man tumbling. He hit the dirt and rolled, shouting out in pain.

Not again.

Donavon stood frozen, remembering that night, that windshield, the dark smoke seeping from the sides of the engine.

The drips falling from the edge of the car door, bent inward at a sharp angle. Dropping to the black pavement with a

Plop.

Plop.

At times he could convince himself it was just oil.

Oil spilling out of the driver's side door.

The man Donavon had bowled over stuck a carved wooden cane to the ground like a skier's pole, using it to raise himself up. The handle of the cane was decorated with a snarling wolf's mouth, its ends plated in gold.

"Are you okay?"

It took Donavon a moment to realize Faye was asking him, not the older gentleman. "Fine," he answered. "You came out of nowhere, I'm sorry. Didn't mean to knock you over." He looked back at Faye. "Can you translate?"

"Don't think I need to," she said.

The older man stood, dusting off his slacks with a gloved hand. His grey hair sprouted from the top of his head like wild weeds, barely covering the bare earth beneath. He had a large nose and crooked teeth and eyes so bloodshot Donavon could barely spot the whites.

The man looked at him curiously then twisted his neck to both sides letting loose a series of disturbing cracks. "Do I know you?"

"You're English?" Faye asked.

"British," the man answered. "Though I have dual citizenship." He opened his mouth and picked between two teeth with a long fingernail. "Not Britain and England, mind you, but here, Venezuela. And, of course, back home."

The smell of alcohol hung from him like a cloud. "Now don't tell me, it'll come."

Donavon smiled and the man's eyes lit up.

"You're the, uh, oh don't tell me, the … that's it! You were the guard in Concentration, the one with the accent that was so bloody awful."

Donavon's smile fell though he saw Faye chuckle. "That was one of my first roles ..."

"Ze plane, Ze plane," the man shouted, laughing.

"That wasn't my line."

"Yes, commander, I will go and kill that Jew. Right away, sir."

"Look, you're obviously drunk and –"

"We need a place to stay," Faye said, cutting him off. "Just for the night."

"Well, my darling, you have stumbled onto the right man. Sir William Francis, the third, at your service." He dipped an imaginary hat, almost falling over in the process. "Mi casa es su casa though I hate to admit I wasn't planning on guests."

"Just a roof over our head would be amazing."

"Do we want to talk about this first?" Donavon said, Faye giving him one of her glares.

"I, for one, thought we were doing exactly that." Sir William chuckled, a light frothy sound.

"You're sure you don't mind?" Faye asked, ignoring Donavon.

"A pretty lady such as yourself? I'd have to be insane to mind that. And will the German be joining us as well?" Sir William said with a terrible attempt at a German accent.

"Come on, I wasn't that bad," Donavon said.

"Hail Hitler!" Sir William shouted, saluting. This time he did lose his balance, falling back onto his rear.

The old man beamed up at them with a childlike smile and Donavon found himself offering his hand to help the man back up.

"The German would love to stay in your abode," Donavon said, speaking in a much more authentic German accent.

"My commode?"

Donavon felt himself flush. "Abode! Your house. We'll – yes, we'd love to stay with you."

Sir William clapped once. "Ha-ha, Spree will be so pleased!" He took Donavon's hand and rose back to his feet. "Come, come, it's not far and I have brandy."

Donavon fell in beside the old man, Faye mouthing the words "thank you" to him. Donavon nodded. Hell, it beat staying in a prison.

Verse XV.

Dugan walked the halls of the Facility, his home away from home for the past fourteen months. In truth he had no home to go back to, so what did that make this place?

Una policia acostada, as the Venezuelans referred to them. A speed bump. Just one amongst many on life's little journey.

The Facility entailed three connected buildings, all but invisible by air through clever camouflage and cover of jungle growth. The amount of money put into these buildings was probably equivalent to Venezuela's annual GDP.

The first structure was a carport; the Humvees for his team parked alongside a line of ATV's and dirt bikes for those few civilian employees allowed to visit town. The carport was an open walled steel structure hidden beneath a thick blanket of tree branches and leaves. Their single helicopter stayed out in the open, covered with a heavy camouflaged tarp. Even by satellite it was impossible to notice.

The second building was the barracks. The kitchen with their staff of chefs, laundry, and individual quarters serving an encampment of close to eighty. There was a grocery store the village of Santa Elena would have been jealous of, a movie theater, basketball court and gym, even an indoor pool. When you lived where you worked for months on end having a bit of distraction was a necessity for most.

The center building connecting both barracks and carport was for operations and, much like an iceberg, was larger underground than above. It was through these halls he walked, the hour guaranteeing his thoughts would remain solitary.

He flashed his badge at a security station and turned his face upward toward the camera in the corner. The heavy steel door before him buzzed. He opened it, stepping through into a room the size of a broom closet, a second vault-like door in front of him.

The door behind rattled closed, locking itself firmly in place. The room invoked a sense of claustrophobia on even the most anxiety-free men and women. Dugan stood up straighter, stretching his left arm down with his palm open, fingers spread. He had been told it was unnecessary but followed the practice every time he entered.

A bright flash left him temporarily blinded, the multimodal biometric scanner simultaneously running facial recognition, hand geometry and palm vein authentication. If even one of the tests came up negative the room would remain on lock-down, an oxygen concentrator in the ceiling whisking away the air, leaving only nitrogen and carbon dioxide behind.

The death, Dugan was told, would be painless.

He blinked through the white flashes as the door before him gave its pressurized release, allowing passage. He walked through entering a second hall.

The war hall. Because whether the world admitted it or not, there wasn't a person out there who hadn't engaged in some form of warfare with the only common enemy they shared.

Mortality.

Zephyr stood outside a doorway, one leg propped up against the wall. A thin wisp of smoke rose from a cigarette in his hand.

"You don't smoke," Dugan said.

Zephyr held the cigarette out for him. "Compliments of the Bear."

"He's not coming?"

Zephyr shook his head.

Strange; he rarely left Dugan's side. Dugan grabbed the cigarette and walked into the room. Zephyr closed the door behind them.

The Callis room always made for tight quarters. It was the only board room Dugan had seen without a single chair. A large circular table in the center was the only piece of furniture in the room. Nothing on the walls and of course, being underground, no windows.

"I'll make this quick."

Marcus Stanton stood opposite Dugan across the table, heavy bags under his eyes. He was tall, grey peppered hair and a lean physique, wearing his typical white button-up shirt with blue jeans. Probably had his cowboy boots on as well. Besides Cy he was the only one in the room who looked clean-shaven. If you didn't count his assistant.

Stanton was the official chief of operations for the project here in Venezuela though everyone knew he was only the handset corporate used to reach those with the real power. Seeing as Dugan had no desire to dosey-doe with the executives, the arrangement served them all.

Dugan nodded to Doctor Morley on Stanton's left, the only other man in the room as dangerous as himself. The mad scientist tipped his mug toward Dugan before taking a sip. There was an unspoken agreement between the three of them enabling Stanton to keep some visage of control in settings where a group was involved.

Stanton's assistant, a blonde knock-out at least half his age, handed him a folder. It was common knowledge she assisted Stanton in matters both work-related and personal. If she was as efficient under the sheets as she was with managing the day-to-day operations, Stanton was a lucky man.

"By the end of the month we're going from off-books to on," Stanton said without opening the folder. Though they all knew what that meant, he continued. It's what men like Stanton did.

"Our center will be open for inspection by the CDER and ITOB. We're expecting an immediate EIR to prove compliance, which gives us an estimated two weeks before inspection. Shannon will see you each have a copy of the Regulatory Procedures Manual as well as the CPG, Compliance Policy Guides, for your designated office. Dugan, I'll need your men to supervise any ... flashing." Stanton glanced around at using the word, as if there were ears who might overhear. "No more deep-sea excursions. I'm sorry."

"Son of a bitch!" Morley hurled his mug against the wall. It bounced off without shattering, black coffee slathering the wall and ground. Not quite the effect he had been looking for. "How long have you known?"

Stanton swallowed hard, looking down at his folder now for the first time. Not for answers but an escape.

"How long, you bastard?" Morley shouted.

"Umm, it's been –"

"A few days is all," Shannon replied, cutting her boss off.

Morely was right to be upset. Stanton may not have held any real power, but the stockholders and investors pulling invisible strings? They could make them all dance if they wanted.

Zephyr walked out, letting the door slam behind him. Cy rubbed at his bald head, the deep lines carved into his face multiplying.

"Dugan! Aren't you going to say something?" Morley asked.

"What's there to say?"

"What's there ... What's there to say?" Morley's face had turned beet red. "They're shutting us down! When we're this friggin' close!"

Dugan blew out a stream of smoke then dropped his cigarette, grounding it into the smooth tiled floor. "Shouting at a tidal wave won't keep you from drowning."

"Bullshit. This is bullshit. Bullshit!" Morley stormed from the room.

Cy bent down to retrieve the fallen mug, holding it out for Shannon to take. "No matter where you run you're a cog in someone's wheel," he said.

Stanton shifted uncomfortably. "Dugan, I'm sorry. You know if I could do anything ..."

Dugan's glare stopped him cold. "A few days?"

"I ..." Stanton tossed the folder onto the table, throwing his hands into the air. "I've been up to my eyeballs swimming in this! Do you have any idea what it's going to require to pass code in this short of time?"

"A graveyard," Dugan said.

Shannon's face went a shade whiter, her eyes darting to Stanton. Though they both knew what went on behind locked doors they preferred to feign ignorance. Who could blame them?

"Find your own Flash team," Dugan said. "My men are busy."

"What, chasing rabid dogs? Newsflash – that's over!" Shannon said.

"We're in clean up mode." Stanton's voice was much calmer than his side kick's.

"*You're* in cleanup mode," Dugan said, pointing with his finger. He felt the anger racing through his veins, pulsing in his head. He needed to hit something. Destroy something. Instead he balled his hands into fists and brought them down to his side. "Give me a week."

"Dugan, I can't ..."

"A week!"

Shannon took a step back, holding one hand protectively against her chest.

Stanton nodded. It wasn't like Dugan had been asking. "Okay but I've got to prep for this, beginning tomorrow," he said. "I wait a week and we'll all be strung up. You understand. Tell Morley I'm sorry. It's ... been a good run."

"You get in my way, and you won't be here by the time the inspectors arrive. Understand?" Dugan said.

This time Stanton's nodding looked like a man begging for his life. "A week," he said. "Then I expect your full support."

"A week and you'll have it," Dugan said. "Shannon." He tilted his head as he ducked from the room, stepping over the ground up cigarette that she would no doubt be cleaning up.

Somehow Oso had known. Dugan had no idea how, but it was the only explanation for why the man had opted not to come. Cy, Zephyr, and Oso made up *his* executive team – their opinions were ones he trusted and they were men he could not only rely on, but that would bring their own unique insight.

A week.

What the hell could he hope to accomplish in a week that he hadn't been able to in the past year? Maybe throw a coup and supplant Stanton in more than just influence.

Coups did seem to go over well in this country.

Dugan felt his hand touching the notebook in his breast pocket. He had given up everything for this. What did it matter if others were asked to sacrifice the same?

Or what did it matter if they were never asked.

Verse XVI.

"Welcome to my humble commode," Sir William said.

The house, if it could be called a house, looked like a complex mathematician's problem. Its base cylindrical with a dome atop, sporting odd sharp angles in some sort of polyhedral equation. Faye was pretty sure the sum of those parts did not add up.

"Looks like a giant golf ball on a tee," Donavon said.

"Maybe a deformed golf ball," Faye said.

"Yes, yes it does."

"What's it for?" Donavon asked.

"The golf ball? Or the tee?" Sir William chuckled.

A low block wall encircled the home with an awry gate that shrieked with their entrance. Off to the side of the yard was a garden with all manner of vegetables in neat planted lines – beans, pumpkins, tomatoes, and a few Faye didn't recognize from their eager sprouts.

Sir William led them to the front door below a stooped perch, unlocking it and gesturing them through.

As soon as Faye entered she was attacked.

Something grabbed her, snagging onto her hair and clawing at her back. She screamed – reaching out to the wall for balance as she batted at her head.

"Get it off! Get it off!"

Beside her Donavon laughed.

The creature freed itself, landing on top of a wooden rocking chair. It leapt from bookshelf to picture frame then disappeared up a twisting iron-wrought staircase. A spider monkey, its fur golden brown with a black tail.

The picture frame fell to the floor with a clatter. There was no glass in it; apparently this wasn't the first time it had fallen.

"You'll have to excuse my flat-mate, I hadn't the chance to inform him guests would be arriving." Sir William closed the door behind him.

"Where's the camera crew when you need them?" Donavon said, still smiling.

Faye shivered, the thought of that thing crawling all over her.

"Spree?" Sir William made a sucking sound with his teeth. "Spree? Oh, now, you've scared him off!"

He dropped his cane against a couch and moved toward the small kitchen in the back, walking with a slight limp. The room was crowded with furniture, old sitting chairs and sofas with tight end-tables between, piles of books stacked across most surfaces. A drooping counter separated the living room from the kitchen. Tiny cockroaches fled into cracks at the kitchen lights coming aglow. A large wrinkled map was draped over the far sofa, partially opened next to a topographical globe, one of the old-school ones, that spins within its casing.

Sir William banged around in the kitchen, pots clanging together as he called out to make themselves at home. Donavon asked about a bathroom and went to the door just past the stairway.

"Don't flush the toilet paper," Sir William shouted after him. "There's a can by the sink! Pipes are sensitive that way."

Something on the arm of the couch caught Faye's attention, a streaked stain that ended in a hardened clump, almost like a mold. She scratched at it with a fingernail, pieces breaking away like clay. She brought it to her face, instantly regretting it.

Feces.

Hopefully the monkeys.

On the way to the house they had told Sir William their reason for being here. Surprisingly he had been almost as excited as Faye herself, telling them how he hated that infernal refinery, his term for the lumber mill. They discovered he had been living in the country for twelve years now, was an astronomer, philosopher, widower, aspiring author, and highly functioning drunk.

Those last two go hand in hand, he had said.

The 'Sir' came from marrying well, though he hadn't been inclined to expound other than to tell them when his wife passed he had felt the need to lift the chains of responsibility and flee to the remotest place he could find.

He had been here ever since.

When Faye had mentioned what had happened with their colleagues, Sir William casually stated he was friends with the governor of the state. He'd place a phone call in the morning that would see their friends released from prison. Faye hoped that wasn't the booze talking.

With Donavon out of earshot, she sat at the counter, their host preparing a drink in the kitchen. A concoction of fresh vegetables, juice and a lot of brandy.

"Have you met any other Americans here in the past two years?" Faye asked, trying for casual conversation.

"Some. Most tourists never get down quite this far South, less lately though who can blame them."

"What about someone who's not a tourist? A scientist, named James Dugan. Have you heard of him?"

"I make it my practice to know as few people as possible. Safer that way. You should try it." He turned the blender on, its mechanical roar keeping the conversation from continuing.

When Donavon returned he did so with a friend. The spider monkey sat atop his shoulder, one arm wrapped around his thick neck, its tail flicking across his back.

"You name him Spree for the candy?" he asked.

"Candy? No, for the trouble he's caused me," Sir William answered. "One continual destruction spree after another. Last month he sent my computer monitor down the stairs. Honestly I don't know why I have anything nice."

As Donavon sat next to Faye, the monkey jumped down onto the counter and scrambled across, jostling dishes, before climbing up their host. Once comfortable, it bared its teeth at Faye and hissed.

"Now, now, manners," Sir William said, filling four glasses with the green mulch-like liquid from the blender. He set one in front of each of them, leaving the fourth by the sink. Spree hopped down, overturning the glass and began to slurp it up with both paws.

Sir William uncorked a bottle of rum, emptying its remains into his glass. "Cheers!" he said, eyes heavy and red but all smiles.

After a light meal of crackers, salty and wet cheeses, and fresh deli meats, along with several more glasses of "magic juice," as Sir William called it, he led them up the winding staircase.

Faye caught her breath as she entered the room above. The odd angles and sharp faces of the dome outside came together in an intricate design, its black ceilinged walls reflecting an array of stars like she had never seen before. It was like watching the galaxy form around you.

She spun in a circle, staring up at what could have passed for sky, only hundreds of light years closer.

"It's amazing," she uttered.

Donavon moved over to a network of telescopes aimed up through an open slat in the ceiling. "How did you …"

"I've always had an affinity for sleeping beneath the stars," Sir William said, a tinge of sadness to his words.

Beyond the telescopes and computers networked to a globed projector, a mattress lie in the corner almost as an afterthought. One worn dresser and a desk crowded with overturned books, papers and drawings.

"Look here," Sir William said, using a laser pointer to circle an array of stars displayed on the ceiling. "The constellation Scorpius, the only scorpion you'll find in these parts. Those three stars in a row form its head, then we follow it down with the curve of its tail here. Proof that our ancestors had imaginations, no? This brighter red star in its center is Antares, fifteen times the size of our sun. Can you imagine? And here, this shiny cluster near its tail almost in the shape of a butterfly? That's M7, commonly referred to as Ptolemy's cluster. Astronomers have been staring at these same stars, these exact formations, for centuries. Nothing like the heavens to ground humanity."

"You built this?" Donavon said.

"Engineered it, yes, though the benefit of having some money enables me to delegate the physical labor. I'm sure one day you'll get there, chap," he said, clapping Donavon on the shoulder. "If the blinking lights on the ceiling keep you from sleep, this lever here will close the window above." He pronounced the word '*leever.*' "There are fans in the corner, I'll see to some clean sheets. It is a bit drab. I'm afraid I've never had a need for more."

"It's amazing," Faye said.

"Where, uh, should we –"

"The bed, of course," Sir William said. "It's not often I have a celebrity and a beautiful woman grace my home."

"You don't have to …" Faye began.

"Oh, shush, I prefer the couch. Just don't be surprised if Spree joins you at some point in the night. He loves to spoon."

Once they settled in, new sheets on the mattress and Sir William shutting the lights out below, Donavon held Faye's hand as they lay next to each other staring up at the brilliant stars.

After a while, Faye spoke. "It's just like the rainforest; looking up at all these stars. You don't realize how big it is until you see it. Makes you feel small but … important. Like your part of something bigger. Connected."

"I wonder if I could hire whoever built it for him," Donavon said.

"Stop." Faye hit him lightly on his chest. "Some things are so beautiful you can't replicate them."

"Like you?" he asked.

"That was reaching, even for you."

He barked out a laugh beside her.

"We are like these stars, though," she continued. "You put one of us out there in the dark, all alone? You won't even see our glow. But put us all together and we make the heavens shine. We're making a difference here. Tomorrow. You'll see."

Soon Donavon's breathing became heavy, his grip relaxing in her hand. Faye finally dozed off, her thoughts flitting like the gaseous streaks of a thousand suns regarding the incredible potential of humanity. For generosity and kindness, even to complete strangers. And also its potential for cruelty and destruction.

Verse XVII.

Dugan watched the monitors scroll from screen to screen, crouched beside a computer terminal. One of the IT tech-heads, a runner by his lean physique and thick calves, navigated at the computer, a scowl on his face.

Oso sat to the tech's right on a fold-out metal chair, sharpening one of his curved long blades on a whetstone. Dugan still wasn't sure what the blade was made of, its metal dark and black, almost liquid in appearance. He could almost see the invisible threads where the sheets of metal had been folded into itself, layer upon layer, like a samurai's sword.

"I'm not finding anything," the tech said, running one hand through his bed-head hair. "I'd almost have to repurpose the software ..."

"We've done it before," Dugan said, blowing a cloud of smoke toward the wiry man. He and the technician had already resolved the issue of the 'no-smoking' policy in the control room.

A stream of formulas appeared on a new blue screen, the technician typing away then looking to the second monitor on his left. "The FV-5 is a sedative not a homing device. It's not meant to track animals but bring 'em down."

"You're wasting my time," Dugan said with an air of finality. "Can you do this or do I need to get someone more competent?"

The technician's mouth pulled to the side, a nervous twitch or tic he was probably unaware of. His fingers rattled against the keyboard. "Yeah, I can do it."

While the majority of the employees here were kept in the dark as to his team's real research, Dugan's reputation was such that when he asked, they jumped. Only afterward would they inquire if it was high enough.

Oso slid his long knife onto the tech's desk, the bleary eyed man pausing only briefly before continuing. Oso pulled the marker from behind his ear, his small notebook open on his lap. When he had finished writing he ripped the sheet free and handed it to Dugan.

Something wrong

"With what?" Dugan asked.

The technician turned around. "What?"

"Not you." Dugan turned back to Oso. "Not him, right?"

Oso shook his head once.

The tech pulled on the collar of his shirt nervously. Dugan couldn't blame him.

"You don't think we should go after him?" Dugan asked.

The lines in Oso's face crinkled. He wrote:

Not that

Then what? Dugan thought.

If he hadn't held Oso's instincts in such high regard it would have been easy to dismiss him out of hand. But experience had made Dugan a believer. At least in trusting the native's intuition.

It was strange having a mute as your confidante but Dugan had never known anyone who could understand his thoughts as clearly as the native. Sometimes he even found himself wondering if Oso, like many of the supposed aboriginals, didn't have some spark of telepathic ability.

Oso began writing then tore the page out, crumbling it into a ball and tossing it at the waste basket below the desk. His next message he handed to Dugan, his eyes wide, head shaking.

Can't explain

"Is he still out there?"

Oso nodded. He knew Dugan wasn't talking about Guayanata.

"He knows we're looking for him?"

Another nod.

"What kind of animal'd you say it was?" the technician asked.

Dugan watched as the closest monitor revealing a map started diving in, an after image of each screen shot morphing into a closer and closer view. Finally the screen settled, a red crosshairs blinking at its center.

If only you knew how appropriate that was, Dugan thought.

"I had to re-triangulate the coda, capturing an increased expression in isoforms of haptoglobin caused by the serum's blotting of protein –"

The tech cut off as Oso stood, leaning over him to jot down the coordinates.

"I don't need to know what happens when I flick a light switch," Dugan said. "I just need the light to turn on."

Oso's hair fell into the man's face, the tech turning slightly while trying not to make it obvious. As Oso finished, he grabbed his knife from the desk, the side of the blade brushing against the tech's arm. The tech gave an almost imperceptible squeak.

"Wake the others," Dugan said. "I need to see Morley before we're off."

As Oso turned to leave the room, Dugan reached down and grabbed the crumpled paper the native had tossed away, unfolding it as he followed the man out.

"You know you could at least say thanks!" the technician shouted after them. "All the crap we do for you, at your beck and call regardless of the hour … do you even know my name?"

The thud of Dugan's boots coming to a stop on the tiled floor seemed to quiet even the tower of servers buzzing behind him. Cords and wires floated to the ceiling before snaking invisibly through the rest of the facility.

On the discarded note were written the words:

Maybe a trap

Dugan turned back, the technician wilting beneath his stare. "Trust me pal, you don't want me to know your name."

Verse XVIII.

The prison was more like a horse corral: dank, dark, and eerily deserted. Windows within each cell allowed a drift of light into the long corridor, enough to see you didn't want to see more. The smell of the place was overpowering, like the mortar between blocks had been crafted from human excrement and re-applied daily. It required all of Faye's efforts not to turn around and march right back out.

The guard who led them swung a rusty iron gate to the side, opening the way in. She hoped it would remain open on their way out.

Eight cells, four on either side.

More than the hotel rooms in town, Faye realized.

"Oh gawd that's foul," Donavon said.

The ground was covered in matted and muddy straw, sticking to their feet as they trod through. Further in, the smell only worsened.

Faye pulled her shirt up to cover her nose and mouth. Ordinarily the act would have made her feel foolish, but this was no ordinary stench.

As the guard passed the second cell on the right, liquid sprayed out as if thrown from a bucket, sloshing between the bars and catching him by surprise. It splattered his uniform, dripping down the side of his face and coat arm.

Donavon extended one arm out in front of Faye protectively. This was new territory for both of them.

The guard turned toward the cell without even a change in countenance. A bubbling laughter spilled from the other side of the bars, rising like a monkey's chortle, definitely the voice of a woman.

That's the sound of insanity, Faye thought, wishing there were some moments you could take back, voices you could erase from memory.

It wasn't the first time that wish had crossed her mind.

The guard spun through his ring of keys pulling a baton from his side belt then dug the key in to the side door. The gate swung out and he stepped inside, Faye losing sight of him. She closed her eyes at the sound of his club striking flesh again and again, another violation she didn't want in her head.

Thwack – thwack – thwack.

It continued long after the laughter subsided, the whimpering began, and the howls followed. It continued until whoever was in that cell was incapable of making a noise.

Thwack – thwack.

Donavon held Faye's arm just below the shoulder; she wasn't sure when he had grabbed hold of her but was grateful he had.

Minutes past. What felt like days.

When the beating finally stopped, the guard exited. He didn't even bother closing the gate to the cell, instead nodding for them to follow. He continued as if nothing had happened, moving to the final cell in the back.

Donavon brought his arm around Faye's waist, keeping her away from the cell. "Don't look," he said.

They stepped around the sloshed liquid, Faye once again covering her nose and mouth. No wonder the guard had been so upset. She was sure now those clumps of matted straw sticking to her shoes were not mud.

Despite Donavon's warning, and her better judgment, she couldn't keep herself from glancing inside the cell as they passed. The first thing that struck her was how bare it seemed. No toilet, no sink, no mattress or cot, just an overturned bucket and lumpy pile of discolored blankets on the ground. The straw here too was stained with liquid, but not feces; blood.

It was spattered all around the blankets, the woman trying to ward off the blows with a thin layer of cloth. And then Faye's mouth dropped.

She looked away, her breath catching.

There were no blankets in the cell – that lumpy form huddled into a misshapen mass of spoiled color, was the prisoner. The only thing that kept her from going to her knees was Donavon at her side. Still, she had to swallow the bile slipping up her throat.

Inside the last cell three faces stared out at her, all ghostly pale. The big guy, Kenny, looked like he had been crying. The intern was the only one standing, the exhaustion in his eyes a clear sign he hadn't sat since entering last night. Both Kenny and Grey were hunkered on the floor, Grey's knees brought up to his chest, both leaning against a filthy and probably disease-ridden wall.

"Hey," Grey said.

"Hey," Faye answered, followed by a sharp intake of breath. The guard rattled through his ring of keys.

"Come to join us or we joinin' you?" Grey asked.

Faye nodded, Donavon catching her inability to speak.

"We're getting you out," he said.

"Thank God," the intern said.

Grey swallowed hard, nodding. "Find a place to stay?"

Faye felt the tears break through the dam, rushing down her cheeks.

She wiped at them quickly, callously. "You're okay?"

"No," Grey said. "This was not okay."

"Come on, we're leaving here now." Donavon extended his hand down, pulling Grey to his feet.

"We going home?" the intern asked, his voice like a child's asking his parent for permission.

"Yeah," Donavon said.

Eventually, Faye thought.

Verse XIX.

"'In the beginning, God created the heaven and the earth.'"

Josue repeated the words but in Spanish, switching from the worn King James Bible to the smaller Reina-Valera Spanish translation. He always read from both hoping to instill a desire to learn English in any who studied with him. Not that there were many who did.

Or any, ordinarily.

A small group of children sat at his feet, their parents watching from a distance in their partitioned four-by-four cubicles made up of stained sheets and faux-marbled floors. Natural disasters and tragedies often had a way of bringing people to God, but the parents of the families who had come to the church for shelter weren't yet ready to seek a deity who had so recently struck them down. Remmy couldn't blame them.

One of the children, a girl with light skin and eyes too large for her face, raised her hand before Josue could continue. He called her by name, asking what she wanted. Remmy didn't understand her response, the Spanish spoken much too fast for his old ears.

Instead of answering, Josue turned to Remmy. "She has a question that I do not know the answer. What was there before the beginning?"

"By definition, the beginning is the start," Remmy said.

"But did God exist before the beginning? Or how could he have created everything?"

"The scriptures don't talk about it, neither should we."

"Did he create the earth from nothing?" Josue asked.

The absolute innocence and faith staring back at him made Remmy want to answer. Even if it was a lie. "I don't believe God is a magician. But maybe to us, what he does looks like magic. I believe he's bound by the laws of science, even if we can't comprehend them. Like the first cavemen. They were in awe over fire, almost worshipping it. Its science, they just didn't understand it yet."

"Were the cavemen after Adam and Eve?" Josue asked.

Remmy realized he was opening more doors than he cared to close. "God probably created the earth and the heavens using ... materials that were here just ... unformed. He fashioned them, so to speak, put them together. Took chaos and put it in order."

"So chaos existed before the beginning?"

And ever since the beginning, Remmy thought.

"Theologians have debated these things for centuries, Josue, but no one knows for sure. Why don't you use the picture books for the young ones? They'll understand them better."

He pushed past the small group, leaving before Josue could ask him another question. Questions to which there were no answers.

In the adjoining classroom where the kitchenette resided, two motherly women were busy at the gas powered stove. A pot of black beans and another of rice. Cachapas cooking in a frying pan filled with grease.

The contents weren't enough to feed half of the mouths in the church and their small storage shelves held little more than what was being used. Funds were almost non-existent; he wouldn't be able to support this many people for long.

If there was ever a time for miracles, this was it.

Remmy squeezed by the two women, thanking them for their help, then went through the back kitchen door. He closed it behind him with effort, the cut of the oversized door scraping against the bottom frame.

Once outside, he leaned back against the stone wall of the church, sucking in gasps of air. The sun beat down on his face and he closed his eyes against its affront.

It was important, on occasion, to recognize that the prison bars around you weren't there for decoration.

The panic attack finally ran its course, Remmy's breathing returning to normal. Or at least what amounted to normal when stuck behind a life that wasn't his.

"In the beginning, God created heaven and hell. The earth, that was hell," Remmy said. He wiped at the sweat on his face before turning back to the door, jostling it with his shoulder to get it to open. "And God saw that it was good."

Verse XX.

Grey unzipped a pocket on the waist strap of his Kenmore pack removing a pair of Rayban sunglasses. The sun had already crept over the trees in the East and was enough to give him an early headache. That and the smell of feces with every breath of air he inhaled. God, what he'd give for a shower.

He and his band of unlucky desperados marched down the dirt road leading back to the center of town, luggage and equipment in tow. At least most of it. The emergency supplies and food were gone; Faye had been told the local police would be distributing them. Grey suspected not even the officer speaking with Faye had believed that tall tale.

One of their camera bags had also vanished as well as every iPad and cellphone. At least they had recovered a few of the laptops, though Grey's MacBook and Malcolm's Dell had gone missing. Luckily, Grey had backed up his content on several zip drives. Malcolm had been livid, but Grey convinced him not to bring it up. When the mob steals from you, you don't ask for your money back, you just thank God you lived to tell about it.

And then you never tell about it.

Several baby chicks darted beneath a crumbling fence on the side of the road disappearing into patches of weed and snag-grass. Kenny hiccupped loudly, a long drawn out chortle that was unlike anything Grey had heard before. Grey quickly decided against asking him what was so funny. The biggest realization of how dejected they were came when he noticed not a single one of them had thought to film their walk from the prison. Maybe it didn't matter anymore.

"I should never have come here," Malcolm said. "I don't even like Mexican food."

Despite everything, Grey laughed.

"This ain't Mexico, bro. You seen any Taco Bells around?" Kenny asked, followed by a loud hiccup. The large rolling crate of camera equipment he dragged behind him left a jittery trail in the dirt.

"Helicopters ready?" Grey asked. "They're still here right?"

"One of them, yeah," Faye answered. The bag hanging from her shoulder pulled her beige collared shirt down, revealing more of the tattoo than Grey had seen before. It made him wonder where the rest of that calligraphic beast had wound itself.

"Only one?"

"The other left soon after we arrived," Faye said.

"So how do we call it back?" Kenny asked.

Here it comes, Grey thought.

"We have to wait until it returns. Besides we haven't accomplished what we came here for."

Both Malcolm and Kenny stopped, a loud hiccup escaping from Kenny. They both turned to Grey, the silent and unanimously-chosen ambassador of the film crew. Though that vote had apparently been taken without his knowledge.

This was a battle, however, he was ready to fight.

"Do you have any idea what we've been through?" He kept his voice calm. Something that required an immense amount of effort. He let his pack slump to the dirt road. "We could have been killed in there and no one would have known. Do you honestly think anyone would notice a few more missing bodies amongst the wreckage from this earthquake?"

"There's not that much wreckage," Faye began.

"You don't get it – these people, they don't have rules! They locked us up because we're American. What do you think'll happen when we try shutting down their plant? A nice civil conversation? Open negotiation? No! They're likely to shove machine guns down our throats!"

"He's right," Donavon said, folding his arms. "It's not worth risking our lives over."

Faye let her bag slip down off her shoulder, not bothering to straighten her shirt. A white tank top poked out from beneath. No one else spoke, yet she looked at each of them in turn, her barrel of a boyfriend included.

A loud hiccup escaped from Kenny's open mouth.

"That's it? One setback and you're ready to jump ship? After everything it's taken to get us this far, two years of planning, preparing for this day, this event! I mean did you really think we wouldn't encounter some opposition? That we'd march in to cheers on the streets, streamers in the air? That we'd be heroes? Is that what you thought?

"Well get over yourselves! This is bigger than you or me or any one of us. I don't care if I have to set up a tripod and march around in a circle filming myself, I am going to get this footage and I am going to shut this plant down even if it's just for a single day, a single hour, because I believe in our cause. And I believe there are millions of others who would fight right alongside us if they just knew how; knew that others cared. That they could … make a difference."

She waited for a response but no one had one.

"There's a reason our campaign is called *Regener–Nation*," Faye continued, speaking softer. "We can't do this alone. We need a nation, an army, the whole world on our side, but if you make me, I'll do it alone. I'll try. I'd die trying."

Twenty minutes later Grey found himself standing in front of the road to the lumber mill recording a now disheveled looking Donavon as he told the story of how they had been thrown into prison. Dirt had been applied to his face like makeup before a scene, his clothing torn. He carried it off like a hero, jaw set, his eyes full of sparkling hope.

"No obstacle will stop us from doing what we came here to do," he said. "Because each of us, no matter our circumstance, can make a difference."

He just needed someone to give him his lines, Grey thought. Maybe they all had.

He smiled back at the performing actor, giving a thumbs up and said, "Perfect."

Verse XXI.

A great big splotch of green crème fell from the pastry Zachary Morley bit into, hitting the ground with a disgusting splat. Ear buds hung from the top of his faded Aerosmith t-shirt, dangling down between the flaps of his lab coat.

Dugan flicked his fingers impatiently against the leg of his Columbia pants, the fabric making a flitting noise. Not surprisingly the screen on the wall display Morley tapped at was filthy with dried swipes of oily food from whenever he had last entered the Freezer.

The section of the hallway they stood in rocked side to side briefly, a precursor to their descent. And then a four foot section of flooring began to lower, Morley stepping away from the wall. As soon as they passed beneath the ground level, a replacement floor slid into place.

The faux flooring was eight feet thick, all but guaranteeing it would go unnoticed by any casual observer in the Facility. Not that anyone with access to the area above could be considered casual, but with the stakes as high as they were, no precaution had been deemed unnecessary. Not even Stanton knew where the entrance to the Freezer was located.

"When were you gonna tell me?" Morley shouted at Dugan once the flooring overhead had sealed completely. His words echoed in the thick polycarbonate tubing they rode through.

"You think I knew about them pulling the plug?"

"Screw the plug, we just find another outlet. Plugs are universal." He made a ring with one hand, sticking his finger in and out. "I'm talking about your man. Escaping. Flying the coop."

"We'll get him."

"You're gettin' old, Dugan," Morley said. "Losing your touch."

"Yeah? Well if you had your shit together I wouldn't be forced to look for alternatives. God knows we have enough guinea pigs for you to work on."

"Ah, I don't believe that for a second. You'd find some reason to keep up the hunt. It's what men like you do." Morley stuffed the last of his pastry into his mouth, wiping his fingers on his coattails. Green goop clung to the front of his beard.

"At least one of us gets results," Dugan said.

"Man, the stuff we're doing down here? No one'll come close to in twenty years. If I could publish this I'd be set for life."

"You'd also be in prison."

"Eh, to each their own. Remember, no smoking."

Dugan felt the drop in temperature immediately as the platform lowered into the center of the dark warehouse. Even without being able to see much there was a sense of vastness here, like you had entered a huge cavern with no end. The air felt electric; alive, as if unimaginable creatures were pressed to the very edges of where the light failed.

"Be a shame to see all this go to waste," Morley said absently. He pressed a button on a small penlight keychain, grabbing a remote from a pillar next to the landing.

Dugan followed him through a winding path in the dark.

"You haven't asked what I'm about to show you," Morley said.

"You're about to show me. Why should I ask?"

"New guy working out?"

"The Kid? Yeah, he's alright."

"You should have seen the knockers on the assistant they sent me the other day. Would've made Dolly Parton look flat!" Morley said, his breathing heavy from their walk.

"What, was she tripping on them?"

"We all were!" Morley said, laughing.

They stopped in front of a number painted on the ground. D-114. Reflecting off of Morley's light, the numbers seemed to glow with an eerie luminescence. Morley pulled the remote from his pocket, a device that looked like a smartphone. Keyed something in.

A sharp light broke through the darkness from overhead, shining down on a lone hospital bed. The body of a small native child lay prone upon it, cords and wires zipping from his arms, neck and head.

He was unconscious, eyes not even roaming behind his closed lids. Only the slight rise and fall of the sheet above his chest gave sign that he was in fact alive. The bed dwarfed him, making it feel as if the white sheets and mattress were slowly consuming him.

In a way, Dugan thought, *they were.*

The machinery and hospital equipment surrounding the bed were half cast in shadow, humming softly in a language no human understood.

Morley stepped to the edge of the bed, pulling the sheet back from the boy's body. He was naked beneath, a grotesque scar like a maniacal smile crossing his lower abdomen.

"You know we don't even bother stitching them anymore?" Morley traced the jagged curve of the scar with one finger. "I mean look at this, after two days? The acceleration of fibrous tissue and collagen equates to almost four weeks of recuperation."

Dugan remained where Morley had left him, the light passing just over his head. "Now I'm asking. I know you didn't bring me here to admire your artwork."

Morley's finger continued sweeping across the boy's skin, his face enraptured. "We broke new ground with this one. Removed his pancreas, intestines and stomach."

"How long?"

"I told you, two days ago. And he's still here, clinging to life. But it's the organs, Dugan, that I'm really proud of – they're still alive! Repairing themselves almost as fast as they're dying! We're close." Morley put his face next to the child's skin and inhaled deeply. "I want to do a heart next. See how long it'll keep beating."

"Congratulations. You're a modern Doctor Frankenstein. Now while you're busy diddling your ex-experiments do I need to hire someone who will actually do what needs to be done? Isolating whatever it is that gives these primitives their regenerative abilities?"

"There is no way to isolate it! Not when there's no *it!* If you were a little smarter I would go into the pathogenic mutations in their millions of genomic variants and the billions of microbiomes unique to their exome sequencing. The homozygous variants we've identified through SNP microarrays during the prioritization process contain more potential causative mutations than horny school girls at a Justin Beiber concert. In layman's terms, it's like looking for a particular person with squinty eyes in China."

"So much for being close."

"Oh, man, really? You're really gonna go there? You and your band of outlaws searching for a mythical sasquatch?" Morley left the bed, coming over to stand directly in front of Dugan. The overhead light shone on the top of his head, highlighting his greasy brown and greying locks. "Even if you found him – *if* he even exists – what makes you think he'd sign up to help you, this Shaman? Your profound reciprocity?"

"He exists. And trust me, he'll have no choice. Not if he wants to save his people."

"What if he doesn't?" Morley asked. "I mean, if he was out there don't you think he would've shown himself by now? If for no other reason than to stop you? Look around, Dugan. I'm surprised there are any natives left."

A squawk sounded from the walkie-talkie on Dugan's belt. He turned away, using it as an excuse to break from Morley's terrible breath. "Yeah."

Zephyr's voice came from the small device. "Boyscouts're ready."

"Be there in five," Dugan said.

"Copy."

Dugan clipped the walkie-talkie back in. "We're going to find this Shaman and he's going to break open whatever code you and your boys have missed and then you and I and everyone involved with Umner Corps are going to change the world. Morley?"

Dugan stepped around the man who stood as if frozen in place. He was only semi-conscious of his own mouth dropping open.

The native child in the bed was sitting up.

Dugan unholstered his gun, a semi-automatic Glock, in a single motion, raising it to point at the child. He glanced from side to side. Of all the monsters creeping in the dark one had just woke. How many others were conscious?

"No way, man, no frickin' way. This can't be happening," Morley said. "It's impossible."

"If the past year has taught us anything, it's that that word has … limitations," Dugan said.

The kid twitched violently, body going taut. His back began to arch, head staring straight up. It looked like he was being controlled by invisible strings, his body torquing in ways Dugan had believed only possible in the movies. Movies like the Exorcist.

Morley was panting. He kept blinking and rubbing at his eyes, maybe wondering if he wasn't hallucinating. Dugan knew the man was wont to the occasional acid tab, finding occasions with some regularity. Maybe he thought he was just on another trip.

"Why isn't he bound? Morley!"

"I, uh … I must have forgot." Morley hit into the metal shelving, having backed up as far from the bed as he could. A scalpel and thin pair of forceps fell to the floor with a rattle.

Still staring up at the darkness above, the kid opened his mouth as if preparing to speak.

Instead he screamed.

Shrill and unearthly, his cry was worse than a siren's blare. Morley moaned, squeezing his head with both hands.

Dugan shot forward to put an end to the hysterics when the boy's head whipped around, his scream silenced. He stared directly at Dugan. Looking but not seeing. One arm stretched out toward him, a finger extending. Then the child began to chant.

"Shan'ti K'lompi Lia'hona K'lan Malaki-ahkan …" The kid

continued speaking almost without breath.

"Get Oso down here now!" Dugan shouted.

Morley's feet skid on the tiled floor as he turned and fled. Dugan unsnapped his walkie-talkie. "Zephyr, get the Bear to the war hall asap. Doc's on his way." He didn't register whatever Zephyr said in response, listening instead to the monosyllabic message spilling from the kids' mouth.

"... Bela'aal Shan'tu-kompi Inktomi ..."

A penetrating alarm sounded from everywhere at once, bleating in rhythmic pulses. One by one every overhead light flickered on, the entire room awash with an artificial glow. Dugan blinked, letting his eyes adjust.

"... Fehener Takushkansh'kan La'a'ione ..."

Takushkansh'kan.

The name of the Shaman.

Dugan stared into the vacant eyes of the child wondering who was looking back at him. Like staring into a camera lens trying to glimpse whoever was on the other side. His heart pattered at an accelerated rate, his throat tightening. Without looking away he pulled the worn pack from his back pocket, shaking out a cigarette and bringing it to his lips.

Looking into those unseeing eyes, he shouted, "I'm coming for you. You hear me in there? I'm coming for you!"

Around him row upon row of hospital beds now had lights shining down on their occupants – men, women, children, their names in the only book Dugan believed in.

The book that would change the world.

The book in the pocket of his blazer.

"Tell him if you can," Dugan said. "I'm coming."

Verse XXII.

The perimeter around the lumber mill was cordoned off by a thick fence of standing logs dug deep into the earth. Totem poles, one lined up after the next, bolding pronouncing the sins of a corporate machine fed by greed and avarice. It created an impenetrable wall twelve feet tall or higher, blocking all but the tallest of structures within from sight.

The dirt road leading into the mill was wide, a thick metal gate pulled back on both sides of the fencing. Even from outside the noise was overpowering – saws screaming, engines rumbling, heavy equipment and machinery in constant motion.

Sir William stood at the entrance leaning heavily on his wooden cane. He wore a dark silver suit with a ruffled white shirt beneath and looked more like a has-been rock star than a philanthropist astronomer. Faye was surprised to see him.

"You came," she said.

"My dear, was there any doubts as to whether I might?" Despite the early hour, the smell of sour brandy poured off his breath. "I see you managed to save the day?"

"You're the one who deserves that credit. Meet the rest of our group," she said, introducing them one by one. Grey came to her rescue with the name of the intern. *Malcolm.* She needed to remember that.

"Sir William was kind enough to open his home to us last night," Donavon said, sensing the group's questions. "He also pulled some strings to help us get you out this morning."

Grey nodded, Kenny and Malcolm offering awkward thanks.

"I should have mentioned he might be joining us," Faye said. "He liked the idea of our protest and wanted to help." She didn't mention she had thought he'd be too hammered to remember.

"So do we have a plan?" Sir William asked.

"Storm the gates?" Kenny said.

"Try not to get arrested again?" Grey added.

Faye frowned at him. "We stick together; that's the plan. And whatever happens, do not stop filming."

They entered the dirt path between the two fence posts, Faye making sure Grey and Kenny both got shots of the log fence. Kenny recorded the group walking while Grey's camera roamed over the large yard. Malcolm carried a microphone attached to a long pole he had assembled from one of their bags, a boom mic, they called it.

Along the perimeter of the fence were bundles of stripped tree trunks. Strapped together, they were easily wider and taller than a house. They were bound with thick metal wire then stacked atop each other in pile after pile. Thousands of trees lying inert. Helpless.

"Most milling companies claim to plant a tree for every one they cut down," Faye said, facing the camera. She raised her voice to be heard over the chaos around them, despite Malcolm's mic hanging overhead.

Donavon moved in next to her, his jaw set as he looked off in the distance.

Faye continued, "From the sheer amount of deforestation taking place around the world we know those numbers are an impossibility. According to the FDFAO, approximately five thousand acres of forests are disappearing every hour, victims to the kind of butchery you see before you. And for every thousand trees that are torn down for consumption, a single sapling will be planted. Considering the average maturation for a tree to yield enough lumber for harvesting is between twenty to forty years, we're looking at a cycle that is unsustainable, cannibalizing itself within the next two decades."

"Unless something changes," Donavon said, giving the camera his best soap opera stare.

As they walked, Faye pointed across the lot to where the finished timber was stored beneath aluminum canopies. Each covered canopy stretched further in length than a football field.

"Most mills such as the one here in Venezuela convert their logs into lumber for easier transport. Over half of the world's timber and almost three-fourths of the world's paper goods are consumed by just a fifth of the world's population: The United States, Europe and Japan."

Faye and her team moved off the road as several heavy duty trucks rolled past and out the gates. Wood chips and sawdust flew into the air with their passing. Faye rubbed at her eyes, trying to remove the microscopic slivers.

Some of the trucks dragged open inverted trailers meant to transport logs; others carried smaller yet more dangerous vehicles, the ones with twisting arms and angular saws, mechanical centipedes that were always hungry and never satisfied.

Grey shouted, "It's too loud – let's just pick up the shots and we'll overdub voice work."

"Probably better to have Donavon saying this anyway," she said.

Grey nodded in agreement.

Large cranes bowed overhead with the load of logs, transporting them to where their dissection would begin. Sawdust spit from a giant tower connected to one of a series of buildings. A dump truck below whisked the pulp to an incinerator manned by several Venezuelans all wearing heat masks, the two rising plumes of smoke they had spotted the previous day being vented out of two shafts.

Other workers moved about ignoring Faye and her companions, forklifts trucking past, men – and even women – all wearing heavy gloves, plastic goggles and earplugs. She was surprised there were no hardhats.

"Where to?" Donavon bellowed.

Faye barely heard him over the sheer level of noise, the sounds of industry at war with the peacefulness of the jungle beyond the fences.

"Is there an office?" she yelled, looking about.

Sir William shrugged nonchalantly. "It's Venezuela, darling."

It was answer enough, she supposed.

"Then we go inside. The conveyor lines!"

They moved toward the main industrial building. Roll-up gates wide enough for tractors revealed a labyrinth of machinery inside. A few workers watched as they passed, not a single one coming to investigate their reason for being there.

Well if you don't come to us, we will certainly go to you, she thought. Donavon clamped his hand on her shoulder and she knew, that in this moment, they were about to make history.

Verse XXIII.

Footfalls echoed in the Freezer, the sounds of someone being chased. At the end of the long row of hospital beds and occupants, a haggard Dr. Morley appeared. He bent down, hands resting on knees. Even from this distance Dugan could see the heavy rise and fall of his chest, his heart working overtime.

Oso quickly appeared, passing Morley without pause. Another man and woman were a few steps behind him, both in lab coats.

None of Dugan's men had ever set foot in the Freezer before, content to play their part and nothing more. They all knew what happened down here to some extent. Rumors of this place were alive everywhere in the Facility, a security issue Blake was not only aware of but encouraged. Hushed whispers and dark secrets spreading from ear to ear created an environment of fear and exaggeration, the perfect combination to keep employees in check. In most facilities those rumors would grow to overshadow any of the actual work being done. Here, Blake wondered if they even came close.

The young native sitting in the bed began to convulse. The IV lines and tubes running from his body carried those tremors up to the machines they were attached to, metal racks and equipment rattling around him. His chanting never ceased.

"Te'lakum Shyan'do'hal Inktomi Ma'falak."

"He keeps repeating part of it," Dugan said as Oso arrived.

Oso brought out his notepad, grabbing the felt marker from his ear. Dugan stood over his shoulder, reading as he wrote.

End beginning

Oso slashed through the words hurriedly.

Beginning ends

He paused as if unsure how to interpret what he was hearing, then turned to a new page.

Destroy the world

He crossed out the first word and replaced it.

Create

Is the same

He circled both the word he had crossed out and the new word written next to it. Destroy and Create.

Oso flipped to a new page.

Darkness comes

Death becomes
Life
Oso's face suddenly went pale. He tore at a new sheet.
Stop him now
"Who? The Shaman?"
The child
Stop him
NOW!!!
Dugan had never seen Oso use punctuation in his sentences. Ever.
He looked from the native beside him to the one on the bed, this child in
the throes of some power beyond himself.

"Get me a tranquilizer," Dugan yelled.

The two scientists had joined them during Oso's writing, the woman
moving quickly to the long metal cabinet alongside the bed at Dugan's
command. She threw open a drawer and began searching through it.

"What's he saying?" the other scientist asked.

"The end is coming," Dugan answered.

"Not very original," Morley said, having just arrived. His breaths
were labored, sweat running down his face.

Dugan noticed Oso writing again and glanced down at the notepad.
No new message; Oso was underlining the word "*NOW*" repeatedly.

Frantically.

His marker wearing through the page and beginning to scribble on
the blank one beneath.

"The tranq!" Dugan shouted.

"Here!" the woman said, holding a capped syringe high. Instruments
on the metal tray next to her began to rattle, though it wasn't attached to
the child on the bed.

Morley stepped forward, almost falling. He braced himself against the
bed's rail then immediately pushed back, abhorred at having come that
close to the ranting native.

The woman scientist's eyes roamed the room, a look of abject horror
on her face. Every bed on the aisle was now shaking, the noise like being
trapped in some elaborate pinball machine. The native child's eyes had
risen into his head, the soft white of his sclera interlaced with red weepy
veins.

"Just another tremor," Dugan said. "Hold on! We ride it out."

Dugan heard the Shaman's name again from the child's lips just
before Oso held a fresh page before him, a haunted look in his eyes.

Too late

The jolt that hit was like a bomb exploding from beneath them, a geyser of rock and concrete displacing everything within its path. Bodies flew – equipment tumbling, beds colliding, from the pressure of some unseen force. A god swatting at a fly.

Verse XXIV.

Faye stood atop a motionless conveyor belt, the husks of tree trunks no longer moving toward the fifteen ton machine at the end of the line. The wicked blades and discs jawing outward like crooked fangs from a gaping mouth had finally fallen idle.

As they should be, Faye thought.

She waved the red banner above her head, its tail trailing, aware of both cameras pointed toward her. Below, the intern marched with Donavon and Sir William as well as a few workers who had surprisingly abandoned stations to pick up signs. Bright signs that would contrast beautifully with the dull metal of the machinery around them.

STAND – UNITED
STAND – FOR OUR MOTHER
STAND – FOR OUR CHILDREN
STAND – FOR OUR FUTURE

In thirty two milling operations throughout the US, Canada, Asia, and South America, protests just like this would be video-recorded and broadcast over the internet and news stations across the world. It was a massive undertaking, the coordinated effort of a small army and more years than Faye wanted to admit, but Regener-Nation's voice in a dozen countries would spread to the entire world.

With a little luck that voice would be heard for generations.

Grey tracked his camera between the rusted scaffolding supporting the weight of tracks and bins filled with slats of lumber. The sheer amount of machinery and moving parts, conveyor lines whisking trees through the automated process of dissimilation, was incredible. The workers standing before them were more for quality assurance and maintenance than anything, a human hand not even needed to turn a tree into a sheet of plywood.

"We're here, today, because our earth can't wait for tomorrow," Donavon said as Grey brought the camera forward, microphone hanging just overhead. "We're here, today, because we want there to be a tomorrow!"

He was good; Faye couldn't keep the smile from her face. Frantz would see – despite what they'd had to go through, this would be worth it in the end. Even if she didn't get what she had really come for.

Three men approached from the back of the building, their confident strides at odds with the shuffled walk and confused faces of the gathered laborers. Faye recognized them immediately, despite their lack of formal apparel.

These were "the suits." The ones in charge.

She was surprised it had taken them this long. Two of them looked local, though well off; Venezuelans who had gladly exchanged the rape of their countryside for a small pot of gold. The third was probably American. Whatever his title might be, he would be the one they needed on camera. You had to put a face to evil in order to rally people against it, and his was a face people could hate.

Faye leapt from the conveyor belt to the ground as the men pressed through the small crowd before them. Kenny came around behind her in a wide shot. Now was her time to shine.

"Donny Hughes," the tall executive said as he approached. "It's an honor to have you here on our yard!"

The executive's face was freshly shaved, grey hair sharp and cut short. His eyes were small, like they had been pressed too far into his head, the arch of his eyebrows jutting out disproportionately. In a tucked-in white polo shirt and khaki pants he stood with perfect posture, one arm outstretched.

Donavon seemed taken aback that he had been recognized so quickly but Faye knew they probably had cameras trained on them from the moment they had entered the yard.

"We were hoping you could join us for a conversation somewhere a little cooler. We have an air conditioned office – believe me, it's a novelty down here." The man held a soft friendly smile on his face that never rose to his eyes.

"We're not going anywhere," Faye said, moving to stand next to Donavon.

"Miss Moanna, please, we'd love to address any concerns you might have; in fact bring the cameras with you. We have nothing to hide."

Kenny let his camera fall from his face. "How does he know ...?"

"Oh, I know everything about you, Kenneth Moore, and your little group. Grey Peters, Malcolm Wu. You even recruited the town drunk into your retinue I see."

"I'm not drunk," Sir William said, his words only slightly slurred.

The man continued, "What is painfully obvious is that you know nothing about us. How, for instance, we are in full compliance with the APPCDLA, the Action Plan for Prevention and Control of Deforestation in Legal Amazon. How every truck that enters or leaves our plant does so with numbered plates. How this tiny village's economy has been reinvigorated by our presence. Did you know we employ over forty percent of the town's population?"

Donavon deferred to Faye, taking a step back and glancing around. This was not going to plan.

"Who you should be targeting are the dozens of illegal operators set up just miles around us, those heating wood and falsifying papers. We are as horrified at such groups as you are. Illegal logging is a bane we have donated millions of dollars towards thwarting, though not with the results we all would want. We are more than willing to help in any way we can."

"Those are nice words," Faye said, "and I'm sure rehearsing them helps you sleep better at night but your conscience is far from guiltless. We're here to put an end to the abuse."

To Faye's surprise, the man before her smiled. "You and your kind are all the same. Decrying pollution while taking commercial jets to your next conference; bewailing the decadence of this generation while purchasing your latest iPhone; screaming the world is ending, the sky is falling, without ever lifting a hand to hold it in place.

"Well, I have news for you. The world is not ending. But the seven billion people who make up the habitants of this planet have needs which are not going away. We are part of a sustainable logging operation that sees to those needs."

"There's nothing sustainable about what you people do," Faye said.

"There's a saying," the man began, "if a tree-hugger yells in the woods and no one's around to hear, is it any different than when they're in front of a crowd?"

"I thought it was, 'does it still make a sound?'" Donavon said.

"Exactly."

Faye felt her face flush. "You're wrong – people are listening. They want change, they just don't know where to start."

The man took a step back, sniffing loudly as if dismissing them. "Señor Madrid, call the policia. These people are trespassing on private property. Maybe another night in a cell will do them some good."

"How did you know –"

Faye extended one hand, cutting Malcolm off and hoping to calm the others. "We stand united," she said, "not as a few people making a stand but as nations, decrying the desecration that you and others like you have subjected –"

"Forget the police," the man said. "Call in the watchdogs. God knows Dugan owes us a favor."

The world stood still, Faye barely able to take in a breath. "Who did you say?"

The man looked down at her derisively. "I wouldn't wait around to find out."

"You said Dugan. James Dugan?"

The man's eyes widened just a fraction. "What are you really here for?"

Before Faye could answer, an audible rumble rose in volume around them. The sound of an avalanche.

The legs of scaffolding and metal racks began to vibrate, shaking violently, sawdust spilling from grates in the tracks above. A forklift rattled nearby, lines appearing in the dirt beneath where its shifting tracks were visible.

Faye heard one of the workers shout "terramoto" as the crowd began to disperse, fleeing toward exits in a panicked rush. Others took cover beneath machinery and scaffolding. Though they had a few moments warning, no one was prepared for the quake that hit.

The ground shot forward, Faye's feet flying out from beneath her, her chin cracking against the hard earth. The taste of blood swarmed her mouth. Groans from machinery and equipment swaying were overshadowed by screams.

Nearby an overhead track rattled loose, heavy tree trunks careening to its edge. A cable snapped with a deep wiry twang and the thousand pound trunks slammed into railings on their way down. Rather than stopping their fall, rails shrieked beneath the bending of metal, debris showering outward.

One worker caught a metal shaft through the throat, his body trampled by those around him, and then the first of the logs hit the ground. Indecipherable shouts as hands were raised to ward off a tidal wave of lumber, and then the bodies simply were no more, flattened as easily as a swarm of beetles beneath stampeding hooves.

As the logs continued to amass they rolled over each other, tipping and overturning heavy equipment. Like a line of falling dominos, one triggering the next, the destruction spread.

A metal tower swayed then collapsed, a leg dropping out from beneath it. A man screamed, coming down with it. A landing platform smothered the suits, burying them in a cloud of dust and rubble. An arm protruded from the cracked and broken platform as the swirling dust settled, the only evidence that three men had stood there just moments ago.

Faye cried out in shock as she was lifted again from the ground, a ragdoll callously kicked by an uncaring child. She slammed into a metal rail, the breath knocked from her body. Flames erupted to her left, the heat washing against her.

Where was Donavon?

The chaos in the building was at its apex, bodies everywhere – running, fleeing, others clearly unmoving. Overturned equipment and fallen logs. Laborers trampled by others attempting to escape. The air was thick with heavy mulch and sawdust, the rain of dirty particles that never fell but continued to float indefinitely.

"Donavon?" Faye yelled, choking on the air.

A loud crack sounded behind her, metal creaking, breaking. She turned in time to see the assembly line tilt toward her, its long tracks and metal beams like arms preparing for an embrace. One that would be her last.

Verse XXV.

Dugan rolled from the shelving unit he had landed against, covering his head with his fall. Tiny pebbles of concrete rained down like scattered hail.

Hospital beds screeched against the tiled floor as they slid, clanging against metal cabinets. Overhead lights wavered as they swung, their intended targets no longer stationary while beneath them bags of fluid burst, IV lines breaking. A steel pipe fell from the ceiling, clanging against a bed or cabinet.

A few yards away the native child directed his mad orchestra, arms outstretched, his words spilling out in that monotonous chant. It seemed to Dugan that the child's bed was the only thing not moving, as if the epicenter of this earthquake, the eye of the storm, began and ended with him.

Another hospital bed had slid from somewhere, colliding with the young native's, the lifeless body of an adult male lying in a heap of sheets. Dugan might just be able to reach it.

He turned at the sound of a woman's cry – a heavy white pedestal that reminded Dugan of a dentist's X-ray machine, toppled toward her. Oso appeared, barreling into the falling machine, its crane-like arm barely missing the woman scientist. It crashed against the ground, sending tiles flying.

The woman stood on shaky legs, supporting herself on Oso when a metal drawer flying through the air struck her in the face.

She went down, legs no longer shaking.

Oso caught sight of Dugan and with his lips pointed toward the child. Dugan nodded. He looked about for Morley but couldn't find him. The tranquilizer the poor woman had found could have been anywhere by now.

Fortunately there were other ways to knock someone unconscious.

Dugan leapt toward the second bed, grabbing hold of the railing. The earth rolled beneath him, his body momentarily rising in the air. A naked native woman missing both of her eyes collided into him as he hit the ground, her limp body slung halfway beneath the bed. Those sightless dark sockets seemed endless.

He wondered on what page of his book he'd find her.

He also wondered what Morley had done with her eyes.

Breaking his gaze from those black pits he rose, leaning heavily against the bed. He used the rail to make his way around, the end of this bed perpendicular to the child's. If the young native was aware of him, he didn't make it known.

As Dugan reached the end of the bed he noticed a capped syringe caught within the sheets.

The tranquilizer!

The rattle of a tray or nearby table being overturned caused him to duck. Instruments flew like shrapnel from a grenade, something slicing into his left calf. Other objects struck him in the back and shoulders, several whirling past. He braced himself for something heavy to find its way to him. It never came.

He opened his eyes and reached out to grab the syringe when the body of the male native lying in the bed jolted upright. Bloodshot eyes met Dugan's, mere inches away.

The thin native opened his mouth – sharp teeth that had been filed to pointy ends jutting forward, a line of spit hanging from the roof to the bottom of his mouth.

Dugan remembered this one.

With one flick of the thumb he uncapped the syringe and brought it up, plunging it deep into the native's neck. His eyes lost their focus and then his body fell back toward the bed.

Amidst the popping of glass and the sound of another cabinet crashing, Dugan barely registered the cough ripping from his throat.

Verse XXVI.

The screams of men, women, and children.

They often came to Remmy in his sleep, whether he had partaken of the forbidden fruit or not. And while he had finally shot himself full of that sweet yet damning nectar, he recognized that these cries weren't echoing in his head, but coming from the neighboring assembly hall.

Panic. Fear. Hopelessness.

Not the feelings one should ascribe to finding in a church.

He knelt beside the toilet in his quarters, his arms wrapped around the porcelain throne, as he listened to the destruction taking place. Loud thumps and clangs; pews sliding, crates from the storage room breaking, and – whether he wanted to admit it or not – the sound of bodies colliding. Falling. Breaking. And the wails that accompanied their shock and pain.

He cringed at the thought of children being tossed to and fro, like a ship with no rudder, on the waves of a sea.

An angry sea.

From an ancient and angry God.

It's my fault. I've failed you.

A shelf broke somewhere in his room, books clattering to the ground with the sound of a vase shattering.

Please, don't punish them for my mistakes!

The ground kicked; Remmy was thrown forward into the bowl, his forehead connecting with a solid thud. Water sloshed out as if children were inside, splashing and playing in the bowl.

Never again. I swear, I will forsake it all if you spare these people.

"Please …" Remmy croaked.

But he knew his words were in vain. What good were the promises of an addict to a god who had heard them a thousand times before?

Verse XXVII.

In the time it took for the section of assembly line to go from tilting to falling, Faye was able to draw in a single breath. Within that breath thousands upon thousands of regrets swarmed over her, a colossal infestation seeking to rip apart her mind. Black gnats, darker than night, tearing at memories and filling the gaping holes with their defecation of doubts.

She should never have come here, should never have broken Frantz' trust, should never have sought to do something so much bigger than herself.

Why had she thought she could change the world? and that that change would make her feel again? fill the black hole she forced herself to squirm out of every morning of every day?

And then the gnats tore deeper, their vociferous buzzing increasing in volume and strength.

She is a little girl again, brushing her teeth before bed, walking past her parents' room to tuck herself in. Her door, which always creeps closed, propped open with a pair of sparkly pink Keds shoes. The lights off in her parents' room. Dark downstairs. Six years old and home alone, but routine – there has never been time to be a child.

Then a startling noise from downstairs.

Glass. Breaking.

Faye, unsure whether to stay put or go investigate.

The silent collaboration of her dolls nestled on a shelf.

She has her father's spirit and her mother's lack of fear, the rustling from downstairs something new, something different. A puzzle to solve.

A flip of a switch and the hall lights come on.

Nothing there.

Her stuffed bunny with the disproportionately long arms and legs is held close but not because she is frightened.

Faye is never frightened.

She has to reach up to hold the wooden banister as she walks down the curved stairs, her fingertips fitting between the inlays of the bowed wood. Her bare feet are silent on the soft carpeted steps.

Through the living room to the back kitchen where the glass-paned French doors are missing a pane of glass.

She smiles, realizing how well that rhymes with "pain in the ass." The door is closed but unlocked.

The door is never unlocked.

Her smile flees, her heart thumping as fast as if she had finished a race and before she can turn around, a shadow swallows her.

A shadow in the shape of a man.

A large man.

For the first time in her young life she recognizes fear.

She is not alone.

She is so alone.

And there is no one there to save her.

She closes her eyes, the drowning drone of the gnats so loud she feels she might vomit, the poisonous warmth of the dark hands reaching out to take her when –

A body slammed into her from behind, driving her forward.

"Come on!"

Donavon!

She ran, almost tripping on the banner she still carried, the arm around her suddenly at her lower back. She was shoved, her feet leaving the ground, body propelled forward. Bracing herself, she hit, her elbows skidding across rough bits of bark and sawdust.

The towering line collapsed, hitting the ground with a tumultuous thud, more sawdust and dirt puffing from the ground in a thick cloud. It now looked like a roller coaster where part of the track had inexplicably collapsed, the jagged edge of the remaining line ending abruptly.

Faye scooted herself further beneath the remaining rail, her breath ragged. She wiped the water from her eyes – from the dust, not the memories. The buzzing, she realized, had come from the electrical lines that were now severed in so many places.

"Are you okay?" she asked. And then she realized the man next to her – the man who had saved her – was not Donavon.

Grey wiped blood from his eye, huddled beside her. "I'm, yeah, I'm … okay." He had a gash on his left eyebrow that continued to seep.

More equipment came crashing down further away in the building, the ground below them not finished with its quaking.

Grey glanced at the rickety legs they sat beneath, metal railings extending to the conveyor line above.

"We can't stay here," he said.

Faye tore off her shirt, buttons ripping open, and reached out, pressing it to Grey's swelling forehead. "You're bleeding badly."

She wore a white tank top beneath but it wasn't her figure Grey was staring at, it was her tattoo. More of the demon she carried with her at all times was now visible, wrestling down her right shoulder and continuing beneath her shirt. "It's just ink. It won't bite, I promise."

Grey breathed out a smile, putting his hands over hers for a moment as she let him take the shirt, applying pressure. He was looking at her as if studying her eyes, her face, her hair – so out of sorts at the moment.

As close as they were to each other it was easy for her to lean in and kiss him full on the lips. He sat up straighter but she broke the kiss before his eyes had adjusted to his shock.

"Thank you," she said. "You saved my life."

He nodded, struggling for words. "We're not out yet," he finally managed.

As if on cue, a low rumble sounded behind them, different from the throaty roar of the earth. Saws and blades came to life above in a deafening thrum, attached to the gaping mouth of the machine the assembly line fed into.

"No!"

Faye scrambled from beneath the legs, shielding her eyes with the banner from the wood chips which sprayed down at her. The last tree on the assembly line was being devoured by the machine above.

"No, no, no!"

A ripple in the earth spilled Faye forward, her feet giving out. She clung to the railing of the line she had stood upon only moments before. Tears made her vision blur.

They were failing. In epic proportion.

Something chugged above her and Faye was suddenly swept off her feet, the sensation not unlike being pulled from a boat on skis. She rose into the air, eyes wide, her side banging against the rail, knocking the breath from her.

Her banner – it was caught in the machine.

Spinning discs and blades several feet in diameter buzzed their death chant as the banner began to disintegrate between them. Faye heard Grey shouting but couldn't make out his words.

She released her grip on the pole but felt the polyvinyl fabric wrap around her hand, cinching it in, her arm almost pulled from its socket. Still she rose toward those grinning metallic teeth.

"I'm not afraid!" she shouted, ripping at the fabric with her other hand. Her whole body was raised high enough that she could see the pounding of metal teeth, the gnats back in her ears in the form of rotating blades.

At the last second the fabric tore free, releasing her from its grip. She fell, hitting again against the rail before tumbling to the ground on her back.

She laid there, the world breaking around her, waiting to see if her body would allow her to move. Above, shredded strings of red ribbon floated down like tufts of falling snow, the remnants of all she believed in, the death of innocence.

Like watching blood fall from the sky.

Verse XXVIII.

Dugan gripped the railing of the bed, his chest heaving harder than the ground around him. He felt like he was vomiting glass, vaguely aware of the wet chunks flying with every forceful cough. His throat, lungs and gut spasmed, seeking to expunge an entity that wasn't there.

Or that was everywhere.

Despite the burn in his larynx and his lightheadedness he pressed on, moving in front of the native child. To his surprise, the boy turned, looking directly at him.

His eyes were swallowed in white, as if his irises and pupils had been removed. The sutures from the scar on his stomach were broken open, fluid leaking like the trickle of gasoline from an already full tank.

Another coughing bout seized Dugan like a sneeze, taking the reins out from under him. It took everything he had just to continue holding on to the hospital bed.

White spots swam before his vision. He wasn't getting enough oxygen, every attempt to suck air back in met with an explosive assault.

In his peripheral, he saw the child turning his outstretched hands upward, palms facing out. The muscles in his twig arms looked ready to pop from his skin, as if he were holding a heavy weight, his hands shaking.

A large crack shot down the wall at the end of the walkway, dust and rock from the ceiling beginning to fall. Dugan felt like he was coughing up burning coals, flames licking upward from his insides.

This is hell, he thought, *and it's everything I deserve.*

He swung at the child with one arm, missing and nearly collapsing to the floor. Unable to straighten his body, he knelt at the bedside, the shreds of his throat coming up with each cough.

I'm coming, he thought. *I'm coming!*

He staggered to his feet, head bowed into the sheets where splotches of blood and mucus congealed in growing pools. He needed ... needed to ... quench ...

Dugan bit into his left hand, tearing through skin and muscle and lapping at the blood that sprung from the wound. He sucked, fighting back the compulsion to retch, until he was able to swallow a second, and third mouthful, the thick blood slowly coating his throat on its way down.

"I'm coming," Dugan said, his voice throaty and harsh. "And there's nothing you can do to stop me!"

This time when he swung, his whole body was behind it. His fist struck the child in the side of the head, his forward motion rocking the kid's neck and body to the side.

The chanting came to an abrupt halt.

Immediately the room settled, ground no longer shaking beneath them. The occasional thwump or clang of metal continued as heavy beds, workstations, and equipment, settled into their new placement.

Blake's fist burned where he had connected with the boy. He wasn't sure if he had ever hit anyone quite that hard and yet the child was still sitting, not yet unconscious.

Oso strode to the bed, overturning a chest of metal drawers in his path. He glanced uneasily around at the destruction that had taken place. Or maybe it was the sheer number of native bodies that now lay on top of, or buried beneath, odd equipment.

Dugan coughed into his arm, only vaguely aware of the blood dripping down the fingers of his left hand.

The child traced the scar on his belly with one finger, raising it up to look at the seepage. His eyes met Dugan's, no longer all white, dark pupils beading at their center.

"Inktomi," the child said calmly, barely more than a whisper. "Fehener Takushkansh'kan. La'a'ione."

With the words he sunk back to the bed, eyes still open but no longer seeing. His chest remained still, just another lifeless body amongst hundreds.

The crashing of equipment continued as men and women scrambled out from beneath machinery throughout the room. Dugan heard his name being called.

"What'd he say?"

Oso stared at the dead child in the bed with an eerie reverence.

"Oso? What'd he say? Something about the Shaman."

Oso broke his gaze with effort, reaching for the marker behind his ear which was gone. He brought out a pen from a pocket and began writing in his book, ripping the page free.

Cannot trust his words

"I still need to know what he said." Dugan lit a cigarette, holding the nicotine-filled smoke in his lungs as long as he dared. He dabbed the side of his hand against his vest, a splotch of blood remaining. "Fehener Takushkansh'kan, find the Shaman, right? What's the rest, Oso?"

Oso looked down before finally writing.

Not find

Found

"Found the Shaman?"

Laaione is Death

"Death found the Shaman. Or is it a threat? Our death if we find him?"

Maybe both

Dugan turned his head to the side, blowing out smoke. "He wants us to think he's dead. After all of this, seems a little pointless. What about Inktomi?"

A series of shouts caused Oso to whip his head around, his hair flicking into Dugan's face.

"I'll see to him," Dugan said. He left the native, moving toward the noise which had progressively gotten louder.

Two bays back he found Morley lying on the ground, a large ceramic basin crushing his lower half. Amongst the wreckage of cords and equipment that had toppled onto him, a native's body hung, face down yet arms extended toward him as if reaching.

"Ah, thank God," Morley said, flinging one of the arms of the native away. The arm only rolled back, fingers brushing at Morley's belly. "Get this thing off me!"

"What, the equipment or the native?"

Morley gave him a deadpan stare.

Dugan's eyes kept returning to the native's limp body until he finally realized what was wrong with it. From the angle he laid, Dugan had thought at first that the native's legs had been buried by debris as well. But not so. His torso had been cut clean in two.

He turned back to the scientist that he both revered and loathed, one of the few men he was frightened of. The man was a monster. A genius, sure, but one of the most dangerous men Dugan had ever met.

Not so different, are we, he thought, a trail of smoke spilling from his nostrils.

"I thought I told you ... no smoking."

Dugan smiled, despite himself. "D'you do that to the body or is that from this quake?"

"What do you think?" Morley said. Each time he tried to wiggle free from the weight atop him, the native's arm flopped back down. He swatted it away. "Come on, this hurts like a bitch! Think my hip's shattered ..."

"Oh, I'll help you, as soon as you tell me."

"I don't know!" Morley shouted. "His incision ... they're all a blur."

"Still think we're chasing shadows?"

"Damnit Dugan," Morley said, his face red with pain.

"Well, do you?"

The native's arm flopped back toward him. This time Morley let it stay. "Look, Dugan, if your man did this? God help us if you actually do find him."

Verse XXIX.

Although the ground had stopped shaking, Grey took every step with a measure of caution. He felt like he did after riding one of those flat moving escalators at the airport and then stepping off onto normal ground – the surprise at having to lift your feet in order to move.

Standing at the roll-up door of the building he had come from, he surveyed the lumber yard. He wasn't sure if he had ever seen this scale of destruction.

Dust and smoke still swarmed up from the ground like an early morning fog. The tower that had been spraying sawdust had toppled, its bent metal scraps like a giant's carcass splayed out on the ground.

Cranes had overturned, their loads either falling or rolling free from the standing stacks of uncut logs near the front. Tree trunks had collapsed onto buildings, crushing vehicles and laborers alike. A fire burned in the distance, visible flames no incinerator held contained.

He wondered if this was what it felt like walking the streets after a war. An almost out of body experience. The corpses lying around you nothing but decoration, like props on a movie set.

Voices yelling, screaming, in distress, were heard but unregistered, as if he had buried himself beneath a body of water; all of the noise and chaos taking place above might as well have been in another realm.

Laborers roamed the grounds like zombies, staggering directionless. A woman, leaning heavily against another man, paused briefly, turning to look back at Grey. Half of her head was caved in. Her skull looked like a pumpkin that was rotting from the inside, her forehead dimpling inward. One of her eyes, he realized had turned blood red. Despite everything he had seen today, he couldn't stop from staring.

Grey felt something grip his insides. And then he vomited.

He stumbled past the pile of puke, noting the woman and man had continued on. Then he caught sight of Donavon moving toward him. He had one arm wrapped around Sir William's shoulder, his other held close to his chest as if injured. A gash ran down his cheek that looked more like makeup than the real thing. Add in his limp and he looked just like a warrior strolling out from a battle he should never have survived.

All that was lacking was the triumphant background music.

Grey reached up and wiped at the blood on his own eyebrow with Faye's shirt. His whole left eye was stuck closed, sticky with the gore. But unlike Donavon he probably looked like an injured imbecile.

Sir William gave him a sweeping grin, his suit now covered in a thick film of dust.

"That was incredible," he shouted with a hoot. "Utterly incredible! Imagine the headlines – *Mother Nature Strikes Back*! *The Earth Avenges it's, uh, Whatever*! It's bloody brilliant. Theatrics, pyrotechnics, the world is going to love it."

As they drew closer the lanky Englishman wrinkled his face, squinting at Grey. "Your head is bleeding, chap."

Grey brought the beige, crumpled shirt up – now more black than beige – and pressed it hard against his head.

"Have you seen Faye?" Donavon asked.

Grey managed to nod and pointed over his shoulder. "Inside. She's fine," he said, but Donavon had already moved past. *Your welcome*, he wanted to add.

Thinking of Faye made his heart beat faster. He felt a flutter in his gut and wondered if he was going to vomit again but no, this wasn't that kind of anxiety. He pictured her tearing her shirt open and ripping it off without a second's thought; the way she had moved into him – deliberately. In control. And God, that kiss.

Once the earthquake had finally ceased, Grey offered her his hand to help her up but she refused, brushing him off. As if the moment they shared had already been forgotten.

"Where's your camera?" she had asked.

He didn't know.

"You mean you missed all of this? Me almost dying!"

"I was too busy saving your life!"

It's what he should have said. What he would have, if he hadn't been so confused by the complete reversal of her attitude towards him. Even now he felt his anger and desire mix together, a slew of emotions he could no more control than the ground that had been shaking mere moments ago.

He had to be careful.

He supposed they all did.

"What about the others?" Grey asked. "Malcolm? Kenny?"

"The, uh, larger fellow made it beneath a cab and chassis; seemed to be alright. I never saw the Asian, thought he stayed behind with you," Sir William said.

Grey pushed past the old man, searching in the debris filled yard. He counted six bodies before seeing Kenny wriggling out from between two giant wheels. The loader he had huddled beneath seemed to be intact.

Kenny spotted him and shouted, "Dude!"

"You seen Malcolm?" Grey asked.

Kenny scrambled out only to fall back to the earth, tripping over a dislodged sheet of metal. He got back to his feet. "Dude I got it! The money shot!"

"What are you talking about?"

Kenny held up his camera triumphantly like a trophy. "Donavon! He totally saved some dude's life – came out of nowhere and caught this tumbling block. I got it all on tape!"

Of course you did, Grey thought, knowing no one had filmed him risking his life for Faye. Would she even tell them? Probably not.

"He looked hurt," Grey said.

"He's gonna be a hero after this! Hold on, I wanna shoot some of the wreckage." Kenny brought his camera up to his shoulder then paused. "What happened to your camera?"

"Long story. Did you see Malcolm?"

"Nah, man, I was just hauling ass, you know."

Grey nodded, circling back through the yard. The intern couldn't have gone far; Grey just prayed it wasn't his body lying beneath one of the scattered logs or twisting metal rails.

He passed two Venezuelan workers who shied away from him as if he were the one who caused the damage. Others ignored him, heading toward the front gate, seeking escape rather than to help their fallen brethren.

Grey headed back to the building he had left, Sir William still standing sentry at the front. "Lord I need a drink," the old man said beneath his breath. "And you need a bath."

Grey ignored him, reentering the labyrinthine maze of fallen scaffolding and collapsed machinery. He stayed hidden as he spotted Faye huddled in Donavon's arms. The movie star kept his left arm back, holding it away from her protectively.

"And he caught it on camera?" Faye asked. "You're sure?"

"Yeah, he caught the whole thing."

"Oh, thank God!" Faye grabbed his face with both hands and kissed him. "This is perfect!"

Grey suddenly felt the urge to vomit again.

Or break something.

Or someone.

"We should leak some of the footage immediately rather than holding it for the documentary," Donavon said.

"You may be right. I've got to check with Frantz first, we may want to coordinate ..."

Grey left them, wandering further into the building.

That kiss.

The taste of puke on his breath.

When he found Malcolm, he recognized him not by his face but by the clothing he wore – his long striped basketball shorts and Adidas shirt, his neon blue tennis shoes. Where Malcolm's head should have been, however, was nothing but the pulp of a grape that had been squished. Caught beneath a log or rail that had since rolled off, his brains and skull had splattered in a crest extending out from the bulk of his chest that hadn't been flattened.

It was the first time Grey could remember thinking how grateful he was he didn't have a camera. Still, he knew this image would be forever engrained in his mind.

He kicked a piece of timber out of the way and sat beside the body trying to remember how to breathe.

None of them had signed up for this, to risk their lives for a cause. It was just a paycheck, a way to pay the bills while that low-budget film project they were all working on – because what videographer didn't have a project they were secretly working on – got a little closer to being ready.

He reached out and touched Malcolm's outstretched hand, his arm undamaged. He was surprised and disturbed to find it still warm.

"Oh, man, I'm sorry," Grey whispered. "So sorry."

Sorry he had chosen the wrong person to save.

To look out for.

But who was looking out for him? For any of them? Certainly not Faye. And if she remained in charge, how many more of them would end up dead?

"I'll tell your parents. Tell 'em what a bunch of assholes they were for not understanding ..." Grey picked up a thick bolt lying at his feet and threw it against the crumpled rails nearby. It twanged loudly, a deep resonant sound. "But maybe they were right, you know. You should have stayed in school, should have realized this dream was just that – an impossible wish. Everyone wants to be famous until they are and then, well, they just want to take it back. Like you. Now you're famous. Or you will be; I'll make sure of that. It's just – no one ever tells you what it's going to cost, you know. And I think it costs everything. Everything we have.

"I don't want to be famous. And I shouldn't have to be, to be treated with … respect."

Just like the metallic twang still vibrating, Grey felt an inner note inside him thrum to life. A dissonant chord, struck with distortion and rage, only this note grew louder with every passing second until even thinking was an impossibility.

Only one thought remained in its wake, pressing through the pounding in his skull and the beating of his heart.

Someone has to pay.

End of Chapter One

"In a time of destruction, create something."

--Maxine Hong Kingston

> "And God said, Let there be a firmament ... And God called the
> firmament Heaven."
> *Genesis Chapter 1, Verses 6-8*

AXIS MUNDI

Chapter Two

Verse I.

In Defense of "Pre-Shocks" – Crisis in Venezuela
– *Associated Press*

Just days after the first earthquake in recorded history in the Canaima
National Park, located in Southeastern Venezuela, a second quake struck,
decimating the region. The U.S. Geological Survey says the magnitude
8.8 tremor struck at precisely 8:43 in the morning, local time (UST).

"This really is unprecedented," said Dr. Skip Krocher, director of the
USGS Earthquake Science Center. "We expect aftershocks to follow an
earthquake, not precede it. The fact that something of this magnitude
could take place within a week of the former event; well, it just shows
how little our understanding is when it comes to seismology."

Effects of the quake were felt as far as Boa Vista, Brazil, an estimated
two-hundred-and-twenty-four miles from the epicenter of the quake.
Government officials have asked for support from foreign countries,
though President Maduro has made it clear they will not accept help
from the United States.

All satellite activity and communication near the quake have been
disrupted, preventing both imagery and communication with the
immediate surrounding towns in the area. Spectacular rumors abound,
from the region becoming a new magnetized pole to a testing ground for
experimental weaponry.

The USGS says they expect hundreds of aftershocks to occur in the next
several days, though of much smaller magnitude.

Verse II.

There is a quiet beauty to destruction, a serenity that takes place after the tumult. When the crossbeams and mortar of fallen houses have settled, furniture and cherished keepsakes sinking within a petrified wave of debris; when the howls and shrieks of parched throats have silenced, pandemonium replaced with dull acceptance; when a warm breeze tosses scattered relics against a cold arm ending in block and rubble, loose papers fluttering while the arm is not.

All that man has made, all he has accomplished, and yet how little he has learned.

Guayanata stood amongst giant sentries. Their army of leaves dangling from heavy boughs swayed today just as they had yesterday, before the earth quaked. Nature acknowledges destruction only in the moment of its passing.

His wrists were pink and tender, the deep gashes worn from yesterday's escape already healed. Like the kapok or fig tree, he too had already forgotten, pain becoming a distant whisper of leaves blowing in the wind.

What he had not forgotten, indeed, could not forget, was the man known as the Spider.

Inktomi.

The white devil.

His calloused web still clung to Guayanata.

He felt it in his blood, moving through his veins, in the slowness of his thoughts. There were no marks where the Spider's darts had sunk into his flesh, but its poison took time to disperse. Soon it would be but a slippery dream one cannot grasp upon awakening, and then Guayanata would return. Return to crush the Spider. And protect what he had sworn to protect.

What they had all sworn.

A pair of red macaws with yellow and blue tipped feathers darted from a branch, frightening another dozen smaller birds. They disappeared in the hanging guaco vines.

So skittish. As if they were afraid.

Of him?

He was one with Nature; they could no more fear him than the branches on which they settled. But Guayanata recognized he too was afraid.

He collected the warm sap from the base of the chicle tree, where his small gash in the bark was visible. Rolling it in his hands, he moved quickly through the jungle growth, a shadow travelling in darkness. In the trees, in the plants, in the dirt beneath his bare feet, he felt his world tremble and quake.

Not as before.

This was not a physical tremor, nor was the earth quaking. It was the trembling of a child before the raised hand of an elder. Knowing punishment was just and must be delivered. Or unjust, yet a rite of passage from child to something more.

The quivering of fear.

Nature didn't care for what had already passed, but it trembled before what was coming. Yes, there was a quiet beauty to destruction, but when Nature contemplates its own mortality even men who do not fear begin to tremble with it.

Verse III.

A thin layer of dirt and dust, displaced only by the tread of panicked footfalls, covered the concrete flooring. A few fallen tiles from the ceiling, an overturned plate of spaghetti, meat sauce slowly inching down a corridor wall. Here, a woman's loafer; a sheaf of papers, like an incomplete collage, trampled and spread across several sections of hall space.

In other parts of the Facility, entire wings had collapsed from the earthquake, steel beams and plaster burying lab equipment, terminals, and the occasional unsuspecting worker. Most of the colossal structure had fared better than the underground graveyard where the epicenter of the quake had begun, that epicenter coming in the form of a possessed native child.

James Dugan continued through the empty corridors barely listening to Zephyr's report of damage. His left hand throbbed from where he had bitten into his own flesh, a thick bandage slapped over the wound. His right knuckles ached, in turn, from striking the young boy in the Freezer. Yet they were small prices to pay for putting an end to the perverse earthquake.

While signs of upheaval were everywhere, they were fortunate the underlying structure of the Facility hadn't been constructed under Venezuelan standards.

Dugan wondered how the town of Santa Elena had fared.

Oso silently tromped along beside them, Zephyr continuing his report. The carport and garage were intact but their helicopter had apparently seen its last flight. A dislodged block of concrete from the outer barracks had buried itself within the copter's hull.

What a mess, Dugan thought. It would take weeks to get back to some semblance of normalcy though, he supposed, the inspection would likely be postponed. At the moment, however, that seemed the least of his concerns.

Only he and a handful of individuals knew the true source of the earthquake, or that it had been brought about by very *unnatural* causes. Which meant there was a reason for it happening now.

Fehener Takushkansh'kan. La'a'ione.

The last words of the dying native child.

Death finds the Shaman; Finding the Shaman brings death.

Whatever the message, it was clear the Shaman intended to slow them down. Which only made Dugan more determined to catch him.

They approached an intersecting hallway. A large circular mirror in the corner revealed not another soul in transit. Most of the scientists and workers had been corralled in the gymnasium, open tennis and basketball courts providing plenty of space. Search parties had been sent out for anyone missing from the staff roster.

As for Dugan and his team, they had their own search to conduct.

Zephyr continued, "Eighteen in the infirmary. Most injuries were minor; a few concussions, only one consigned to a wheelchair who shouldn't have already been in one ..."

Dugan smiled at that. Everyone knew there was no love lost between Dr. Morley and Zephyr.

"... two deceased, a Brittney Cass and a Samuel A. Wells ..."

"You'll –"

"Here are their names," Zephyr said, holding up a sheet of paper. "Cass didn't know what hit her; her body was found in the freezer."

Dugan remembered the metal drawer flying through the air, striking the woman scientist in the face.

"Wells passed about an hour ago; internal bleeding."

Dugan grabbed the folded sheet from Zephyr. He pulled out his leather bound journal, placing the paper inside, then tucked it back into the inner pocket of his vest.

"Could have been a lot worse," Zephyr said.

"Nothing is worse than having your enemy catch you by surprise. I've underestimated him."

"No one can predict an earthquake."

"That was no ordinary earthquake."

Dugan was aware of the doubts many of his men carried regarding the supposed native they sought. A man who, if alive, was past his two hundredth year. Who communed with spirits, living off the land and purportedly walking between two realms. A man who had chosen one clan over another, abandoning the Pemoni tribe while granting supernatural healing abilities to the Makuxi.

Rumors circulated like the chaff brought in from a wind-swept storm. Not everything they heard was true, but there were whispers of truth within each story, hints that led them closer to an understanding of the man that would change the world.

Takushkansh'kan. The Shaman.

But if Dugan had underestimated this shadow of a man they were pursuing, he took comfort in knowing the Shaman had also underestimated him.

"Make sure I have the names of any others they find," Dugan said, knowing these two wouldn't be the only casualties.

"What about the people who died in town?" Zephyr asked. "You wanna add their names? In fact, I heard a local lumberjack died the other day when a log fell from a loader. Want me to track his name down?"

Dugan stopped walking. "You have a problem with the way I run business?"

Zephyr remained silent; Oso, of course, couldn't speak.

"You think my book's, what – a waste of time? Proof of my senility? Or the overwhelming burden of my own conscience?"

"Forget it – it doesn't matter."

"No, I want to hear. Go ahead, tell me."

"That book makes you look weak. Memorializing every man, woman and child who get in our way? It's like putting up a plaque of each pig you kill in a slaughterhouse. No one cares. No one will remember them. People are only concerned that the bacon is crisp and the sausage is fatty on their plates come Sunday morning. You can't pretend it'll be any different with what we're doing. No one will care what it cost to produce the miracle drug you'll bring them. They'll just want to know where they can get in line. So put the damn book away Dugan, before somebody uses it against you."

Dugan stepped up to Zephyr, looking up into the black man's eyes. Zephyr was only a few inches taller but probably had Dugan beat by a good hundred pounds, every ounce of it muscle. But Dugan had never been one for intimidation.

"Let's get one thing clear. This book – these names? They're sacred, but not for the reason you think they are. See I know you, Zephyr. Michael Gillian Brown. And just because you don't have a conscience, don't assume it's a weakness to those of us who do. Some of the greatest men in history accomplished what they did not because they were great, not because they were psychotic, but because they had to. Because there was no one else to do what they knew they could. But these people deserve to be remembered. Not because they gave their lives for a cause; any asshole in a uniform can do that. But because they weren't given the choice. See, we made it for them. Determined that their life wasn't greater than the thousands of lives that could be saved. The millions that could be healed.

"So no, Zephyr, this book – it's not for me. I accept the loss of every one of these names, and I won't hesitate to add however many more to this list we need to add – even yours if I have to. But I'll be damned if all those who benefit don't even know the names of those who lost their lives. Don't even know they existed. That's why this book is so important. To remember. That a miracle always has its cost."

"You're more insane than Morley, you just don't know it."

In a single motion Dugan snatched his notebook from the inner pocket of his vest and brought it up against Zephyr's neck. "That could've been a knife."

Even his men forgot how quick he was on the draw. Sometimes it was good to remind them.

"Are we through?" Zephyr asked. "Or are you going to try and papercut me to death?"

Dugan slid the notebook back into his pocket, stepping away. "We're all just a name away from ending up on the pages of someone's book."

"That a threat?"

"Just a reality. At least those in my book will be remembered."

"You can put your toys away," Zephyr said.

Oso slid both of his blades back into sheaths, the dark metal disappearing in leather folds. The man had Dugan's back even when Dugan didn't know he needed it.

Both Zephyr and Dugan's walkie-talkies suddenly squawked in unison. Dugan unclipped the portable device, his words coming back in stereo through Zephyr's unit until the man dialed his off.

"Dugan, we're heading to control. Go," he said.

"Cy, there's no need," came the voice on the other end. "We've got the coordinates for the Snipe. At least where he last was. Trace has worn off. Go."

"Copy," Dugan said. "Map the Snipe's last location and get the boyscouts ready. Full uniforms, neckerchiefs and all. Go."

"Copy," Cy said, the transmitter going silent.

"I thought Stanton said no more deep sea excursions," Zephyr said.

Dugan began walking, ignoring the man's attempt at levity.

After a moment, Zephyr said, "I just don't want to see you fail."

"It's okay, Zephyr. No apology necessary."

"I wasn't apologizing."

"What are your thoughts, Oso?" Dugan asked. "Think this could be a trap?"

The native whipped out his pen, writing quickly on his notepad without missing a step.

Too soon

"I agree. He expects this earthquake to slow us down, which is why we hit him now, before he has a chance to catch his breath. But just in case? Tell the men we're no longer collecting samples."

Zephyr glanced at Dugan, looking him up and down. "You want us to leave the tranqs behind?"

"I want the Shaman to feel pain – real pain – and if that means butchering his people, so be it. We're going to fill some empty pages today. Find out what these bastards can't heal from."

For the first time that morning a smile broke across Zephyr's face.

Verse IV.

Faye Moanna sat at the bottom of the winding staircase lacing up her boots, a double knot for each of them. She wore her pink running sweatshirt over her shorts and grey tank top, a loose fitting cover that provided more protection from the sun than cold. She hoped it wouldn't raise too many questions.

Sir William's bungalow – Faye didn't think of it as a house – had fortunately been intact after the earthquake, at least structurally. The British astronomer's toys had not been so fortunate. Glass had littered the auditorium upstairs when they had returned, telescopes and equipment lying in shattered pieces on the floor.

"See what happens when I leave Spree to himself for a day?" Sir William had said. While his pet monkey certainly hadn't caused all the damage, Faye was pretty certain he had helped.

They assisted in cleaning, salvaging what they could. Both Grey and Kenny had taken to the computer equipment and network system Sir William had rigged to project the stars onto the ceiling in his atrium. Despite several hours, they weren't able to get it working. Quite the loss, considering only Donavon and her had seen the masterpiece of their host's efforts the previous day.

Sir William did take the time to let the two techies peer through one of the unbroken telescopes, a cylinder almost as large as a cannon mounted to the auditorium floor. Strangely, it wasn't until after showing them the stars that Sir William really became rattled. Faye didn't fully understand, but something had clearly bothered him last night that had nothing to do with broken equipment.

The front door opened, Sir William entering with a half dozen chicken eggs cradled in his arm. The monkey leapt from his shoulder, bounding across furniture in the room. "Ah, you're up early! I was out sequestering our breakfast."

"Thank you but I'm not hungry." Faye began to stretch, lifting one leg onto a raised stair. "I'm sure the others will be delighted."

Sir William harrumphed, moving past her and into the small kitchen, opening cupboards seemingly at random. Pots and pans clanged wildly. Spree clambered up onto the counter, overturning a tumbler with an ounce of amber liquid at the bottom, lapping it up.

"Thank you again for your hospitality. I don't know what we would have done without you."

"The pleasure has been all mine."

Another cupboard slammed, Sir William rising with a blackened frying pan. "Butter, butter …" he said, lifting odds and ends on his cluttered countertops.

"In the fridge. I moved it there last night."

He opened the fridge, one finger tracing lines in the air as he searched each shelf.

"Behind the Ketchup. Sorry," Faye said. "Force of habit."

In truth habit had nothing to do with it. The tiny cockroaches that fled every time an object was adjusted in the kitchen had been all the convincing Faye needed.

She glanced up the staircase to make sure no one was on their way down. Sir William had given Donavon some pills for his wrist which had knocked him out so hard he had actually snored last night. The footage Kenny had captured of the movie star deflecting a falling beam at the lumber mill was going to play extremely well. Donavon had saved one of the millworker's lives despite the fact that they had been there to shut the mill down. No one would be able to dispute the footage, and the amount of PR it would create not only for their foundation, but every other eco-conscious group out there, would be enough to justify any costs of their last minute diversion to Venezuela.

She couldn't wait for Frantz to see it.

"At the lumber mill yesterday one of the men mentioned a man. A James Dugan? I think I asked you about him before, but I sensed you might know him?"

"Ah, damn!"

Sir William pulled one hand back sharply as butter sizzled on the pan. "Like I told you, darling, I know the name of the two barkeeps at the tavern and that's pretty much it. And often I even forget their names."

"Just seems like you would hear about another foreigner living here. With your contacts in the state? The man I'm looking for, he makes waves everywhere he goes."

Sir William stared at her with his weepy and bloodshot eyes. "You accomplished what you came for, yes? The destruction of the mill? You should be celebrating, not moping about like a spoiled child who wants the red *and* blue balloon."

"The way I was raised, having a single objective was seen as poor foresight."

"Were you an army brat?"

"Might as well have been. Where would someone stay if they didn't live in town?"

Sir William poured what looked like yellow flour out of a paper carton onto the pan. "Did you know I didn't recognize one star in the sky last night? Not one!"

Spree pounced on a tiny cockroach, a spoon and stack of magazines spilling from the counter to the floor. The monkey lifted one paw, surprised that the beetle had escaped.

"A master conversationalist is someone who can change the topic without anyone taking notice. But Sir William, forgive me for saying so, it's hard not to notice."

"Well then, speaking of stars, is our action hero feeling any better this morning? I'm making a special breakfast; I'd hate for him to miss out on my home-made cachapas."

"Sounds like a disease," a man's voice said.

"Well if it is, it's certainly contagious – believe me, you'll love them," Sir William said.

Faye pulled her foot from the stairwell as Grey sauntered down. He wore his black pajama bottoms and nothing else, the tuft of hair on his chest hiding a quiet definition beneath. A butterfly bandage was wrapped tightly over his left eyebrow, covering the gash from whatever had struck him during the earthquake.

"Morning," he said, walking past Faye, not even meeting her eyes.

It had been a mistake to kiss him.

She still had more questions for their host but they would have to wait. "I'm running into town, be back in a bit," she said, squeezing past a wooden rocking chair and moving toward the door.

"What's in town?" Grey asked. He sat at the bar, spinning a glass tumbler with one finger.

"I'm just ... I wanna find the pilot, make sure everything's ready to go."

Grey spun on his stool, finally looking at her. "I thought you said you spoke with him yesterday. After we left. What might have changed between now and then?"

"Nothing."

"She's, uh, helping me with something," Sir William interjected. "A little errand."

Grey turned back around, pounding his fist lightly against the deflated counter. "You know we won't be able to use any of the footage. Not with what happened."

His words caught her by surprise, stopping her in front of the door.

"What do you mean? It's not like we have much from the earthquake and what little footage we do, we need."

"I'm not going to use Malcolm's death as a marketing ploy," Grey answered.

Faye felt her face flush. So much planning had gone into the coordination of that day, lumber mills being shut down all across the world. It was no one's fault that an earthquake happened to strike while they were there, that the intern had been unable to escape the resulting ruin.

You wouldn't have escaped yourself without Grey's help. Maybe she needed to go a little easy on him.

"You don't own the rights of the footage you've recorded. This entire trip was funded by Frantz and Regener-Nation, including your cameras, film, equipment; the list goes on and on, so let me remind you – it's not your choice!"

So much for going easy.

"Yeah, we'll see." Grey sniffed at the air, turning back to the kitchen. "It's burning, old man."

Sir William jumped, having been too caught up in their conversation. He cursed, batting at the flames now rising from the pan. Faye used the distraction to open the door and step outside.

It took every effort not to slam it behind her.

A wave of heat hit that made her stomach roll. Or maybe it was just the smell of burning cachapas. Still, she felt so angry at the audacity of Grey. It was like he blamed her for what happened, for Malcolm's death.

He's not angry over that; he's angry over you.

The way he had looked at her when she had stripped off her button-up to place it against his bleeding brow. When she had kissed him – so lightly – to thank him for saving her. Did he really think a moment of panic and a kneejerk reaction entitled him to more?

Probably, she realized.

She accepted that she wouldn't have kissed him if she hadn't wanted to. In the moment, it had felt right.

It was just a kiss. God, are we in grade school?

The door suddenly opened behind her, a figure stepping through. "I'm coming with you," Grey said.

"I don't need you." Faye was in no mood for this show of machismo.

"I don't think you need anyone, but I also prefer not adding to our body count," Grey said. "These townspeople think we're responsible for the earthquake, Faye. They blame us, like we brought some American curse down on them. You know they're superstitious, and with all they've been through that makes them dangerous."

"Look, I appreciate the fact that you saved my life yesterday, I really do. But I'm a big girl and I can take care of myself."

"What is so important that you go marching back into town for?"

"It's not your concern! Go eat your breakfast and have everyone pack up."

"Malcolm is dead, Faye. His parents, his girlfriend; hell, his hairdresser – not a single person back home even has a clue! And instead of trying to do something about it, you go marching off on some other crusade that's gonna put all our lives in jeopardy again!"

Faye shook her head. "I've tried reaching Frantz – not even the sat-phone's working! Maybe that's why I'm going into town, you ever think of that?"

"Maybe," Grey said. "But it's not, is it."

Faye looked away.

"You don't give a shit about anyone but yourself and that's okay. I get it. It's … who you are. But don't lie to me about why we're really here. You at least owe me that."

Faye watched two black and yellow birds dart from tree to tree beyond Sir William's estate in an exaggerated game of chase. "My whole life I've tried to make a difference. Accomplish something – I don't know – beyond myself. It's not a popular path. Half the time I end up destroying something, or someone, I care about in order to accomplish something better. But it still hurts." Faye rubbed her hand against the shaved side of her scalp.

"So saving the world isn't easy, huh?" Grey said, causing Faye to smile.

It felt good, that smile.

"I guess what I'm trying to say is that I'm doing what I feel is right. I won't put anyone's life at risk but some things are out of our control. I get you're angry about Malcolm, but there's no one to blame! If anything be angry with God. If you believe in that sort of thing."

"I don't know what I believe," Grey said.

"If what I'm doing is more important than the cause I've dedicated the last five years of my life to, you know it's something big. We can make a difference here. If you only knew."

"So tell me!"

"I can't," Faye said.

"Whoever you're looking for knows – maybe not that you're here, but that people want to find him. I didn't have a chance to tell you, but that's why we were arrested. Not because we're American, because people heard you were asking around."

A surge coursed through Faye, her weariness disappearing. She placed her hands inside the front pocket of her light sweatshirt, fingering the eleven-ounce Beretta inside. It's cold steel so alien to her touch. At only eighteen millimeters wide, it had been small enough for her to pack inside one of the camera bags, equipment they had been given clearance not to run through scanners.

Two .380 caliber bullets were loaded into its steel chamber. All it could hold; one more than she would need.

"Do you see why I'm concerned? Not for you," Grey added, almost too quickly, "but for us. Your actions affect us all."

"Everything will work out fine."

It was Grey's turn to look away, staring off into the landscape around them. He shook his head. From within the house there was a loud crash followed by a screech. Sir William, yelling, "Spree!"

"I'm gonna change, but don't leave without me."

"You're not going to try and stop me?"

"If helping you means we get out of this godforsaken country faster, then okay, I'll help. But you've got to let me help and that starts by telling me the truth."

Faye nodded. She could tell him, at least most of the truth. But no one could know her real motive for being here, the driving force that had guided her more persistently than anything in her life. The desire to look her father, the man whom she hadn't seen in fifteen years, in the eyes.

Eyes that were no longer seeing.

"Come if you like. Just don't get in my way."

Verse V.

The trees beyond the river barely rustled with the breeze, their limbs and vines, branches, even leaves, carrying a weight to them which seemed to hold the wind at bay. They were like the tepuis – immovable. Permanent. Indestructible to all but the human hands that would one day ravage as far as this remote part of the jungle in exchange for a few pieces of lumber and a multi-million dollar contract.

Dugan stood at the bank of the Icabarú river, studying the foliage beyond with a cigarette in hand. Chupa laughed behind him at something one of the men said, the noise blending in with the cries of birds and chitter of spider monkeys.

The bridge here was collapsed, whether from the earthquake or sabotaged by natives he wasn't sure. In truth, Dugan believed it was one and the same. The Humvees were more than capable of passing through the river, its depths typically less than six feet, but these days were feeling less and less typical.

"What do you think?" He asked, without looking away from the opposite side of the river.

Oso, of course, couldn't vocalize his answer, but he also didn't write one. Maybe he sensed Dugan's question had been rhetorical; the native had been the one, after all, to stop the vehicle and get out, observing quietly their surroundings. Oso had a strange intuition that Dugan had learned to trust and right now the native's apprehension was making him nervous.

Kendall approached, stretching his arms wide and groaning loudly. Dressed in his camos, he was only missing a beige hardhat to complete what would surely be a Ken doll safari outfit. Though Dugan doubted Mattel outfitted their dolls with fully automatic rifles.

Further down, where debris from the bridge had gathered in the water, the Kid was taking a leak into the river. A few of the others had gathered nearby.

"Should we pull out the picnic blankets?" Kendall asked, swatting at a mosquito on his arm. "Or you want us to build a rowboat?"

Dugan ignored him, glancing again at his handheld GPS coordinator. They were less than two miles from where the native Guayanata had fled; no wonder the men were antsy.

A sharp scream sounded, Dugan following the noise.

The Kid toppled into the water with a huge splash, Rojo and Chupa laughing at the river's edge. The black Somalian handed Rojo a joint. Weed was like candy down here. Not that much different from where things were going in the States, from what Dugan had heard.

The Kid came up, slapping water at the two of them. "Come on, man, my dick was still in my hand!"

"It's always in your hand," Rojo said, to more laughter.

Kendall left to join the others, shouting something Dugan chose to ignore. His attention fell back to the river. It was a dark turquoise, greener at the shores with moss and growth. Giant Amazon water lilies, Victoria amazonica, stretched across the river just north of them; deceptive stepping stones, each up to four meters in length. Thick vines passed in the currents, though they might have been snakes. They were in anaconda country.

The men roared with laughter. Dugan started toward them.

"I think the Kid just earned his name!" one of them shouted.

"That ain't funny," the Kid yelled, pulling himself up the shore.

"Leech! Leech! Leech!" the men shouted in uncoordinated unison.

The Kid was covered in them, black masses like tumors sticking to his flesh. He ripped one from his forearm, blood squirting out with its suction-like release.

"You want, we can help," Chupa said. "With these." He flipped open a large serrated steel blade.

"Oso's a whiz at slicing away skinny little leeches," one of them said.

"Especially white ones."

The Kid yanked another leech from his stomach with a sickening squelch. The skin beneath it looked like it had been covered in ointment, oozing a thick viscous fluid with trails of blood.

"What you get for dressing like a —"

Dugan raised his Glock and fired into the air, silencing the group. The jungle seemed to hold its breath, animals and birds silenced, if only for a moment.

The men parted for him as he stepped in front of the Kid. His busted lip and black eye from where Zephyr had hit him the previous day truly made him look like a hick.

Dugan held his cigarette out and pressed its tip into the fat body of a slug on the Kid's neck. There was a sizzle and then the leech dropped off, the Kid brushing at it on its way down.

"I want to thank each of you personally for guaranteeing this operation is a bust. I think the Pemoni's in Brazil are aware of our location thanks to your debacle."

The men looked like school children being scolded by their teacher. Some avoided eye contact, others shrinking at his words.

"It wasn't my ..." The Kid cut off, the tip of Dugan's Glock pressing against his temple.

"It's always your fault. I don't employ people who can't accept responsibility."

The Kid nodded, his Adam's apple bobbing in his long neck. "Sorry, Dugan. My bad; won't happen again."

Dugan lowered his pistol. "See that it doesn't. Leech."

Around him, the men smiled. Rojo passed the joint to their newest member, even Cy coming up and slugging Leech on the arm.

"Welcome to the club," he said.

Dugan started toward the water's edge. "Leave the vehicles. Bring what you can carry." He sat at the ridged bank and began unlacing his boots.

The men immediately fell into action, not a single one questioning why. Leeches or no leeches, they would follow him.

Oso waded into the river not needing to unlace shoes; the soles of his bare feet were as thick as a leather hide. He raised his belt with several long knives over his head to keep from getting wet, as well as a black AK74. Dugan recognized Oso's notepad as well, nestled in his raised palm.

Chupa dove into the water behind him with a small splash, his twin Sigs held high above him. "Maybe those leeches only like little white skinny kids."

Halfway across, Oso suddenly wrestled in the water almost dipping completely beneath. He came up, eyes wide, holding one hand outstretched toward them.

Stop.

Chupa slowed, water settling around him. Cy, who had now waded in to his knees, also halted. Oso continued to press his hand out toward them, the ends of his belt dipping into the water. His long black hair flowed around him like a wilting wreath.

The native tossed his belt and gun to the other side, knives scattering on the shore then dove beneath the murky water. After a moment he came back up, his eyes following the length of the river. He continued across lengthwise, raising his hand behind him every so often to tell them to wait.

The clack of a round being racked into a barrel sounded beside Dugan. Zephyr held an SRM Gen2 tactical shotgun pointed at the ground, one of the only shotguns capable of accurately firing over two hundred yards. With its detachable magazine holding sixteen rounds, it was a formidable weapon. His Vektor assault rifle was slung around his back.

Zephyr's narrow eyes tracked Oso's every move. "Just in case," he said.

"He's one of us," Dugan whispered.

"You're the one who sensed a trap," Zephyr replied.

The air felt electric, thrumming with the anticipation of action, the men feeding off that energy like the mosquitos swarming around them. Not even Kendall slapped at them now.

Oso arrived on the far side of the shore and staggered up. He flung his neck to the side, his long hair whipping after it, then began to pull off his vest. Leeches clung to his thick limbs but he seemed not to notice.

"Oso?" Dugan called. "What is it?"

The bulky native leaned against a thin tree trunk, extending his leg and lifting his foot for them to see.

A long gash ran across the bottom of his foot, blood seeping out and dripping from his heel.

"That it?" Chupa said, starting forward again.

Oso's hand came up again in warning. He trailed a finger, pointing across the width of the river.

"There's something down there," Dugan said. "Did they do it? To stop us? The Makuxi?"

Oso nodded.

"Alright, so keep your legs and balls tucked in," Rojo said, treading into the water.

"And put that shotgun away," Dugan said, in a more hushed tone.

"Guess you were right," Zephyr said.

"He is one of us," Dugan said.

"About leaving the vehicles," Zephyr finished.

Leech walked past the two of them. "Some club," he said.

By the time they made it across, Oso's foot was wrapped with a torn piece from his vest, the unused remnants lying on the ground. Dugan didn't ask if he was okay; Oso would take offense to such an inquiry.

As the men dug at the leeches on their bodies Dugan stuffed his leather book back into his breast pocket. Oso reattached his belt, spinning his knives like a gunslinger his gun before sliding them back into their sheaths. Despite his injury he walked without revealing the slightest discomfort, his bare feet crunching on the broad tufts of gamalote grass by the bank.

Dugan looked over his men, sliding his sunglasses in place. "They know we're coming," he said.

"What does that change?" Leech asked.

Rojo and Zephyr, the other men around him, all smiled.

"Nothing," Dugan said.

Verse VI.

Two dogs chased after a third hairless mutt, cutting through the hard packed dirt road. The one in the lead carried something dripping in its mouth. Faye kept her eyes on the road. Better not to know.

The small huts and make-shift-homes on either side of the road looked like a leveled graveyard, aluminum siding and tin roofs jutting up from the ground at odd angles. The fields were littered with wash bins and filthy mattresses, dressers and collapsed tables and chairs; small and seemingly trivial possessions, when compared to what was buried alongside them.

Bodies. Or body parts.

A shirtless man's sightless gaze, staring up beneath the sharp-edged metal roof separating his upper half from his clothed lower one. A child's bare feet and legs protruding from the remnants of a kitchen sink now lying perpendicular to the ground, an open microwave where his head should have been. Heaps of clothing pinned to the earth by metal scraps, concrete blocks, or furniture turned deadly. With enough convincing, Faye could believe that was all she was seeing – the forgotten laundry of people who had escaped, not their forgotten bodies within and beneath.

To distract herself from the carnage, Faye related to Grey what she could about the man she was looking for. His background, his uncanny ability to get results and the wake he left wherever he went.

"Don't get me wrong, this changes nothing of my passion for protecting nature and changing the world, but by the same token I can't sit back and let this man, this … evil, continue to exist under the guise of commerce and science. He, and everyone like him, must be held accountable for their actions! Horrors masquerading as progress."

As they approached Main Street, which lead to the town square, and further down to the alcalde's office and prison, Grey reached out, grabbing Faye lightly by the arm. His touch surprised her, and she almost apologized for her jumpiness, until that touch began to hurt.

"Let go."

"Wait. We need to talk."

"Then let go of my arm."

Grey glanced at where he held her, seeming to be almost as surprised as she was by his actions. But he didn't let go. "I brought you out here so that we could talk, without the others overhearing."

"About what?" Faye said, her anger now flaring.

"Yesterday, this ... whole trip, the earthquake; everything!"

"You're hurting me."

Grey finally let go. Faye took a step back, rubbing at where he had grabbed her. Grey followed her movement, keeping her close.

"Not everyone is so spellbound by you that we believe every word you say. Has anything about this supposed Dugan character been true or is it just another one of your fabrications in order to keep us all in tow?"

"I'm not lying to you!"

"Well then it's worse! Because if it is true? You're knowingly risking our lives this time."

"This was why I wanted to come alone," Faye said.

"So that you could put our lives in jeopardy without any of us knowing?"

"Can you even hear yourself? You're blaming me for an act of God, as if I personally caused the earthquake! Besides, the only one who got hurt —"

She stopped, but not before the damage was done.

"What? Not going to finish your thought?"

Faye looked away. Main Street within sight, but far enough away that there was no one out to witness their argument.

"The only one who got hurt was the intern?" Grey said, finishing her sentence for her. He took another step toward her, matching her retreat.

"That's not what I meant."

"I'm taking over. You're no longer calling the shots or making any decision regarding our stay or leave, and that begins this instant. Which means you and I are turning around and marching back to be with the others where we will stay until the helicopter's ready to take us home."

"I told you I didn't need you."

Grey rushed her, shoving her back with such force her legs lifted into the air. She landed on her tailbone with a twang of pain that shot up her spine as she slid onto her back. But this time Grey wasn't attempting to save her life.

He lumbered over her, driving one knee into her chest and pinning her to the ground, then slapped her across the face. The shock of what was happening, and how quickly things had turned, kept Faye from reacting other than the defensive gesture of her upturned hands.

Grey pressed his body on top of hers, ripping at her running shorts which slid down with ease.

"Stop!"

He hit her again, this time palm closed, then grabbed her by the shoulders, slamming her back against the ground and locking her arms in place.

Something flashed across his face, a moment of recognition, of doubt, of the realization of the atrocity he was about to commit. And then it was gone.

"This is for Malcolm," he said, releasing one of her arms so he could unlatch the belt of the jeans he had changed into. "And for every one of us that would have died had I not shown you your place!"

Faye is a little girl again, transported back all those years when she has gone in search of her parents in her own house.

The noise that wakes her.

The shattered pane of glass in the French doors of their kitchen.

Bunny, falling from her arms as someone grabs her from behind.

She screams but a hand clamps over her trembling mouth as she is lifted off the ground. She can't see the man's face but she can feel his whiskers against her skin, smell his sour breath. The stink of his sweat. A droplet rolls from his face to hers, curving down the side of her face and continuing down her neck.

The first of many violations to come.

"This is for your Father," the man says.

He carries her toward the living room, his thick hairy arms squeezing her so tight she can barely breathe. Her kicks are futile.

He tosses her over the back of the couch, the hard edge ripping into her gut, then yanks on her legs so that she is teetering, halfway over. She hears the man's belt unlatch, the jangling of the metal prong against the belt's buckle.

Faye is sobbing. She has forgotten how to scream. How to fight.

She is only six.

"You tell him he had this coming," the man yells. "He'll know why. This is his fault!"

A shrill cackle sounded from the trees, rising above the peripheral noise of birds and animals speaking their minds. Commentating on the animalistic scene that was happening before them. Nature taking its course. But Faye was no longer only six.

She had just enough range of motion with her free arm to reach into the front pocket of her sweatshirt. She wrapped her hand around the grip of her Beretta. As Grey finished pulling his pants down on top of her, he turned back to face the small twin barrels hovering an inch from his skull.

"Like I said, I don't need you."

His breathing haggard, Grey stayed atop her for several seconds before his face broke. He rolled off her, weeping and wiping at his face, not even bothering to pull his pants back up.

"Oh god … I don't know what came over me … I don't know –" He let out a guttural cry, striking the ground beside him.

Faye stayed where she was as well, though she did reach down to cover herself with her underwear and shorts.

The sky above was an intoxicating blue, so rich and deep Faye felt she might fall upward into it, like diving into a pool. Not a single cloud in sight. She wondered if it would even make a ripple, that fall upward.

Grey sobbed beside her, unable to find anything to say. An apology, they both knew, would never go far enough. And so Faye spoke for him. To him.

"This never happened." Her swallow sounded harsh to her own ears. "But I swear to God if you ever look at me again, I will put a bullet through your head. And if you ever contradict me in front of the group? Or tell them I'm here for any purpose other than what I tell them – whatever that might be? I'll tell them everything."

This little encounter could prove to be worthwhile after all, she thought.

She rolled over on top of him, her knees spread over his body as if she were riding him, the short metallic barrel pressed deep into the side of his head.

"You are mine, now. Do you understand?"

He looked up at her, the shell of the man he had been but moments ago, and nodded.

She shifted her running shorts and panties and, with Grey's pants already down, guided him inside her. Not once did she remove the pistol, from start to end.

Grey began to cry anew but Faye made sure his eyes were connected to hers the entire time. He had to know who was in control; who was on bottom and who was on top.

When she was finished with him, she rolled back off, panting mildly. She hadn't been gentle; she knew if it came to it she'd have the evidence now of what he'd done.

"Come on," she said, already moving back onto the path that connected to the main road. "We have someone to find. And if you're thinking of killing yourself, at least do it after you help me."

She left him there, lying in the dirt. Both eyes closed, tears leaking down the sides of his face. But she wasn't worried. He would catch up. Fall in line behind her.

He no longer had a choice.

Verse VII.

The dense jungle leveled out to bedrock covered in soft clay dirt, each step forward met with a half-slide back. The forest opened up, trees dotting the landscape like lampposts a city street interspersed by brush and rocks.

Dugan was surprised they hadn't yet seen the Parai-Tepui; though a good hour-and-a-half from their location, the table-top mountain should have been visible by now. Dark clouds spread across the eastern skies, some part of the Amazon already enveloped in rain. A storm was coming.

It had been coming for some time.

His men moved in silence, the noises of the jungle continuing as if they weren't even there. Hand and facial signals were all the men required, broken into two squads, Dugan and Oso forming a third.

In the distance a filter of white noise began to grow from a whisper to a shout. They were drawing near.

Without a command, both squads moved out in opposite directions, flanking their destination. Dugan and Oso quietly drove up the center toward the last coordinates their escaped captive fled.

Guayanata.

The only name in Dugan's book that didn't belong.

At least not yet.

They came around a large outcropping of rocks, water spilling from the top into a shallow emerald pool. There was no source for the water – the river was a mile or two to the west – but natural springs out here, like cenotes, were not uncommon, underground rivers running for miles both unseen and unheard.

In a large clearing before the waterfall the remains of a camp were in evidence. Spits hanging above coals with leather hides strung from the branches of trees, still in the early stages of tanning. Ceramic bowls and cookware abandoned. Skinned carcasses of what looked like a jaguar and several boars stretched over wooden stakes, a few only partially degreased and unhaired.

Dugan's boot fell next to a child's doll, its faceless head dyed black. He bent down, picking it up.

It's dress was a mix of desert-colored reds, oranges, and maroons. He brought the doll closer, unable to see past its faceless head. No eyes. No mouth. No possibilities for expression, communication, emotion.

Betrayal.

An odd thought occurred to him, that when they finally found the Shaman, he would be like this doll – featureless. Unable to tell them his secrets because he had no mouth with which to speak from.

The simmering of coals broke Dugan from the doll's sightless gaze. Oso stood on top of one of the rings of coals barefoot, except for the strap wrapped around his injured foot.

The coals – they were still warm.

"Left in a hurry," Zephyr said, leading his squad in from the north, Kendall and Rojo with him. A giant anteater broke from behind nearby foliage, lumbering off with a young pup clinging to its back.

"They haven't gone far," Dugan said. "Fan out. A brick for the one who finds something that leads us to them."

The incentive was unnecessary; his men would respond out of duty but even Dugan felt the anticipation of a long hunt coming to an end.

Cy appeared from the other side of the rock formation, his squad somewhere behind the waterfall. His face was stern, jaw clenched. "You need to see this."

"Find them?"

Cy shook his head. "I don't know what we found."

Lighting a cigarette, Dugan followed the one-eyed Vietnamese former lieutenant. The rest of the men fell in behind him.

A glimmer of light reflected out from near the top of the waterfall, like the sun reflecting off glass. Dugan squinted, even with his sunglasses. He stopped, looking up at the wall of rock when the glint disappeared.

He moved back and forth but the shimmer was gone. The water that fell landed on a black rock only five or six feet from the top, from there scattering into equal parts spray, equal parts dribble, as it both trailed down and dropped the remaining thirty feet.

"Dugan?" Cy asked.

"Yeah. Coming."

They continued past the falls. Several young Huasui trees had sprouted in their search for sunlight. A type of palm, they typically grew closer to marshy areas within the basin. Dugan noticed that most of their berries had been picked, a delicatessen amongst the natives.

Past a cluster of walking palms, their stilt-like roots spreading out like tangled tripods, he spotted Leech and Chupa. They stood next to each other, backs turned to Dugan and the approaching men.

Before them a thick wall of fog stretched outward in either direction, running in an endless line. Over twelve feet high, its dark grey wisps circled in revolving patterns. It was unlike any fog Dugan had encountered. Not a single strand stretched beyond the boundary of the wall, as if this fog were made of brick and stone, as stationary as a sentry's gate.

Dugan unholstered his Glock as they approached, registering Zephyr bringing his tactical shotgun up beside him. The men stopped in an almost perfect line with the other two. After a moment the other men who had been searching the perimeter joined the group.

"Fifty yards south, we found the same thing," Kendall said. "It keeps going."

"What the hell is it?" Leech asked.

"Maybe it's a warning," Rojo said, lobbing a glob of tobacco onto the ground.

"It's black magic," Chupa said. "We shouldn't be here."

"It's just fog," Zephyr said. "Probably from the storm."

"You seen fog do this?" Kendall asked.

Dugan blew out a cloud of smoke that hit the wall of fog, intermingling until the two became one. "Anyone gone in?"

"Hell no!" Leech said. "Could be monsters and shit in there. I swear we seen faces moving in the clouds."

Zephyr suddenly fired his shotgun, knocking out four rounds as he rotated the angle of his weapon. He twisted the chamber beneath the barrel, firing another four, shell casings dropping to the ground.

The gaping holes where his rounds had punched through slowly reknit as tendrils of fog stretched and refilled the gaps. Everyone listened – not a sound beyond the soft roar of the falls behind them.

"You hear any monsters in there?" Zephyr asked.

"Go ahead in and I'll tell ya," Rojo said, with his crooked grin.

"Oso?" Dugan asked.

The native swung a black blade into his hand and stepped into the fog, immediately disappearing.

"Oso, wait!" Dugan said, pulling back just before entering the fog himself. The fog pressed in around where the native had entered, once again appearing whole. It was as if Oso had been swallowed.

"Damnit!" Dugan shouted.

Kendall stuck his fingers in his mouth and whistled loudly, a few of the men clapping or continuing to call out Oso's name.

"Maybe not the smartest move to send in the one guy who can't call for help," Rojo said.

They waited a minute. Then a minute more. With each passing

second Dugan's stomach knotted tighter.

"All jokes aside, this just feels … wrong," Rojo said. He waved the tip of his gun into the fog, a line swirling like water being displaced.

"They're finally learning to fight back," Chupa said.

"No," Dugan said. "They're not fighting, they're fleeing. All of this – the earthquake, the fog – it's the blanket the magician tosses on the table so he can escape unseen."

"They're trying to slow us down," Cy said.

"Exactly."

"And it's working," Zephyr said.

Kendall cleared his throat loudly. "No offense, Dugan, but what if you're wrong? Think about it – the spikes in the river, now this? We could walk straight into a trap; who knows what could be hiding in there?"

Cy stepped up beside Dugan, speaking softly. "Let me take the new guy, run back to the HV's. We've got a FLIR monocular …"

"How many?" Dugan asked.

"Just the one. We didn't prep for a night raid."

The FLIR was a multi-sensor thermal lens able to detect heat signatures in the darkest of environments. It would see straight through the fog as if it wasn't there. It was a smart play.

"We'll grab the ropes while we're there. Make sure no one … gets lost."

Dugan heard the missing word as if Cy had said it.

Make sure no one else *gets lost.*

"Two miles there, two back; I'm not sure we can afford the delay," Dugan said.

"We'll be fast. Whatever time we lose will be more than made up for with the FLIR alone. I agree with Kendall, I think we should use caution."

"If this fog is more than just a delay tactic, we'll all be glad we waited," Rojo said.

"Go," Dugan said.

Zephyr stepped away, shaking his head. Cy and Leech both unstrapped any extra weight, each keeping only a small handgun before taking off in a near sprint.

"This is bullshit," Zephyr said, once they had left.

"I didn't see you volunteering to go after Oso," Kendall said.

"What if this is part of their plan? To keep us separated? Hell of a lot easier to take out two men than a small army."

"Least it's just Cy and the new guy," Chupa said, crouching down beside a large thin tree trunk.

"Yeah, we've been trying to get rid of them for who knows how long?" Rojo said, his comment followed by laughter.

Dugan moved away from their conversation, walking parallel to the fog. It did feel … wrong. They knew so little about the people they were hunting short of their miraculous ability to heal. Did they also have an uncanny ability to kill?

He drew in another lungful of smoke before flicking his cigarette into the curtain of fog. He touched the notebook in his inner vest pocket, subconsciously aware of the souls he carried with him.

How many more will I be adding before the day's end? Or will the Shaman be adding our names to a book of his own making?

Verse VIII.

Conversation had been nonexistent since Grey had rejoined Faye. Small talk would have been an affront and they both knew there was no justification for what had almost taken place.

Or for what had taken place.

The calle they had followed connected to Main Street, one dirt road replaced by another. Grey didn't so much as glance at her, though every so often he would stop to wipe at an eye or a nostril.

The homes here were more intact, all concrete and block; each exterior painted in a bright swath of colors – reds, oranges, yellows and greens. The occasional blue. One of the homes had only the door still standing, blocks lying in rubble around it, but for the most part the damage from the quake seemed superficial. Of the few townspeople they had encountered, not one appeared friendly.

Across from the town's center, the public square where Faye and Donavon had faced the soldiers, a large crowd was gathered before the church. Raised voices and shouts echoed both from inside and without.

"We should try the church," Grey said.

"I don't think Dugan's the church-going type."

"No, I mean, to see if anyone there knows him. Pastors, Reverends, Bishops – whatever you call them – they have a handle on who's who in a town this size."

More shouting came from inside the church.

"It's worth a try," Grey said.

"I think we may be safer asking the police."

"Try staying there overnight and then say that."

Faye sighed. She hated going to a church more than a visit to the dentist. "Alright. But try to steer clear if that turns into a riot."

A handful of children ran toward them as they approached the stone building, Faye unable to tell if they were the same ones that had helped with their luggage. Maybe just being white and not covered in filth was enough to warrant being asked for a handout.

She shook her head. "We don't have any money. No dinero."

They swarmed Grey instead, latching onto his legs and pulling at his shirt. He almost tripped with so many underfoot. A plump girl no older than three clung to his pant leg while sitting on his shoe, her short black hair no longer than a boy's.

"Try asking them if they know this guy," Grey said.

"They're not going to know him."

"It doesn't hurt to ask."

"Grey."

It was all she needed to say. He ducked his head subserviently. She wasn't sure she had ever broken someone so completely in such a short amount of time.

As the children pulled at their legs as they continued through the street, Grey pulled out a pack of gum. The kids gathered before him like puppies expecting a treat.

"Here, here!"

He tore each piece in two, placing them in grubby hands. It wasn't long before he was out.

"That's all!" he said. "No more!"

"No mas," Faye said.

"No mas!" Grey repeated.

The stout girl with the boy's haircut still clung to his leg, burying her face into his pants. Grey kicked out lightly in an attempt to get her off. The girl only latched on that much fiercer.

She said something into the leg of his pants, her words muffled.

Faye bent down, asking her to repeat what she had said. Upon hearing it, Faye stood, glancing around the desolate street. She wiped at the sweat on her brow, her stomach sinking. "We need to go."

"Why? What'd she say?"

"Nothing, just pull her off."

"What'd she say, Faye?"

"It doesn't matter – we can't help them."

"Please, just – tell me?" Grey said.

"She asked if ... if you would be her father."

"God ..." Grey said, voice breaking. He closed his eyes, swaying slightly. "This place ... It's so much worse than I thought. How do they live like this?"

"It's all they know."

As they drew nearer the church the children fell back, disappearing down an alley. All but the small child, who was still wrapped around Grey's leg.

"I can't help you," he said, peeling her fingers off and lifting her back to the ground. "I can't even help myself."

Faye wasn't sure if she was meant to hear that last part.

The girl sat on the dirt ground, fresh tears running down her cheeks.

"At least ask her if her parents are alive," Grey said. "She may need help."

Faye shook her head. "We don't have time."

"We can't leave her —"

"Are you gonna help me, or not?" Faye asked.

Grey wiped at his face, turning away from her. "God! It's like a bad dream …"

Faye waited for him to compose himself before realizing it was going to take him some time. She said, "I once heard a story of a man walking a beach where hundreds of starfish had been swept up onto the shore. This couple passes, watching as the man bends down and picks one up, tossing it back into the sea. Does the same with another one. So the couple asks him, 'Why bother? What you're doing won't make a difference.' And he answers, 'It made a difference to that one.'

"I always had an issue with that story. Partly because the couple didn't join him in helping after his answer, but mostly because what the couple said was true. It didn't matter. Helping one person, one starfish, at a time? There are no lasting effects; no changes. But if you go to the source, fix what's causing the real issue, that's when change happens. That's when you make a difference."

She tugged at Grey's sleeve. "Come on."

He left the child there, walking slowly with her to the church. "So how do you stop the tide?" he asked.

"You can always pull down the moon."

The doorway to the church was blocked by a handful of men, one of them shouting so fast even Faye couldn't understand his Spanish. Spit flew from the dark skinned Venezuelan, his hands moving almost as quickly as his mouth. Wooden pews were stacked alongside the church's exterior, two children no older than three climbing atop them, one dangling off. A few of the men gathered at the entrance noticed Grey approach. They turned their backs to him without a second glance.

"Excuse us," Grey said, patting one lighter-skinned Venezuelan on the shoulder. "We need to get through."

The man shook Grey's hand from his shoulder, shoving him back. Grey was caught so off guard he lost his footing, colliding into one of the plastered pillars out front.

Before Faye realized it, she had removed the pistol from the pocket of her sweatshirt and raised it in the air. The POP of the hammer striking ammunition wasn't nearly as impressive as she had hoped but it got the crowd's attention.

Someone inside the church screamed, imagining the worst.

"Let us through," she said in Spanish.

The men by the door immediately backed away, several with hands raised. A few others filed out from just inside the building, ducking their heads, children with them. Faye wasn't sure what was going on inside the chapel but knew it wasn't a religious service.

Grey followed her into the building, watching her as carefully as the men who had made way for their passage. Once inside it didn't take long to realize a gun would be pointless, especially a gun with a maximum capacity of two rounds. She had never seen a room this size with more people crowded into it – no club or concert or sporting event even came close.

Grey looked back toward the door. "I get ... claustrophobic."

"You're staying here," Faye said.

The smell of so many bodies crowded together was overpowering. Faye tried to squeeze past a woman in front of her. A stout Venezuelan with curly black hair and a face like a troll, she toppled into the man standing next to her with Faye's movement, that man leaning into the body next to him. It was like a line of dominos. Shouts and curses, arms jabbing; no one was getting through this crowd. It might as well have been a living wall.

Faye rested one hand on Grey's shoulder, asking the man in front of her if she could use him for support. His deer-in-headlights look convinced her to act and apologize later.

She boosted herself up above the crowd, her arms locked on their shoulders, ignoring the grunt of the Venezuelan man. At least Grey had the courtesy to pretend she weighed nothing.

A head or two above the milling crowd, Faye was able to see the entire room. Doors had been broken off an adjoining room, cots or tables set up inside. Partially covered bodies lay on them, more lying on the floor.

A sick room, maybe? Now that she thought about it, she hadn't seen a hospital in town. There had to be doctors here, didn't there?

Near the entrance to the sick room two boys were managing the crowd. They handed a package to a woman in line, ignoring her shouts and gestures. One of the boys with a deformity on his face took her by the arm, ushering her and her three children into the sick room. It must lead to an exit.

Before the woman disappeared around the corner, Faye caught a better glimpse of what she carried – the object the boys had delivered. It was the emergency supplies Faye and her team had brought down.

Freeze dried food, blankets, and clothing, together in a tightly wrapped bundle.

The man whose shoulder she was balancing on buckled beneath her and Faye came down hard crashing into Grey who made an attempt to catch her. They both ended up on the floor.

More bodies shuffled in to the church from outside, the gunshot already forgotten.

"This is pointless," Faye said.

"Did you see a pastor?"

"No, just a couple kids. Let's go."

Grey cupped his hands together. "I need everyone's attention! We need to speak with the pastor or priest here! It's a matter of life and death."

Dirty faces stared back at them with blank stares.

"It's not going to work," Faye said.

"We need to speak with the head of the church!"

A soft voice rose from the back of the room. "You can wait in line like everyone else." The English was good, but it wasn't a man's voice; it was the voice of a child.

"Lift me up again," Faye said. "On your shoulders."

Grey ducked down for her to climb on top. He stood, a little shaky at first, before getting his feet beneath him.

Faye looked out over the sea of heads, the two boys continuing to deliver their goods while pointedly ignoring her. "What you're handing out? I brought that! Those are my goods," she shouted.

The boy with the face that was half black, almost as if he were wearing a mask, glanced at her briefly.

"We only want a minute of his time," Faye continued. "Please?"

Not even a glance this time.

"Crowd surf," Grey said beneath her. "Just ride on top of them." His sentences were getting shorter, his breathing shallow. He hadn't been joking about the claustrophobia.

Bodies so tightly packed together with barely enough space to shuffle a half-step at a time. It just might work.

"I always wanted to be a rock star," Faye said, before shouting for the group to raise their hands. "Levantense las manos!" she repeated.

The men and women directly in front of her must have thought she was about to bring out her gun again as their hands shot upward.

"Please, help me," she said in Spanish as she stretched her upper body over the first group of people, her legs still wrapped around Grey's head.

They caught her. Grey shifted his body, grabbing and pushing her butt as he lifted her from his head, helping her glide forward.

Faye smiled inwardly.

Slick, Grey, slick.

Her body rolled – shifting, falling, rising as the hands beneath her kept her afloat. Her smile only grew wider. What a rush. She slipped between two individuals, her head landing against someone's shoulder and then she was back up, riding the crowd until she came to the far end of the room.

The landing wasn't nearly as graceful as the voyage, and even that had been wobbly, but Faye picked herself up, standing before the two young boys. They gazed at her as if she had appeared out of thin air.

"Take me to the priest," she said.

This time she got a nod.

Verse IX.

Zephyr finished tying off a rope wound around a six-meter thick kapok tree, its grey bark protruding in gnarled spikes. A second rope had been secured around a fallen boulder the size of a small house. He pulled against the rope, rippled muscles on his arms and shoulders revealing thick veins beneath.

"We're good," he called back.

Dugan spun an outstretched finger in a circular motion. *Let's get on it with it, boys.*

Zephyr snapped a carabineer onto the rope, attaching it to the webbing he had stepped into, then tossed the rope's end to the men standing at the edge of the fog. "This ain't spelunking cable; three to a line. No more."

Leech picked up the fallen rope, attaching his webbing to the knotted loop. "Should we hold hands too?"

"Kumbaya my Lord, kumbaya," Rojo sang, his grainy voice barely keeping to the melody. A few of the others snickered as he took the rope from Leech.

Cy snapped his own carabineer in to the second rope, handing it off to Dugan. Dugan let the rope fall, without hooking in.

"You staying?" Kendall asked, replacing a canteen onto his belt and picking up the fallen line.

"I'll take my chances without stumbling over all of you," Dugan said.

"You're a real boy scout."

Rojo stood at the edge of the fog, raising the FLIR monocular again from his eyes. "You sure it's not the batteries?"

"They're lithium-iodide, not Duracell," Cy said.

Night vision goggles were useless when it came to seeing through fog; their sole design was built around the magnification of light. The problem was that the tiny particles in smoke or fog reflected light, so all you ended up doing was trading a grey cloud for a green one.

Thermal imaging however was different. Because fog gave off no resident heat, one could simply see through it as if it weren't there, the intense heat signatures of anything living lighting up with no obfuscation.

At least that was how it was supposed to work.

Dugan still saw a flash of white behind his eyelids every time he blinked. The wall of fog had been one massive towering entity of heat, breathing in and out with every tendril's swirl. A searing white light had blasted from the FLIR's view, blinding Dugan and each of the others who had looked through it. What they were seeing, according to the laws of physics and nature, simply couldn't be. Then again they were dealing with a people who were skimming the edges of immortality and a prophet who could summon the earth and sky at his command.

"You think it's alive? The fog?" Rojo asked.

"If it is then there's a way to kill it," Zephyr said.

"No guns," Dugan said. "Be too easy to get turned around in there and start shooting each other. Bring them but I want them holstered. And if you see a Makuxi you damn well make sure it's not Oso before you bring him down or don't bother coming back out. Understood?"

He could see the apprehension in a few of their faces. In truth, he could understand. They were facing something that had no explanation. And by the time they made out more than the form of a person within that dense fog, it might be too late.

He continued, "I don't care how deep this goes, or what it does to us. We press through till we find the other side. Once you're through, wait for the others. We move on as a team."

"Dugan?" Cy came over and slapped a hard cylinder into his hand. It was a handheld signal flare, its tube casing protecting the signal carrier that would launch with an initiated charge. "In case we get separated."

He handed a flare to each of the other men.

"I'd feel better knowing whether Oso had screamed," Kendall said.

"The only one screaming will be the Shaman. He's here. And I can guarantee he's more frightened of us than we are of this."

Dugan unlatched his hunting knife, its ivory handle expertly molded to the shape of his hand. The blade curved like a wave, serrated teeth grinning darkly. "Stay grounded."

He stepped into the fog.

Immediately his senses felt heightened. A blizzard of ash enveloped him, shapes and shadows swirling in a hypnotic, dizzying effect. He had seen shapes within the fog while they waited for Cy and Leech to return, but dismissed them for the imaginings he knew they were. Now he wasn't so sure.

His eyes stung and began to water. He held a hand directly in front of his face, the fog so thick he saw only a shadowed outline. Vapors crawled through his nostrils, reaching down his throat. He wondered if those wispy tendrils would suddenly solidify, smoke becoming substance, killing him where he stood. He should have at least lit a cigarette before stepping into this madness.

"Stay grounded!" he shouted.

His words were hollow, dissipating before they had a chance to carry, as if the fog itself had clamped an invisible hand over his mouth. He glanced behind to see if anyone had followed. If they had he would never know.

Turning back around he realized he was no longer certain which way was forward. He stumbled, one foot kicking against some inanimate object he couldn't see. Distorted faces slunk just within grasp before disappearing back into the fog. A tree trunk appeared causing his heart to leap. If there was a coordinated attack in this fog his men wouldn't have a chance.

Something suddenly pressed into the small of his back.

Dugan froze. This was no hallucination.

A man's face slid within inches of his own. Dark skin, pale colorless eyes.

"Doog."

Zephyr raised his shotgun between them, rotating its barrel with a clack that should have been much louder before continuing past. He was instantly lost in grey shadow.

So much for Dugan's charge regarding the guns.

He stepped on the rope trailing behind Zephyr, almost tripping over it. Brambles of brush tore at his feet, an invisible branch scraping the top of his head.

How far had they come? And what were they being led to?

Dugan pressed one hand to his vest, feeling the weight of his notebook within. The tickle in his throat was becoming an itch he couldn't scratch; he cleared his throat in an attempt to keep it at bay.

A high-pitched screech broke through the fog, directionless. Not a scream of agony or pain, but one of surprise.

And fear.

Dugan turned about, trying to pinpoint where it was coming from. The scream seemed to pull back, whisked away like the noise of a passing train.

"Watch for sinkholes!"

He realized, with the words, they couldn't see their own feet let alone the ground before them. He wasn't sure anyone could hear him anyway.

A slight buzzing sound vibrated up from the ground around him. Something moving. Quickly.

Dugan gripped his knife tighter, ignoring his sweaty palm. Without being able to see the flare he held in his other hand, he flipped open the firing cap. Now he'd only need to apply pressure to its end to send the flare soaring.

That and cover his eyes.

"Dugan?"

Zephyr's voice, close. Or far. He had no way to gage.

"Here!"

"I'm gonna —" *Thwoomp*.

Zephyr's voice cut off as if someone or something had hit him hard. He cried out, his voice trailing off as if he were being dragged away at unimaginable speeds.

The buzzing noise amplified all around Dugan, vibrating. He crouched down, preparing to slam the flare's end into the ground when something pulled taut beneath him, sweeping him from his feet. Dugan fell, one leg caught in the contraption that now yanked him forward, his back sliding against the hardened earth.

A trap.

His head hit into a rock or tree trunk as his body was propelled along, dragged across the down-sloped terrain. He rolled in the dirt, coming loose from the winding rope only to be snagged by it again. It shot him forward as if wound by an electric crank. A shark on a line.

Dugan flailed, his knife lost, hand battering at the ground, trying to keep with the speed he was being pulled. Just ahead he heard Zephyr's cry go from anger to a tremulous yelp.

Dugan slammed the butt of the flare into the ground, light bursting around him, then behind him as he was pulled forward.

It was enough to see what was coming.

Enough to see what wasn't.

Dugan grasped at the rope biting into his leg but too late — he was launched into the air, the ground dropping out from beneath him, propelled off the edge of a precipice that should not have been there.

Verse X.

The child with the growth on his face led Faye not through the sick room, but past a hanging sheet on the other side of the wall. It opened up into a short hall. He had to be no older than nine or ten, his arms so thin Faye wondered if there was any muscle attached to the bone. He had an innocent look to his face despite the deformity which was impossible not to stare at. By not looking at it, Faye felt she was drawing even more attention to it.

"What's your name?" she asked.

"Josue," the child answered.

"Do people treat you differently, Josue? Because of your face?"

"They used to."

"Don't let them. You see this?" She pointed to the side of her head, the curved tattooed claw raking against her whiskered skull. "It's to remind me. That our pains? The abuses people inflict upon us? They can be used to make us stronger."

The boy turned away from her, continuing down the hall. "God is my reminder," he said.

"You speak English very well."

This time he didn't answer her.

Josue stopped before a curved wooden door. A thick woven rug hung from the adjacent wall depicting a bald man with a light shining from the back of his head in an arc. He held a dove in one hand and what Faye assumed was the bible in his other. She had always hated churches that glorified ordinary men, creating an air of impossible righteousness even the most pious of churchgoers could never attain.

No matter what you ordered when you walked into a church, it always came with an extra helping of guilt when what most people really needed was just to know they were okay. Their faults, their failures, their mistakes? They had all been made before.

And they would be made again.

She'd never understand why these religions oppressed the ones who should have been lauded for their efforts. Crushed those who were already on their knees. Like this poor child with the deformity on his face. He had probably never known a normal life and now, instead of being permitted to go out and gain his own experiences, he was in servitude to some high and mighty priest.

The only thing worse than being a slave, she thought, *was being one and not knowing.*

Josue hesitated before the door, his fingertips bouncing off each other in a strange rhythmic clap. "Father?" he finally said.

On the opposite wall of the door, diagonal to the rug, was an oil painting of another beardless Saint, that ridiculous halo crown surrounding his head, as he stood confidently before a crowd of men and women. Some listened to his words with rapt attention while others turned their faces away.

Even the church knows it it's not for everyone, Faye thought.

"Father?" Josue rapped lightly at the door.

A voice responded from the other side of the door. "I'm in prayer, whatever it is can wait."

Before the child could turn back to Faye, she pushed her way past him, depressing the lever in the handle. She had already noticed there wasn't a lock; one benefit of being in a church.

"What are you doing?" Josue said.

She swung the door wide and entered the priest's chambers. A man in robes scurried on the ground, closing a wooden chest next to the door. In his hurry he knocked over a small Bunsen burner and the metal saucer on top. A dash of amber liquid splashed against a cabinet, the priest sweeping objects beneath his robe in a huff. He glanced about the floor as if there was more evidence he had forgotten to hide.

"That's some prayer."

"You have no right!" The priest was ancient; dark bags beneath his eyes, his skin pulled tight across his skull. White whiskers dotted his chin.

"Might want to turn off your burner," Faye said.

The priest looked past her at Josue standing at the door.

"Father Shumway, forgive me, I did not know …"

"Leave me, Josue," the priest said. "And close the door."

Josue did as he was told, tears welling in his eyes.

With the door closed, the priest reached back and grabbed the burner. For a moment Faye thought he might throw it at her; instead he turned the dial, gas and flame extinguishing. "You have no idea how much damage you've just done."

"By opening his eyes to the hypocrisy of those dedicated to the Lord?" Faye asked. "Some might say I've done him a favor."

"That child …" the priest paused, hand shaking as he held it out. Instead of continuing, he clenched his bony hand into a fist then gathered up the supplies beneath him. Needle, band for his arm, a brass key which clinked against the stone floor before disappearing into a pocket of his robe.

"It wouldn't have taken me walking in on you to recognize what you are. I know an addict when I see one."

The priest's mouth tightened.

"I'm Faye. Moanna. Been clean coming up on two years."

"You're never clean."

"Says the man preaching repentance."

"What is it you want?"

"How about a name? Father Shumway, is it?"

"To some."

"And to others?"

The priest sighed. "Remmy."

"Remmy," Faye repeated. "Which do you prefer?"

"I'm an old man who no longer has time for patience. If you think you can hold this over my head to get me to join your insane cause, you're barking up the wrong tree."

"And what cause might that be?"

Remmy rose, glancing briefly at the tattoo along the side of her head. "I know who you are. Don't think you're the first to come around; you most certainly won't be the last. Carrying your vain and supposed noble quest like some extinguished torch, illuminating nothing but your own ambition, and never once considering the consequences of your actions.

"This town – the people here? They need that lumber mill to survive. The livelihood of hundreds hinging on a grown woman's stepping stone as she moves on to the next conquest. You're not here to create a legacy, Faye Moanna. You're here only to destroy."

"Sorry to disappoint, Father," Faye said, emphasizing the title, "but your God beat us to it. But he's always been aces when it comes to destruction, hasn't he?"

Remmy wiped at the sweat on his face with a thick sleeve. "Despite what you've seen, despite my … weakness, I care about the people here." He looked down, his lips pursed. "They're all I have. And … I'm all they have. We get by without needing more."

"So help me," Faye said. "I'm not looking for your help with the lumber mill, I need to find a man, an American, who I believe is living here or nearby."

"Who?"

"His name is James Dugan."

"I can't help you." Remmy began walking away from her, carrying off his relics.

"You know him! Please, I need to find him. It's a matter of life and death!"

"But whose death, Faye Moanna? Whose death? You think only of yourself, but with the kicks and scratches of your tantrum you would send a boulder tumbling down the hill that will smother us all!"

"You do know him."

"Only enough to not want to know more."

"So he's here? In town?"

"I can't help you," Remmy said.

"How do I find him?"

"You don't! He's not a man you find, he's a man who finds you. The fact that you know him is confirmation enough that I want nothing to do with you."

The gun suddenly leapt into Faye's hands. She pointed a shaking arm at the old priest.

A smile cracked across his leathery face. "I should be so lucky," he said.

"Don't make me cause problems for you."

He looked at her with what Faye thought might be sympathy. "I worry you won't need my help."

Faye lowered the gun. They both knew she wouldn't use it.

"Go back home. You don't belong here," Remmy said.

"He's my father!"

The priest's eyes darkened ever so slightly. One of his eyes twitched as he chewed at the inner lining of his cheek, a nervous habit he probably wasn't aware of. All addicts had them.

"He's my father, a man I haven't seen in seventeen years. And I thought ... he should know the truth. I'm dying, Remmy. I know I'm young, but ... well, that doesn't guarantee us much. There are things I need to make right before that happens. Of anyone, a man like you should understand."

Remmy glanced back at the tattoo alongside Faye's scalp, that clawed hand hovering so near.

She nodded. "I can escape my addictions, but not what's eating me inside."

"Cancer?" he asked.

"Worse. Same that killed my mother."

"What about –"

"There is no cure," Faye said.

"He comes in to town every few days; him or one of his men. They meet with the alcalde. Sometimes his men are at the tavern but –"

"Never him."

"No," Remmy said. "Never Dugan."

"He stopped drinking when I was young. Do you think addictions are inherited? Or the ... propensity towards them? Does he still smoke?"

"I keep my distance. Father or not, I'd advise you to do the same. He's dangerous."

"Then it's more than just addictions I inherited."

"They drive a huge military vehicle. A tank without a turret. I can't tell you when, but at some point, he'll show there, at the aclalde's."

"The prison?"

"The town jail. Prisons here are … much worse."

"Thank you," Faye said.

"You're in over your head, child."

Faye nodded, unable to disagree. "Aren't we all."

Verse XI.

Dugan fell in a freefall, his stomach lurching up toward his throat. Fog swept past like clouds, wind hammering into him from all sides. His pack flew free, banging into something on its descent just above him as he flailed, not even sure which way was up or down, just knowing he was falling. He was dying.

Something struck his head – not the pack; the rope, pulled taut and thrumming from the impact like the cord of a piano. Dugan frantically reached for it, the coiled cable bending his fingers back with his first grasp.

He slammed into something hard, breaking his fall and ripping his breath from his lungs. His body rolled over Zephyr who groaned, unaware of what had hit him before Dugan slipped free.

"Dugan!"

Zephyr hung from the rope by his webbing, his descent at an end, before disappearing in the clouds above.

But Dugan's fall was far from over.

Grasping at air, Dugan finally found the rope again. He snaked one arm over it, bringing his body close, the rope cradled between his body and armpit. The friction of his slowing created a whir in his ears. He felt the rope biting into his flesh, already having burned through his vest and shirt. Still he held on, teeth clenched, eyes shut, not wanting to see what might be beneath him.

His descent slowed then came to a halt. Dugan wrapped the rope around one wrist, clutching on with both hands. The skin under his arms burned to a degree that made his teeth chatter. But he wasn't going to die.

Not yet, at least.

As if by the command of some unseen force, the fog around him lifted, dissipating into the air.

The view was worse than the fog had been.

Dugan hung on the taut line staring at the canyon floor, a good fifteen hundred meters below. The wall of the cliff's side stretched straight down alongside him. Unlike any tepui Dugan had seen, this wall was sheer rock without a single break in it, not formed over time but in an instant. A legend come to life.

Temple of the gods.

The locals spoke of the table-top mountains with reverence. Most

Venezuelans held to some of the native beliefs that the tepuis were formed not through erosion of the sandstone plateaus that had covered this basin however many millions of years ago, but a god raising mountains from level dirt.

Dugan never would have believed there was any truth to the legend. Not until now.

"Woooooh!" Leech dangled from the end of the rope below Dugan, screaming defiantly. "Thought for sure we were done there! Oh, man, talk about a rush!"

"Dugan? You alright?" Zephyr asked above him.

Dugan was certain "alright" was not the word to describe their current predicament.

"I'm good," he called back. "The rope okay?"

He felt a vibration travel all the way down from where Zephyr plucked the cord. Pebbles and loose dirt rained down on Dugan from above. Zephyr's hanging feet and body blocked his view of the upper rim.

"Rojo!" Zephyr shouted. "Don't you dare come over that edge!"

"Agh, you muku!" came the voice of Rojo from above. "You think I'm trying?"

Dugan heard Rojo's feet scraping against gravel, more tiny rocks tumbling down. He closed his eyes, the turning rope making him dizzy.

"Have someone help him!" he shouted.

"Fog's still thick up top," Zephyr said. "Rojo? Can you –"

"Stop your damn moving!" Rojo shouted back, the strain in his voice evident.

Suddenly the cough Dugan had been keeping inside forced its way from his lungs, a stringy wet rasp that racked his entire body. The rope shifted from the new tension, that sway traveling upward. More loose dirt rained down after breaking on Zephyr.

"Son of a –"

Dugan lost the rest of Leech's cursing with another hollow cough that felt like it was raping his insides.

"Can you reach your smokes?" Zephyr said.

"I lost them ... in my bag," Dugan managed to squeak out between coughs.

The rope dropped another three feet, Dugan barely grappling on with the unexpected motion.

"Stop moving or I'm bailing out!" Rojo yelled through what sounded like gritted teeth.

"Shit man, I don't want to die."

Through watering eyes Dugan caught sight of Leech staring down at the ground so far below them. Tree tops that had shrunken down to the size of broccoli. Or smaller.

"We gotta do something," Zephyr said. "Leech, is there a ledge or something you can climb to? Release some tension?"

"Man, there ain't no ledge!"

Wet splatter spilled from Dugan's mouth. He felt lightheaded, a combination of the coughing, fall and potential blood loss from what he imagined the rope had done to his skin.

"There! Where the cliff turns white," Zephyr said. "What's that?"

Along the cliff's sleek wall, a slight indentation made for a small platform not too far from where Leech hung.

"Jump, Leech!" Zephyr said.

"Are you freakin' crazy? That won't hold me!"

"Do it!" Dugan coughed out, barely able to see with the moisture in his eyes.

"You're the extra man on the line – you jump!" Leech shouted.

Another bellow forced its way up Dugan's throat. The rope rocked back and forth from Zephyr's movements above.

"Hold on, Doog. I'm gonna drop a pack. Cigarettes."

Dugan coughed into his arm trying to keep from adding to the movement. "You don't smoke," he said.

Above him Zephyr held a pack of cigarettes in one outstretched hand. "Yeah, but you do."

Just as he let go of the pack, the rope lurched – Zephyr slid sideways, Dugan getting a clear shot of Rojo's foot sliding out over the edge of the cliff. The rope jostled and bounced, Rojo cursing above and scrambling at something.

"Stop moving!" he shouted.

The pack of cigarettes fell to Dugan's left. He could reach them if he spun out on the rope.

Rojo snarled above, and Dugan watched as the pack of cigarettes fell, inches from his outstretched fingertips. His coughing this time nearly caused him to lose his grip.

"He's gonna come over!" Zephyr said.

"No he won't," Dugan said. He reached into his vest and came out with a folding knife – not nearly as sharp as his hunting knife, but it would do the trick. He brought it to the rope just below him.

"What the hell –" Leech began when something else fell free from

Dugan's vest, flapping in the wind as it dropped.

Dugan's notebook.

"Grab it!" he yelled, the knife slipping from his fingers and plummeting down. "The notebook, Leech!"

It's leather string unwound with its fall, whipping in the air as the pages began to flutter.

Leech swayed back and forth like a pendulum, barely managing to snatch the notebook from the air as it flew past. He held it high, triumphantly.

"Ha, I got it! I got it Dugan!"

Dugan breathed in and out through his nose, his coughing subsiding momentarily. He watched as Leech held the book back out as if preparing to drop it.

"No!" Dugan yelled. "I swear to God I will destroy you if you even think about it!"

"Is this book more important than your life? 'Cause I'm dropping it in three if you don't jump to that landing!"

As if to emphasize Leech's words, more dirt and rock sprinkled down from above, the noise of Rojo's grunts echoing down the canyon wall.

"Don't drop it," Dugan said.

"One!"

Dugan cleared his throat, trying to ease the pressure mounting again. "I'll do it. I'll jump."

"Dugan, don't!" Zephyr yelled.

"Two!"

"No, I'm going!" Dugan crept down the rope hand over hand, lowering himself slowly.

"That's close enough!" Leech shouted. "No tricks."

The ledge was smaller than Dugan had thought; not really a ledge but a wrinkle in the stone. No one could make that leap – there would be nothing to hang onto.

"Just like stepping into a ring. Don't think about it, just do it," Leech said. "The consequences will take care of themselves."

Rojo groaned loudly, rope swaying anew. "Hang on!"

A dark shape tumbled from the top of the cliff.

We're too late, Dugan realized. But the rope he held to hadn't budged beyond the slight vibrations from above, so it wasn't Rojo tumbling over.

Not a yelp or cry came from whoever had stumbled over the edge, their apparent descent not accidental but planned. And then Dugan recognized the bare feet dropping toward him. Black hair lashing back and forth like a whip.

Oso fell silently past Zephyr, holding on to the end of the second rope. The arc of his curve brought him back against the canyon walls, his feet slamming into the rock as he bounced back out, continuing his descent. He dropped past Dugan, his line pulling him again into the wall before bouncing back out near Leech.

"Haha! I knew we'd be alright!" Leech shouted, clapping Oso on the shoulder as the native swung back to the rock.

This time Oso stayed there, positioning himself on the tiny indentation of a ledge. He swung the rope back out, one arm cradled in a small divot in the stone wall.

Dugan grabbed hold of the second rope, transitioning himself over. There was a moment of weightlessness, the feeling that he would drop despite his grip. Looking down certainly hadn't helped.

Until Dugan realized what Oso was holding in his other hand.

Dugan's worn notebook fluttered in the native's clutched grip. Leech seemed to realize it at the same time.

"No, no, no, that could have fallen! I wasn't gonna let it go!" He looked up at Dugan. "I swear, I wouldn't have done it! I would've jumped myself – I would have!"

Oso stuffed the notebook into his pants, pulling free a long slender blade from his side. The machete's steel was black except for its edge which shone with a brightened gleam.

Leech instantly had a gun in his hand pointing it at Oso. The second rope had moved further away from the wall when Dugan climbed over, a good four or five feet's distance from the native.

"Don't even think about it," Leech said. "You're staying there till they pull us up or I put a dart through your forehead." The machete twirled in Oso's hand. "I mean it!"

The soft call of a bird sounded from above. Dugan glanced up just in time to see Zephyr release his own machete, the knife dropping straight toward him. It turned in the air, blade flipping awkwardly.

"No, Dugan, don't!" Leech cried.

Dugan barely heard him. He grabbed the blade out of the air by the handle and with the same backward motion brought it to the first rope, sliding its smooth edge against it.

One swipe and the line severed.

Leech seemed to levitate a fraction of a second in the air, his arm swinging up with his dart gun toward Blake, then he was lost. His scream floated up to them, slowly dissipating like the fog.

Verse XII.

A few patters of raindrops became a torrential downfall, the water torrid, strangling in its ferocity. The fog lifted with it, about the only benefit Dugan and his men could derive from such a storm. What would have ordinarily felt cleansing now felt tainted and sullied. How much of the weather could he trust anymore?

How much of his own senses?

He stood at the edge of the newly formed tepui that hadn't existed twenty-four hours ago and placed his notebook back into the inner pocket of his vest. The notebook that now held one additional name.

Kendall and Chupa had already taken off in one direction, Cy and Zephyr in the other, following the perimeter of the cliffs. They had to know what they were up against; what the Shaman had done. Dugan was confident they would meet each other at some point. There would be no way down.

They would reconvene in town rather than the Facility. Dugan wanted to know whether the helicopters that had flown in earlier were still there and intact. It might be their only hope of continuing the hunt.

If the town was still there, that was.

"What are you gonna name it?" Rojo asked.

He sat, leaning heavily against the same kapok tree the rope had been tied to. The rain was just beginning to soak through the shelter of overhead leaves and branches, the Amazon floor base typically not receiving moisture until a good half hour of showers. Dugan smelled the heavy scent of the cigar Rojo was smoking, and though it didn't cause his throat to tighten, it did create an invisible itch.

Rojo looked spent. Drops of rain splattered onto his bald head, leaking down the sides of his face and collecting in his beard. The task of holding their combined weight on the line had taken a lot from the big man. "Well, are you?"

"Name what?" Dugan asked. He sucked on his cigarette.

"The temple of the gods we're all standing on," Rojo said. "You'll be the first to name one in over a hundred years."

Dugan looked back out at the grounds beneath them. The heavy lines of rain falling at an angle blurred the forest below.

Rojo continued, "That is what we're saying this Shaman did, right? Create a tepui from thin air? Raise a mountain from a flat plain with an earthquake? Shit, Dugan, I stood there at that ledge watching you three dangle from a line a thousand feet above the ground and I barely believe it myself."

"Not a question of whether he did it, it's a question of why," Dugan said.

"A grain of a mustard seed."

"I'm sorry?"

"The bible," Rojo said. "If you have faith the size of a mustard seed you can move mountains. What it says anyway."

"You believe that?"

"I didn't this morning."

Dugan breathed out a heavy plume of smoke. "Ask why, not how. Why would the Shaman do something like this? Either he's trying to scare us off, which if he's learned anything about us, would be pointless, or he's trying to flee."

Rojo rustled behind him. "So you think he did this to keep us trapped up here while they're down there?"

"I think he knew we were close and that he's growing desperate."

"I've seen desperate men, Dugan. This ... well, this feels like someone showing off. A man doing something just to prove he can."

Oso stepped out from beneath a tree, holding his notebook out toward Dugan, while shielding it to keep it dry.

"What's it say?" Rojo asked.

Dugan ripped off the page from the small spiral bound pad. "He says you're wrong. Not a man; only a god can do this."

"What, hold the weight of three dangling mukus over a cliff by his lonesome self? You found me out, Oso. I am a god!"

Oso scratched out a new note, handing it to Dugan who smiled.

"He says he didn't know gods were so ugly."

Rojo laughed. "Even the mute's a comedian. Well, what about it, Oso? You always stayed behind when we ascended these things. Is this the first time you've set foot on a tepui? Shouldn't you be throwing yourself off as a sacrifice for walking on holy ground or something?"

A flash of metal danced before Oso's hands, his blade flying out. It struck the ground between Rojo's legs, inches from flesh. Rojo only laughed harder.

"If my ex had been as good at conversation as you, we'd still be together," Rojo said, tearing the knife from the soft dirt and tossing it back to the native.

Blake wiped at the rain on his brow, letting the now useless cigarette fall from his lips. "Beard."

"What?" Rojo asked.

"It's what I'd name the tepui. B-Y-R-D, pronounced beard, after Richard Evelyn Byrd. He was a naval officer, the youngest admiral in the history of the US Navy. A lifelong explorer. The first man to reach both North and South Poles by air. But what's fascinating about Admiral Byrd, along with his ... curiosity, are the rumors that surround his last journey, his expedition to the North Pole.

"They say he had two journals documenting the event; the first was published by the American Geographical Society and expanded upon in his autobiography. The second ... well, that's where the rumors begin. Supposedly he showed that journal to only three men in his lifetime. In it, he described an encounter he was encouraged to leave out of his official report."

"An *encounter?*" Rojo barked a laugh. "You talking aliens?"

"Maybe. Or maybe something else entirely. What bothers me isn't what he found, it's why he wouldn't share it. A man like Byrd, searching for greater truths his entire life, finally discovers the unthinkable and then takes it to his grave."

"Probably knew everyone would say he caught frostbite in the brain or something."

"He wasn't crazy, he was brilliant; a Freemason, a mind like few in that generation," Dugan said.

A crackle of something falling came from a nearby tree, a waterlogged branch or overripe fruit dropping to the mossy floor.

"Whatever he learned, whatever he saw, he never went on an expedition again. In fact, six months after he returned he confined himself to his home in upstate Boston, spent the next seventeen years there. Never left his room, let alone the house."

"You really think he found something alien out there?" Rojo asked.

Dugan took a moment before answering. "I do. But no more alien than what we've discovered here. I think there are truths in this world we can't comprehend. Revealed in one light they might appear otherworldly, godly even. Yet in another light, as common as projecting moving images onto a screen or making glass out of sand. It all depends on where we're standing."

Rojo laughed quietly to himself. "Tepui Beard. Here I thought you were naming it after this little baby." He pulled at the long red whiskers hanging from his chin, glistening with the moisture.

"All depends on where you're standing," Dugan said.

Rojo rose to his feet, stretching his arms and cracking his neck with a quick turn. "Alright, I'm ready. But if the others ask, tell 'em you named it after me. We could even call it Tepui Red Beard."

They started back beneath the cover of dripping trees, the jungle transformed by the wetness. Plant leaves were turned in, water trickling down vines and stalks. Dugan stepped past a pitcher plant, a Heliamphora, attached to a low branch. It was a carnivorous plant that looked like a bloated balloon cucumber, its small opening allowing insects to pass through then get lodged in the water and enzymes at its center. It seemed everything survived by killing something else here in the Amazon.

Oso tapped Dugan on the elbow, proffering his small notepad. One word was scribbled on it.

Inktomi

Dugan glanced back at the native, remembering the word. The child had repeated it in his rantings before the earthquake. And just before he took his last breath. The native that had escaped had also used it, when they first met. Guayanata.

Oso pointed back to the pad with his lips. Dugan grabbed it, flipping the page. He read:

Is what they call you
The Spider

"So I have a name. The spider." Dugan lit a fresh cigarette, oddly excited at his title. You only give a name to an enemy when you know they are a threat.

"Well the Shaman will have to do more than move a mountain to get out of my web."

Verse XIII.

Marcus Stanton walked swiftly through the halls of the Facility, his assistant, Shannon, by his side. Her tan poly-suede skirt swished back and forth with every one of her steps, forced to match his stride. In heels, no less. Neither of them could talk out here in the open, not of what they had learned, nor of what needed to be done.

With Dugan out on some fool's errand, the decisions were now being left to him. Or Dr. Morley and him. Though who could trust that crackpot scientist?

He pulled a small lip balm from the pocket of his sports coat, dousing his lips in an all-natural vanilla bean coating. A few Facility workers nodded hello, others stepping aside to avoid being trampled. Everyone was out of sorts today, the earthquake causing much more than just physical damage.

No answers had come at the control center; communication with the outside world had somehow been disrupted during the quake. It all felt like some giant conspiracy, leaving him as the fall guy, with no one to warn him or help spread the blame.

And holy hell, was there a lot of blame to go around.

They stopped in front of the Gold elevators, Shannon depressing the button. Each stairwell and elevator grouping in the Facility was designated by color.

Except for the elevator leading down to the Freezer, Marcus thought.

That storage room of decaying native bodies, where Dr. Morley conducted his diabolical research, had become more than a stain that needed scrubbing. Because of the earthquake, too many of the workers now knew of it. People had gone down to help search for survivors, never realizing that once you made it down there it was where you stayed. Or at least that was how it was supposed to be.

Now that stain had grown into a disease. And it was spreading.

The elevator doors opened silently. Marcus walked in, Shannon following him and pressing the button for the lower floor. There they would meet with Morley who, with any luck, would be incoherent with painkillers and morphine.

The doors slid shut.

Just as the elevator started to descend, Shannon pulled the knob below the buttons, the elevator shuddering to a stop.

"We need to talk," she said.

"You think I don't know that?"

She turned to him and a hunger raced inside. She was stunning; blonde hair pulled back in a ponytail, better revealing her delicate neck and full upturned mouth. Her small waist was accentuated by her tight skirt, long slender legs he could have nibbled on for days. Her light blue blouse had no frills but showed just enough cleavage to pull the eyes toward it again and again.

"Look at my face," she said.

"You mean that's not why you stopped the elevator?"

"We have a serious problem," Shannon said, all business. "Forget ITOB or the CDER inspection. If word leaks of what has been going on under your watch? It'll be the GRSBA."

Global Regulatory, Safety & Biometrics Agency. Less of a watchdog, they were more an international taskforce.

"We have it contained," Marcus said.

"Not yet, you don't."

"Everyone here knew what Dr. Morley and his team were doing."

"Suspected, yes. But when engineers and IT personnel – even chefs? – were exposed to what happened down there? When they saw hundreds of those … dissected bodies? That shakes your faith a little more than when you just suspect something's going on."

Marcus tilted his head back, staring up at the mirror on the ceiling. *God, this would make a good room to make love in. Why haven't we done that yet?*

"So what do you want me to do, Shannon? I can't flash an entire facility. Not without orders."

"You're right. You have to do more than that."

"Come on?"

"What do you think Umner Corp is more likely to forgive? A swift executive decision that will protect their long-term assets and viability? Or a delayed reaction due to a fault in communication that could level the entire company?"

"I don't know …"

"Your security detail – Dugan still doesn't know about them?"

"No, they've been offsite."

"Maybe it's time to call them onsite."

Shannon reached up and unbuttoned the top of her blouse. She continued slowly, sensually, her garment opening like the petals of a flower to the sun.

"They put you in charge for a reason," she said. "You won them over. Just like you did me."

For the next fifteen minutes, Marcus forgot all his concerns.

The Facility.

The earthquake.

The dead bodies.

All sunk beneath the rising waves of ecstasy.

He rode the wave in an infinite number of universes, the image of their bodies intertwined bouncing between the mirrored surfaces of the elevator for what seemed an eternity.

On and on and on.

Once the tide settled, they helped each other reclothe.

"You're amazing," she whispered, standing on her tiptoes to kiss him on the neck.

He cupped her breast, bending down to kiss her. "We'll do it, but not until Dugan and his men return. It's no good if we put down the rabbits but leave the hounds roaming around."

"You're sure that's the right decision?" she asked.

He glanced at his reflection in the mirror, watching as a thousand other Marcus Stanton's nodded alongside him. "Positive."

Verse XIV.

Faye ran her nails across Donavon's back. His head was bent forward, hanging over the toilet bowl in Sir William's tiny bathroom, about as clean as one could expect from a bachelor's pad. The copper stain spiraling around the inside of the bowl was probably permanent. At some point in the night, with the assistance of the concoction of painkillers and "magic juice" Sir William had given him for his wrist, Donavon had woken with a stomach that was more than upset. It was furious.

Faye had hoped his condition would be a little better upon her and Grey's return. Apparently it had only gotten worse.

"I think I'm good," Donavon said, wiping at his mouth with a rag.

Faye leaned in and kissed the top of his head. "Sorry you were the one to come down with this."

His teeth chattered despite the hot and sticky bathroom. The rain had a way of making the humidity all the more pungent; rather than cooling the place down it had transformed Sir William's home into a sauna.

Donavon clambered to his feet, his left arm raised up in a sling. He turned on the sink, splashing water on his face with one hand. "Go ahead, I'm listening."

Faye reentered the atrium of Sir William's home, the oddly concaved panels of his domed roof less than concentric. Without the presentation of the stars manifested on those walls at night Faye wondered how lonely this place would become.

Kenny sat on a fold out chair, his hands gripped tightly in front of him. Sir William stood near the iron staircase, Grey at a throw's distance, pacing back and forth. A sheaf of papers spilled outward from a desk in the back of the room, announcing the monkey's location.

The sound of Donavon back at the toilet caused Faye to wince. Spree's head appeared briefly, registering the noise, then he disappeared back behind the desk.

"So?" Faye asked. "What's the consensus?"

Grey avoided looking at her.

"Like I said before, you're welcome here as long as you like," Sir William said. "It's not often I get visitors and when I do they're seldom as entertaining as your little group."

The sullen expressions of both Grey and Kenny weren't what Faye would have described as entertaining. "Thank you. You don't know how much that means," she said.

Kenny blew out air into his hands. "The pilot's willing to wait?"

"He doesn't have a choice, with the storm," Faye said. "Look, I want this to be a group decision, not me telling you what we're going to do. It's why I wanted to discuss it in the first place."

"What happens if we do find this man you're looking for?" Kenny asked. "Is he dangerous? A terrorist?"

"He's a phytopharmacologist. It's a big word but not scary." The toilet flushed from the bathroom. Faye continued, "He studies plants, herbs; finds ingredients for drug companies."

"And that's bad?" Kenny asked, picking at a zit on his neck.

"Spree!" Sir William shouted, just before a carved stone fish fell from a shelf on the wall. The monkey was already in the air, leaping to the next shelf.

The statue hit the ground and shattered, a piece of coral reef sliding all the way across the room.

"That damn monkey!" Sir William headed down the metal staircase. "I've got to find a broom ..."

Faye was grateful for the distraction; she had to regroup, come at this from a different angle. "Yes, this is dangerous. But so is anything worth doing. Men like the one we're looking for are paid by the big pharmas, companies with billions of dollars to spend. But when these men are paid for their discoveries? No one asks how they found it."

"So what, he's stealing stuff?" Kenny asked.

"Does Donny know about him?" Grey said.

Faye glanced back at the bathroom but Donavon was still predisposed. A good thing; he hated being called Donny.

"In South Africa there was a small tribe believed to have been descendants of the Khoikhoi discovered by three spelunkers. These caves in South Africa are immense, prehistoric, and apparently this ancestral tribe had been holed up in one of the offshoots for who knows how many centuries. Anyway, one of these cave divers was injured, I think he fell and shattered his femur or pelvis or something, and so his two friends go off searching for something to make a stretcher out of and run into these natives. You can read the whole story in a National Geographic from a few years ago. I can't remember the details but this medicine man ends up healing their friend in a matter of a week. Broken bones stitched back together and all, and this guy ends up walking out of the cave with his two buddies.

"So their story gets published and a year later an investigative journal sends a team back to, you know, interview or whatever these natives but they're never found. I think one of the original guys went back with them too, I can't remember, but where the tribe had been? There was nothing but a boneyard. Blackened and burnt bodies. Like the holocaust. And no one knows what happened.

"Three years later, a new drug is introduced said to combine angiogenesis with bone repair. It's been touted as the next miracle drug, though it's still awaiting FDA approval. But the one ingredient in the drug that's never been used before in modern medicine is a rare, almost unheard of, mineral. And guess where the only place you can find it is?"

"The caves in South Africa," Grey said.

"James Dugan, the man I'm searching for, was stationed in the Mpumalanga region, a stone's throw from the Sudwala caves where this tribe was discovered. And if you do enough research, you find he works for the same company that's submitted the Efescon-H drug, which will more than likely be approved this following year. And now? He's here, in Venezuela, and has been for the past year-and-a-half."

"How do you know all this?" Kenny asked.

"I've been … following him, his whereabouts, for some time. I've just never been in a position to do anything about it before now."

A long silence passed, thoughts Faye wished she had access to rolling through their minds.

Sir William's steps returned on the staircase. "What's your plan if you do catch up with said individual?" he asked, moving past them with a broom. Its bristles were crusted over in mud.

"Same plan we had with the lumber mill," Faye answered. "Let people know the truth. You can't fight evil if no one knows it's there."

"Very Tolkien-esque," Sir William said.

Grey was striking his temple with an open palm repeatedly as he paced. She had hoped for his help in this, in convincing the others. Maybe refraining from speaking his mind was the best he could do.

"So we just record him?" Kenny asked.

"Yeah," Faye said, hoping the lie was believable.

Donavon reappeared at the doorway, a line creased in his forehead. Faye new what that meant. "I say no," he said.

"No to what?" Faye asked.

"To staying. To confronting some madman who's clearly not afraid of using force."

"I know you're sick, you don't have to come –"

"Look, I think it's great you've followed this guy around, Faye, I really do, and I even agree someone needs to stop him, but the right someone. You need the FBI or Special Forces or someone who can go up against a group of killers. I'm assuming he doesn't act alone?"

Faye knew her lack of an answer was an answer in itself.

"We're just likely to get ourselves killed," Donavon continued. "How much evil can you stop in the world when you're dead? My vote's no. We stay here till this storm passes and then we get the hell out of here."

Faye was surprised at how betrayed she felt at the moment. She thought Donavon would be the easy one to convince. With Grey cowed, she knew Kenny would fall in line. One way or another.

"I thought you were with me," she said.

"I am with you, you're just not thinking clearly."

"And Grey, what do you think?" Faye asked.

He stared at her, unseen thoughts tumbling like a waterfall.

"When Grey and I went out earlier this morning, we had this very same conversation, didn't we? As we were walking out by the road. Do you remember what you said, Grey? Before, you know? 'This is for Malcolm,' wasn't that it? How it started?"

Grey broke from her gaze rubbing at his face with his hands. "Malcolm's dead and we have nothing to show for it," he said. "If we use the footage from the earthquake we'll be crucified, exposing human suffering for an agenda, but this ... we could do something with. Something big."

"We already lost one member of our team and now you're getting in line to lose another?" Donavon asked.

Grey didn't even bother looking at him. At any of them. "If Faye tells us we're not in danger, I have to believe her."

"The things a pretty face will do to a man, huh?" Donavon said.

Faye slapped him.

The ringing of that slap hung in the air, Faye's hand imprinted in red on Donavon's cheek. He just looked at her, not saying a word. She refused to back down, refused to be the one to look away first.

"This is what happens when you don't get your way," he finally said. "You just manipulate us until we all come around."

The others in the room had gone completely silent, except for the monkey who was giving off a low mewling sound, almost like a purr.

"Thanks for bringing this before everyone so we could make a *group* decision," Donavon finished.

Half the time I end up destroying something or someone I care about in order to accomplish something better.

The words she had spoken to Grey played through her mind.

But it still hurts.

Only it didn't hurt. It never had. Not when she knew she was in the right. The only damage done was the violent gouging of that image she had created in her mind, who she had wanted Donavon to be.

Before she could tell him what she really thought, Kenny spoke up unexpectedly.

"I'm in."

Faye turned, finding Kenny petting the monkey who had crawled up onto his lap. It arched its back beneath his fingers.

"But I want Exec Producer credits on anything that comes of this."

Faye hesitated only a second. "Done. We don't know when he'll be in town next but we know where he goes."

Kenny nodded, Spree wrapping his small hand over Kenny's thumb. "I helped on a shoot for a documentary on ants few years back, most boring ass thing I've ever done. But you learn the only way to get the shot is to keep showing up."

"Wait, we need to talk this through," Donavon said.

"The lady's made up her mind," Sir William said. "And I don't think she's the type to change it often."

"If we do this – *if* – then the first sign of danger we're all backing out. I won't be a part of some investigation on why our entire film crew was killed while on shoot," Donavon said.

"That's very selfless of you," Faye said.

Donavon didn't catch her sarcasm.

"Thank you, each of you. I know this isn't a light thing I'm asking, but I promise it will be worth it."

Grey was back to massaging his scalp.

Verse XV.

Zephyr ducked beneath low hanging branches, hopping over a fallen tree trunk covered in moss. They were making a good pace, especially with the weather. Just ahead Cy moved as if he were hovering rather than running through the jungle growth. The kook may be the oldest of their group but he was certainly fit.

Less than a meter away on his right the forest disappeared; like walking up to the edge of the earth. They had passed a few trees that had been split in two, roots dangling out over the precipice like severed veins from an amputated arm. Rain drizzled down in a constant barrage, dribbling over Zephyr's face. With every step his feet sunk into the marshy jungle floor, beetles and spiders scurrying underfoot to escape the onslaught.

Cy came to an abrupt halt.

Zephyr immediately brought his SRM shotgun into position, scanning the trees and brush. The noises of the jungle persisted, trees come alive with the heaviness of the water that fell.

Zephyr clicked his tongue against his roof in a call made to imitate a macaw. Cy looked back at him, an emotionless gaze.

"The river," he said.

Zephyr drew forward, stepping over coiled vines. An orange butterfly the size of his fist fluttered past his face.

Between scattered trees the river was visible in spurts, water lapping over the bank like waves on a shore. Considering the sudden downpour, the levels should have risen much higher, the temporary ebb and flow of that line shifting from day to day.

Zephyr followed the river to its end. The source of its dipping level was painfully obvious.

The Icabarú river had become a waterfall.

Cascading from the edge of the cliff, water sprayed out in a wide scattered stream. It was mesmerizing to watch, water disappearing into nothing.

"The birth of a waterfall," Cy said.

"Illegitimate birth." Zephyr snorted loudly, spitting over the edge. "How long before it runs dry?"

Cy blew out his breath. "If we're bottlenecked on both sides? Half a day? Maybe sooner. We could dam it."

"We won't be here on this island long enough for it to matter."

"And the town?" Cy asked.

"Can find their own water."

Something large climbed up a tree nearby, its shaking branches accentuating the rainfall with added moisture.

Cy picked up a small stone and hurled it off the edge. "I keep wondering when I'm going to wake up and realize I've been shot so full of drugs by these natives I've been imagining the whole thing. It's like we're living in a dream."

"That's where you and I differ. I only believe what I see with my eyes."

"Maybe that's why you see so little."

"I see a hell of a lot more than you, Cyclops," Zephyr said, staring at the man's mutilated eye. "Like Dugan said, it's not a question of *if,* it's a question of *why.*"

"I've been thinking about that. When you're trapping an animal that's on the run – or a native muku, we'll say – what's the general rule?"

"Cut off retreat, keep him surrounded."

"More than that. What are the principles that keep him running?"

Zephyr folded his arms, his impatience growing. "You let him think he can get away."

Cy nodded, his one good eye focusing on Zephyr. "Not just that he can get away but that he has a choice. You let him think he's choosing where he's going when all the while –"

"He's going where you want him to."

"I fear this … barrier, that has been imposed upon us? Maybe it isn't meant to hinder our search of the Shaman, but to keep us from fleeing when we do find him."

"Or when he finds us?" Zephyr asked.

"Precisely."

Verse XVI.

The Humvee tore across the flat plains having left the denser jungle behind. Water splashed up from the puddles hidden beneath thick savannah grass, the wipers ticking back and forth without pause. A herd of tayassu stopped, small thin-haired boars, their necks rising to watch the vehicles roar past.

Dugan's notebook was open on his lap, the natural fold in the book revealing the page which had been turned to more than any other. A page that contained only one name.

It was a name he couldn't forget if he had wanted to.

It surprised him how often he did want to.

Selah Moanna.

He had inscribed her maiden name, for reasons that escaped him then and he had yet to understand now. Selah was a Hebrew word found in the Bible, thought to be an instruction to the musicians who played to the reading of the Psalms.

Play louder and with more meaning. Selah! There was no substitute in the English language to adequately translate the ancient word.

Moanna meant Ocean Goddess in her native island roots. Maybe that was the way he preferred to remember her – a goddess, not the diseased doppelganger that had cannibalized her divinity one crippling day at a time.

Selah Moanna.

Play it louder, Ocean Goddess.

"We all die," she had told him. "It's part of the adventure, the climax of all these rising actions that make up the chapters of our lives. But the denouement, my love, is not this."

She motioned to her withered body.

"The denouement is what awaits us on the other side. You can't rob me of that climax, or anyone else. We earn it. We deserve to know how all these seemingly separate strands that make up our existence resolve together in the end. You have to believe, James. Believe that whatever poet in the sky is directing this mad narrative will see those strands resolved into a fulfilling conclusion. Have faith. If not in Him, in me."

Dugan left the very next morning. Without saying goodbye.

His reverie was broken as a military jeep came hurtling over the next rise toward them, a second trailing not far behind. The first cut in at a sharp angle, cutting off their path.

Oso slammed on the brakes, bringing the Humvee to a stop. A cloud of dirt carried on past them, its trajectory continuing like a shadow that hadn't realized its host had stopped.

Rojo lifted an assault rifle out from the back, a casualness to his unhurried action. Dugan rewound the strap around his notebook, tucking it back in the pocket of his vest. He flinched at the pain from where the rope had burned through the side of his pectoral muscle and inner triceps. There hadn't been time to dress the wound; other matters more pressing.

He exited the vehicle, conscious of the driver's door closing. Oso joined him out front.

Several soldiers hopped out of the first vehicle, followed by General Gutierrez who stepped out from the second jeep. He was dressed in grey fatigues, his large gut hanging over his pants which rode low. His ever-present brown fedora clung tightly to his head.

He opened his hands wide as if to greet them with a hug. "My friend!"

He came forward, clapping Dugan on both shoulders and shaking him jovially. Never mind that his men were fingering their rifles.

"Jou are well?"

Dugan stepped back, lighting a cigarette. "As well as can be."

The General reached out to take the cigarette, forcing Dugan to light another for himself.

"Santa Elena? The town still stands?"

"Parts, yes, but de earthquake was, very bad," Gutierrez said.

Dugan wondered if the man knew just how bad it had been; so bad that they had been lifted several thousand feet into the air.

"The, uh, factory is no bueno," Gutierrez continued. "Many peoples smashed dead. Like bugs." The general clapped his hands suddenly together in a squashing motion.

Dugan nodded as if this concerned him. "We saw two helicopters the other day?"

"Ah yes, de, uh, Americans. Dey are, how do you say, tree lovers?" Gutierrez surprised one of his men by grabbing hold of him from behind and pretending to rape him. He barked a laugh, a few of his men joining.

"Tree huggers," Dugan said. "It's their helicopter?"

"No, dey rent but I check it out for you. Is no competition. But dere is bigger problem – dey are asking for you. By name."

Dugan sensed Oso tense beside him. This wouldn't be the first time people had been sent to follow Dugan. He was a proven bet in the big pharma community, an industry notorious for stealing other people's work. If they could swipe what they needed before it got into a laboratory, all the better.

Yet if they were asking for him by name, why hide behind the ruse of a green organization?

"I know where dey are staying," the General said, his grin spreading. He blew a ring of smoke into the air.

"As always, your services are appreciated," Dugan said, handing a white envelope across to the General.

Gutierrez held the cigarette out at a distance, looking at it. "Why you like dese cheapy cheapies? A real man smokes a cigar."

Dugan didn't respond.

"Da last time I smoke a Cuban, has been when you first arrive. Dat was some good flavors, no?"

"I'll see what I can do to come up with another." Dugan had no intention of following up on the promise. Not for this man.

Gutierrez opened the envelope, thumbing through the stack of hundred dollar bills. "Is not cheap to get this kind of information," Gutierrez said. "We had dem arrested, dese Americans, but dey know peoples and our resources are, uh, limited."

Looming over the short fat Venezuelan, his smug smile strapped across his greasy face, Dugan felt the sudden urge to signal Rojo to cut him down. It wasn't the money that bothered him; he would have paid ten times as much for what this beady bastard had already done for him. It was that smile the man held while accepting Dugan's money; that cockiness, as if he were only ever revealing half of what he knew.

"Expect the same tomorrow," Dugan said, turning his back on the man and returning to the Humvee. "And I'll see if I can find you some cigars."

Only if I shit on them first, Dugan thought.

"You no want the location? Where dey are staying?"

"Give it to Oso," Dugan said, without looking back.

"He does not talk!"

"Which is why I trust him." Dugan knew the General would miss the implication.

As he climbed back into the passenger seat, he heard Rojo mutter a sigh. "One day I'd really like to split that muku's head open."

Dugan snubbed the end of his cigarette against the windshield, right over the General's face. "One day I'll let you."

Verse XVII.

Grey clicked through still frames on his laptop, cutting and saving any sequence with Malcolm in it. He wasn't sure why he was doing it, other than it giving him something to do. In most of the photos Malcolm was only in the background, a partial head or body, turned away from the camera. Not important enough to be the focus of any shot.

But Grey had found a few.

Malcolm seated in one of the restaurants the bus had stopped at, pointing at the fried blackened bananas and gravy splattered meat with a closed-mouth smile.

Malcolm crashed out on the bus ride, his knees tucked up against the seat, Knicks hat askew.

Malcolm giving his closed-mouth grin and two thumbs up in front of the helicopter, his eyes appearing as closed as his mouth.

The one shot he repeatedly discovered, over and over, was one that had never been taken: Malcolm lying on the ground, his head completely flattened, an oval arc of pulpy tissue splattered around it like a devil's halo. The image never left his mind.

Grey clicked forward through a long stream of clips, Faye almost glowing in every one. Her candid expressions, the angles of her face, that coy smile. Every movement a lesson in seductiveness.

He slammed the lid closed on his MacBook, shutting the computer down. He didn't want to think about her.

She's all I want to think about!

Rain beat against the house like an angry neighbor at the door. A constant dribble of water fell into the bucket Sir William had placed beneath the leak in the roof, as bad as the annoying tick of a clock.

Ping – Ping – Ping.

Upstairs, the old man was sleeping through it, though Grey was sure his inebriated state had assisted with that task.

Grey stretched his legs out onto the glass coffee table surrounded by mismatched chairs and couches. The others had left on their first reconnaissance mission, Grey opting to stay back when Donavon insisted on going despite being ill. Every time Grey looked at the actor he felt a need to spill his guts, tell him what had almost happened. And what had.

That wasn't me, that monster I turned into. I would never do that.

And yet he knew he would have.

But then what Faye had done to him? How was that any better?

He still wondered if it had all really happened.

This state of confusion, this … infatuation; it wasn't like him. She had a hold on him that went beyond anything he had ever felt before. Like a drug, it was changing him – his nature, his thought process, reactions. And as much as he wanted to never see her again, to stay clear of her forever, he couldn't deny the yearning scraping out his insides.

Would they have another moment together? Had her opinion of Donny-boy changed like Grey thought it had? And if so, did her feelings towards Grey have anything to do with it?

Is she as infatuated with me as I am with her?

He lifted the lid back up on his MacBook, quickly typing in his password. He scrolled through another dozen photos, finding one of Malcolm toying with a ginormous ant with a stick. He dropped it into the folder marked X.

Malcolm X. Fitting in so many ways.

His face, smashed, like a dropped pie.

He decided if it was the only footage he ever showed from this trip, he would make sure the world saw a memorial for the intern. If, of course, they made it out of Venezuela alive.

Grey slid the USB satellite adapter back into the port on his laptop, raising the antennae, for all the good it would do.

Still no signal.

Strange how disconnected he felt from the world while surrounded by nature. But his world had always been a virtual one, born and raised in the cloud.

Over the rattling rain he heard a noise outside, more like a vibration. Maybe Faye and the others had given up on their stake-out for the night; God knew the weather was bad enough.

An image of her walking through the door popped into his head – her hair clinging to her face, wet clothes gripping her so tight they might as well not exist. She would see him sitting there on the couch, her green eyes lighting up.

The noise came again, something scraping against the door.

Grey slid his laptop onto the table and stood when the front door split open with a loud burst, blowing outward.

A large man in a dark camouflaged suit rushed through the open doorway, barrel of his rifle shoved into Grey's face.

"Get down! Get down!"

Grey fell back into the couch, hands raised.

The red-bearded man slammed a foot against the rocking chair in front of Grey. The chair overturned with a racket of noise, one of its spindles breaking at the top. His eyes crinkled beneath his red eyebrows, as he shouted, "Where are the others?"

Grey's hands were already raised above his head. He pointed upward by lowering three of his fingers.

Another body swept past, climbing the curved metal staircase in two bounds, long black hair flowing behind him like a phantom. Grey heard Sir William's surprise as he was woken from sleep.

Or his drunken stupor.

Their host came down the metal staircase, hands waving about. "I'm going, I'm going!" Sir William stopped at the bottom of the landing, looking past Grey. "Oh hell." He trod over to the kitchen bar, pouring Scotch from the bottle into a dirty glass.

At the door a man stood wearing a dark cargo vest and nylon hiking pants. His outfit wasn't what caused Grey to take a step back however; it was his stance, his demeanor. And the man seemed to not even realize it.

He took in the entire room with a single glance, carrying himself with a confidence that would be obscene on anyone else. But this was an alpha wolf, a man who led while standing silently in a room.

The soldier with long black hair who looked more like a Venezuelan than the other two made some kind of movement with his lips and hands, motioning above him on the stairs.

The man at the door nodded. "Hello Frederick."

A hinge from the door scraped lightly against the broken frame with the wind.

"Dugan," Sir William said, knocking back the last of his liquor.

"I hear you have friends who are looking for me. Care to make introductions?"

Verse XVIII.

"You sure you're okay?"

Faye and Kenny hovered over Donavon who sat beneath the awning of a school building situated across from the police station. Despite the location, there was still plenty of graffiti on the walls. Donavon leaned his head back against the mustard-colored brick wall, his eyes closed.

"I'm fine."

"You didn't have to come," Faye said.

"Neither did you," he muttered.

The rain fell in droves just beyond the alcove; even for someone who lived in New York this felt torrential. They would have gone back by now if they had a car, or any way of transporting Donavon without letting him get soaked. The last thing he needed was pneumonia alongside his stomach flu or food poisoning.

The Main Street of the town had turned into a river, water running over the lip of the curbed sidewalk before the school and pooling in the vestibule they had crowded into. It was difficult to tell if evening had arrived or if it was only the storm clouds. Either way, the man she sought wasn't coming today.

They heard a noise back at the station – a door slamming.

The alcalde, chief of police, ducked beneath an umbrella one of his men held, running from the station to the jeep parked out front. He had arrived only a few minutes before. Faye was under the impression he was the type to delegate rather than sit behind a desk.

After safely transporting him into the passenger seat, two of the men returned to the station, the others accompanying him in the jeep. With the alcalde leaving, it was a certainty Dugan wouldn't be showing.

A gurgle sounded from Donavon, rising not from his throat but stomach. He grimaced, rubbing at his side. Faye wondered if the slop he was sitting in was only mud, then instantly regretted the thought.

The jeep started, headlights glowing, giving the rain life. Specters danced in the road, water covering the entire expanse as if a stream had arisen from the ground. Water sprayed out in dual rivulets as the jeep barreled down the road.

"I wish we had a car," Faye said, holding one hand out of the archway, rain pelting it.

It was warm.

"As soon as it lets up, we'll go." Despite her best efforts she couldn't keep the disappointment from her voice.

"Try again tomorrow?" Donavon asked.

"Not with you we won't. You're staying in bed."

Kenny flicked a three-inch long cockroach off the wall. Rather than fall, it sprouted wings, flitting around like a moth.

"We shouldn't have brought the camera," he said. His long hair had frizzed out making him look almost like Weird Al Yankovich. A much heavier version of him anyway.

"I thought you said it was waterproof?" Faye said.

"Water resistant. There's a big difference between a light shower and walking beneath the Niagara."

He brought out a small metal case that looked like it might hold business cards, opening it. He removed a rolled joint, putting it to his lips.

"You want one?" he asked, his words muffled. He held the case out as he searched for his lighter.

Faye shook her head, going back to the archway and staring out at the dark skies. Such relentless anger in those clouds. The thing was, she *did* want one.

You're never clean.

The Priest's voice echoed in her head.

"I'll take one."

Kenny handed Donavon the case, tossing him the lighter and taking his first puff. "They don't call it the rainforest for nothin," he said.

Headlights appeared further down the road, their beams flaring through the curtains of rain. They must have forgotten something. Faye wondered where the alcalde lived; if he required men watching his own home at all times just to keep the people from uprising.

The aroma of marijuana filled her head. She scratched at her arm, an old nervous tic.

The headlights grew, twin eyes of a monstrous beast shining with irreverent light. Faye ducked back within the alcove, the jeep skidding to a halt in a gush of rainwater. But it wasn't the jeep – it was larger, its wheels like giant gears sitting beneath a machine created for one purpose only.

War.

The back door opened and a man fell out. He landed on his shoulder, the water swallowing his head only to spit him back out. The man struggled to his knees, splashing in the water..

It was Sir William.

"Frederick!" Faye shouted.

He bobbed his head, casting about. With the shadows of the covered patio he must not have seen them.

Faye stepped onto the sidewalk, her running shoes sinking in water. "Over here!"

Sir William swung his arm. "Run, Faye! Run!"

The driver's door opened, a Venezuelan with long hair leaping out. He wasn't in uniform and didn't look like any of the soldiers Faye had seen. He yanked Sir William to his feet gripping him by the back of his shirt, a long machete sliding just beneath his throat.

"No!"

Faye ran out into the road, buffeted by the rain and wind. Two men trudged from around the other side of the vehicle. Grey, his hands bound in front of him, face darkened, maybe bruised. He was led by a bald bearded man holding a wicked looking rifle.

"Faye! Get back!" Donavon called.

Both Kenny and Donavon stood at either side of the columned archway. Kenny fumbled with the camera, raising it just as a white light sprung from its top, bathing her in its glow.

She spun back around, her confidence surging knowing this was being filmed. "Let them go!"

The man behind Grey smiled, his beard rising with his grin.

"You're on camera, streaming live to the world!" she shouted. It was a bluff but maybe they wouldn't know any better.

"Only stream here's the one you're standing in, darling," the man with the beard said. "You're the one looking for Dugan?"

Cold steeled through Faye's veins, nothing to do with the rain soaking her. She brushed the hair back from her face. "You'll take me to him?"

The bearded man raised his gun, aiming it now at her. "Uh-uh, stay where you are cowboy!"

Donavon stood halfway between Faye and the school's awning, his unslung hand raised, palm out. "This is a misunderstanding," he said. "I'm an actor and producer; we're scouting for locations."

Grey suddenly brought an elbow back, turning as he rammed the man with the gun behind him. "Go!" he yelled.

Before his words had left his mouth he was falling, the man slamming his foot down on top of Grey's back as he stepped forward, gun positioned to fire.

"Wait!" Faye yelled. "I'm his daughter!"

Grey brought his head up, dirty water spilling from his mouth.

"I'm his daughter."

A man appeared at the edge of the vehicle, his confident gait undeterred by the stream that had replaced the road. A red dot glowed near his mouth as he pulled a cigarette away.

"Faye?" the man said.

His voice, like a glacier splitting in two.

"Dad."

Verse XIX.

Dugan let the cigarette fall from his fingers. It bobbed in the water, floating along the current like a piece of straw.

His daughter stood before him, clothing and hair plastered to her body by the rain. So much had changed – her head shaved on one side, her lean muscular frame, so different from the pudgy girl he had left behind. Yet she still had that spark in her eyes, that fire nothing could quench.

For a moment Dugan regretted the choices he had made in his life. The moment quickly passed.

"Long way to come for a reunion," he said.

Faye's lips quivered. With the rain he couldn't tell if she was crying or just cold. "You bastard."

"You get my postcards?"

He, of course, knew that she did. Dugan paid a lot of money to track his daughter's whereabouts, and to keep her safe.

"I heard you got married."

The man standing beside her with a lineman's physique looked at her sharply. He could have fit the mold for one of Dugan's men – was certainly large enough – though despite his set jaw, Dugan sensed he was much softer than he looked. An egg that hadn't been boiled long enough. The makeshift sling wrapped around his arm certainly didn't help.

"Engaged," Faye said.

"Where's the ring?"

Faye withdrew her hand, clenching it into a fist and shoving it into the pocket of her sweatshirt. The man beside her rested one hand on her arm.

The kid on the ground splashed about, trying to free himself beneath Rojo's boot.

"Tell your soldiers to let them go!" Faye said. "Capturing an old man and a college kid? You must be real proud."

Dugan smiled but didn't raise a finger toward Oso or Rojo. Always wiser to keep pieces off the board that had already been removed. "I heard about your little protest. Still trying to save the world?"

"Are you still trying to destroy it?"

"Difficult to do one without the other." Dugan smiled. God, it had been so long. "It's really good to see you."

"No. You don't get to pretend to be a father, pretend to have missed me. You lost that privilege a long time ago." She was shaking now. "Did you know when she died she was calling your name? You didn't even come to the funeral!"

Dugan continued to meet her eyes without glancing away. He had come to terms with the choices he had made a long time ago.

"You are despicable – you're not even human! What you and your ... syndicate do? Murdering entire villages all to find the next weight-loss drug? To, to make the pharmas their next billions? Oh yeah, I know what you really do. I've followed your movements, the body count you leave in your trail. How I'm the only one who's been able to track you is beyond me."

That's because the others that try are all dead, Dugan thought.

"What did she ever see in you? Or did you give her as much choice as the holy-men you put your guns to in order to get their secrets? She never loved you."

"Are you through?"

"Not even close! You have to be stopped and I am going to be the one to do it."

An odd silence fell with the last of her words, the light from whoever held that camera behind her causing Dugan to squint.

"You've grown into the woman I always hoped you'd be," he said.

Faye brought her hand out from the sweatshirt pocket raising a silver derringer to Dugan's face.

"Don't!" Dugan yelled.

Not to Faye; to Oso and Rojo.

He put his hands out toward them.

Tension zipped through the air like electricity leaping between falling drops of rain.

"Faye, what are you doing?" the man said beside her.

She didn't answer, just stepped away from him, a foot closer to Dugan. Water drizzled down her face.

"This is the only way to stop you," she said. "One death to save how many? Hundreds? Thousands?"

Dugan spoke slowly, carefully. "Exactly why I do what I do."

"Don't do this, Faye," the man on the ground said.

"Shut up," she said, biting her lower lip.

"Dugan?" Rojo said.

"No!" Dugan yelled back. "I've got this."

The pupils in Faye's eyes shrunk ever so slightly. "You never had this."

She pulled the trigger.

Noting the change in her eyes, Dugan dropped a half-second before. Felt the bullet zip past his cheek. Faye's eyes widened at having missed. Dugan lowered his shoulder and slammed into his daughter, following her down as they dropped to the water, her gun flying from her grip.

They hit, with Dugan on top; he felt the breath leap out of her. He swept his other foot around, expecting her quarterback boyfriend to come to her aid. Struck his ankles so hard the boyfriend toppled with a groan, landing beside Dugan on the ground.

Oso was there beside him, his curved black blade falling just short of breaking skin on the boyfriend's neck. Behind them, the Englishman stumbled back against the Humvee, glancing around for a place to flee.

Dugan rose, retrieving Faye's gun from the stream in the road. "I never expected you to understand and I don't need your forgiveness."

He popped open the barrel of the small handgun, both chambers empty, and snapped it back in. "But one day, one day I think you might. Understand."

He tossed the gun back to Faye who had sat up, gasping as air returned to her.

"Consider your lives a gift," Dugan said, slowly backing up. "To make up for the shitty father I've been. And even shittier human being. I would tell you to leave town but I'm not sure you'll be able to. But I do appreciate you letting us borrow your helicopter."

He looked up at the third man hiding near the school's entryway, the bright flash making it impossible to make out his details. "I'll be needing that before we go. Rojo?"

The light from the camera wavered as Rojo stepped off the skinny man they had taken at the house and started toward the school.

"It was good to see you Faye. But next time, call first."

"I hate you," she said staring back at him from the ground, water covering her waist. "I hate you!"

Verse XX.

Faye had never felt more like a child in all her life. Like a little girl that had fallen in a puddle, arms outstretched, waiting for her father to lift her to her feet and tell her everything would be okay.

Though she would be waiting a long time.

She had failed. Had found her father, confronted him, but ultimately failed. And she knew she wouldn't be so lucky as to have another opportunity.

The light from Kenny's camera went dark, bathing the street once again in shadow. A strobe effect suddenly flashed, light going in and out several times before something exploded. Faye turned back in time to see Kenny drop the camera, catching just a glimpse of the ancillary flash from the spark.

She shielded her eyes but too late, a white afterimage burning behind her eyelids. She wasn't certain but she could have sworn the bearded mercenary hadn't yet reached Kenny. Then why had the camera failed?

Several similar bursts sounded, electronics popping with some kind of surge. Donavon shouted, tossing something into the water. A wisp of smoke rose from where it had fallen.

"My cell!" he said, rubbing at his leg where his phone had been.

The Indian-looking Venezuelan with long hair twirled his long machete in his hand, glancing nervously around.

"What is it, Oso?" her father said.

The light above the porch of the police station blew out, followed by both of the Humvee's headlights. Leaning against the vehicle, Sir William jumped at the sudden noise, almost ending back in the water. Faye reached out to Donavon who helped her up.

"Oso?"

Another explosion sounded, the mercenary with the beard stripping off a handheld radio which looked like it had detonated. In the dark it was difficult to tell, but Faye thought his side where the radio had been clipped on was dark with blood. If so, the man seemed unperturbed.

Faye caught a foul smell with the breeze, so strong it caused an instant gag reflex. It was the smell of something rotting. Something that used to be alive.

"Oh, gawd," Donavon said, putting one hand to his face.

Her father splashed through the water, a black heavy pistol replacing the small gun he had taken from her. "What will it be this time?" he shouted to the darkness.

Grey cowered as Dugan stepped past him.

"I'm right here!" Dugan screamed.

Donavon grabbed hold of Faye's arm, pointing down the road.

A strange green luminescence shone through the blurred lines of stinted rain, seeming to grow larger. The rain was the only noise around them, pattering in a steady chant. Everyone quietly waiting for whatever approached. Both of Dugan's men had weapons out and ready, focused on the growing apparition.

Faye blinked through the flash that still hovered over her eyes. Something was in the light, she just couldn't make it out. A form, like a shadow – blurred or out of focus.

And then as if he were stepping through the light into the darkness before it, a man appeared, frail and weathered. The green light was gone as if it had never been.

The man walked slowly, taking quiet steps.

Heavy stone necklaces hung from his long thin neck, sweeping back and forth against his bare chest as he moved. His flesh was wrinkled and leathery, marks on his chest Faye recognized as tattoos. His hair was grey and woven in long bands that hung from his head like the drooping fronds of a plant deprived of sunlight. Sunken eyes, a long bony chin and a piece of reed wood twining through the flesh of his bottom lip. His only clothing was a thin cloth flap, barely covering what most men kept concealed.

He stretched out a frail hand. "Inktomi."

Lightning could have struck the very ground. In an instant everyone was moving – Dugan and his two men kicking up water as they circled around the native Indian, guns pointed toward him. They kept their distance, but it was apparent they had no intention of letting the man escape their reach.

Sir William stepped forward with uncertain footing, his face ghostly pale. Grey finally rose from the water, looking to Faye as if for direction.

For once she didn't have any.

"Inktomi Fehener La'aione."

The man turned in a semi-circle following Dugan's movements. Her father was the only person the native Indian seemed to notice.

"Takushkansh'kan." Dugan said the foreign word almost with reverence. "You underestimated me."

"No," the old Indian said forcefully, his voice gravel scraping against stone.

"Are you here to trade? Your life for your people?"

"No."

Sir William stepped past Faye and Donavon, his head shaking. He was mumbling to himself. "Can it … Can it be …?"

Dugan continued his dance around the man. "Then you're here to give us what we need. Peacefully."

Faye caught only a glimpse of the Indian's smile as he turned away from her, but that glimpse sent a shiver through her body.

"No."

Faye followed after Sir William, moving closer toward the exchange. Something about the Indian was off, like an unfinished painting, one shade away from being complete. And then she realized what it was.

Not a single drop of water fell on the man.

Rain fell as thick as sleet, pelting them all like tiny needles, and yet the drops wound around the Indian. The rain bent as if there were a warp in the air, molecules of water never coming in contact with his person. He stood in the middle of a storm completely dry except for his feet, submerged in the stream that had been a road.

"You must know you can't win," Dugan said, their circle tightening closer around the man. "No one else needs to be hurt."

"No!"

"Wait!"

Faye was surprised the words had come from her but she continued, shooting past Sir William and stepping between the frail Indian and her father. "No more! This has to end!"

Her father stepped to the side, not even looking at her, his gaze falling only on the native behind her.

"Dad?"

"Get rid of her," he said, almost as an afterthought.

The bald bearded mercenary was on her instantly. Faye felt herself drop, her head wrapped in the crook of his arms as he dragged her off to the side, the task like battling a kitten. She beat at the man, pummeling his back and arm with her fists, but knew it was pointless.

"Stop!"

The word spoken by the frail native wasn't a word but a command. And it was obeyed. Dugan and the long-haired mercenary stopped their movements around him like a stalled clock. Faye felt herself released from the bearded man's grasp.

"Little time," the native said, staring only at her father. "End begins … New beginning. Cycle … cracked. Broken. World … does not survive. Inktomi –"

As if someone had paused a show on the television, the native stopped mid-sentence, his mouth hanging open. He suddenly jerked forward, his shoulders pressing in on themselves, back arching. It looked like something was trying to crawl out of him, as if he were about to split out of his skin like a reptile. He spread his thin arms out to either side, forming a cross.

Faye could see the man's cracked lips splitting, blood seeping from the open sores.

"Deceive man … stop … beginning."

The native was no longer staring at her father but through him. He shifted his eyes from Dugan to the other native mercenary with long black hair.

"Inktomi. Ser'apa La'mielke."

With the words, the old Indian suddenly bent backward – his back curving to the point his hands could have touched the ground behind him if they hadn't been raised skyward. Winds lashed about in conflicting directions, rain seeming to come at them from all sides.

Faye held her arm in front of her face to keep from being blinded yet in that moment the green light returned, split on either side of her shadowed arm.

When she finally lowered her arm to look, the Indian before her, the one her father had called Takushkansh'kan, was levitating in the air.

Verse XXI.

Wind wrested Dugan, lashing out and carrying with it rain that felt as if it were penetrating skin rather than breaking on it. And yet, despite the hurricane-like storm, he couldn't force himself to look away. The answer he had been searching for his entire life was within his grasp, embodied in the man before him.

A man who was floating a foot above the water.

The Shaman's bare feet dangled in the air, his levitating trick now at its maximum height. Despite his demonstration of power, Takushkansh'kan did not look like a man in control. He didn't hover like a god, arms held steady at his side, staring down at the ants before him. Instead he looked like a child's doll being carried. His body was limp, head lolling side to side, his arms no longer held up but hanging down.

One thing was certain: this was not a man Dugan need fear.

A few men and women had congregated, locals who consumed gossip as quickly as cerveza. They were huddled together in small groupings on the outskirts of the road or hiding within doorways. Watching. Staring. Even a few of the General's La Guardia were intermingled within the crowd, the soldiers equally agitated.

Out of the corner of his eye Dugan caught sight of Zephyr and Cy both pushing past bodies and moving into the street, their boots lost beneath water. Dugan was glad to see them. Just in case things got ugly.

Something boomed from above the Shaman, a low rumble that shook Dugan to his core. The crowd uniformly cowered at the noise, men and women ducking in fright. Water now pelted the native hovering in the air as if he had become a magnet, rain sweeping toward him from every direction.

Dugan held out a hand to Zephyr, the man sighting his tranq gun on the floating Shaman.

Not yet.

The Shaman opened his mouth. A green mist spouted out like a breath in the winter cold, and then the world flashed white. It was like lightning had struck in front of Dugan's face.

Temporarily blinded, he fell to his knees in the rainwater, trying to blink through the shock.

The earth rumbled with the Shaman's words, Dugan steadying himself with one hand to keep from falling over.

"K'lana Sa'taumn Lia'ona Shan'kaunum."

Gales of directionless wind swept upward to meet the Shaman, a sudden pressure in the air making Dugan feel like his ears were about to pop.

His vision slowly returned. He stretched one hand out, feeling the droplets of water strike his palm. Raindrops that were falling *upward* from the ground. Defying the laws of gravity, the water rose from the stream toward the Shaman.

Okay, maybe a little fear would be wise, Dugan thought.

"Di'aonak Ka'lumnin Ka'logna."

The pressure in the air was building, like stepping sixty feet below water without a chance to acclimate first. Oso looked upward, his face a mask of pain. The black blade slipped from his fingers, splashing to the ground. Dugan realized he was no longer holding his own gun. When had it fallen?

The Shaman's entire body now glowed with a soft green haze.

Dugan's eardrums were about to burst, the pressure at its apex. Dugan signaled Zephyr and screamed above the deep thrum ringing through his ears.

"Now, Zephyr! Now!"

The Shaman spun in the air, turning toward Zephyr. This was the hovering god the Shaman hadn't been moments before.

Zephyr's gun arm shook violently, the muscles on his neck bulging. And then the gun slowly began to turn toward Dugan.

"I can't – Doog!" Zephyr cried.

A THWOMP sounded, a dart firing from Zephyr's gun into the darkness, followed by a second, which struck someone in the crowd behind them. The Venezuelan dropped face first into the muddy stream, those beside him, reaching out to help.

Zephyr's gun was now aligned with Dugan, the barrel wavering.

"I am Inktomi, the Spider!" Dugan slapped his chest, rising back to his feet. "And you are the hunted, not the hunter!"

The Shaman spun back toward Dugan, and in that face, in those eyes, Dugan realized he had never before known fear.

Not like this.

He was a spec, a smudge, the whole of the universe bearing down on him, smothering him beneath the weight of something so vast, so infinite, so eternal, it had no end. Eons crushed against him, endless galaxies compressing upon him until he might as well not exist. If he was the Spider it was because this creature could squash him like the insignificant bug he was. He was nothing. A blot. A blip. Unable to breathe. Unable to move. Unable to think. A strand of fiber that was being unraveled. Disintegrating. Into nothing. He was –

A dart sunk deep into the Shaman's chest.

"Hunted! Not the hunter!" Zephyr shouted, tossing his empty dart gun into the water.

A string of shots followed his cry, Rojo and Cy unleashing their own darts. Three more stuck from the Shaman's torso, neck and arm.

The pressure in Dugan's ears popped, the sounds of rainfall swelling anew, and then the Shaman's body fell to the ground, water cascading over him before leveling back out.

Rain continued to fall. Downward.

As it was meant to.

The Shaman lifted his head from the water and reached one bony arm toward Dugan as if for help and then Faye was beside him, raising his head above the water and heaving him upward. Frederick, the old Englishman, leapt past Rojo, Faye's boyfriend now at her side.

"Bring him! Quick!" Frederick yelled.

Faye's boyfriend lifted the Shaman like a bag of potatoes, despite his slung arm, and then they were racing through the street, tearing through the water as they went.

More movement as the crowd began to disperse, panicked chaos ensuing. A man with long hair ducked out from the school's awning – the cameraman, his hands now empty and raised. After coming to the conclusion he wasn't going to get shot, he started running after his friends.

Dugan began to laugh.

He stared up into the sky, arms outstretched, rain falling around him, pelting him. He was dripping wet and he had never felt so alive. Reduced to nothing, he had survived.

To find the Shaman is death. Or Death finds the Shaman.

Looks like it was the latter of the two. And Dugan was Death.

He brought out his pack of cigarettes, damp but not soaked, and placed one between his lips. When he brought his lighter up he realized the cap had exploded. He laughed even harder.

Verse XXII.

The front door of the church slammed inward, striking someone on the other side. Faye swept in through the doorway, immediately noticing that while the rain had cleared out the crowd petitioning outside, it had done little to remove those already within.

"We need help!" she shouted. "Ayudanos!"

Men and women and children upon children were huddled together in small camps on the tiled floor. Most of their reactions made her think these men and women would be more likely to string her up on a cross than offer a hand.

Remmy, the priest, entered from the adjoining sick room, his face weary. "I thought I told you –"

Donavon trudged through the doorway, the Shaman's limp body hanging over him like a drape. Sir William was right behind him, shouting at someone else outside.

"Who …" Remmy began, Faye cutting him off.

"They're coming to take him! Please, we need your help!"

For a moment the man in robes appeared to wither, his face appearing even older, then he motioned them back. "Come. Hurry!"

He snatched a book from a small case, handing it to the boy Faye had met earlier, the one with the mark on his face. Josue. The child immediately shouted for everyone to make way in Spanish, parents gathering their children in an attempt to create a path.

Faye and her group walked through, stepping carefully to avoid little fingers or toes. God, why did none of the children even have shoes?

Kenny joined them as they moved beneath the cloth hanging in front of the short hallway. "They're coming!" he shouted.

"Your room?" Faye asked.

"Filled with three families," Remmy said. "We ran out of space in the chapel. Come!"

At the end of the hall he raised one of the tapestries that clung to the wall, revealing a crude doorway behind it. They ducked through into a room with only a partial roof. Beams and steel cables extended overhead, the ground hardened cement, not tile. Water covered the floor in a thin film as slippery as it was filthy. In the far corner, bricks had collapsed outward, opening up to the darkened sky. A light rain spilled through the gap.

"We never had the funds to finish," Remmy said.

He pulled a rolled up rug from a table, pushing boxes and crates out of the way. A few of them Faye recognized as supply boxes they had brought. Others had markings that looked like medical supplies, though they hadn't come from her efforts.

Remmy laid the rug on the ground, its cloth quickly absorbing the water beneath like a sponge. Donavon knelt, grimacing in pain as Sir William helped him lay the Shaman down.

"Will they find us here?" Faye asked.

"The police? They don't know this room exists."

"No, Dugan."

Shumway's face fell. "You couldn't listen to me, could you?"

Sir William held the Shaman's wrist in his hand, checking for a pulse.

"So what, we just wait here and hope the men with guns don't find us? How long before those people out there give us up?" Kenny asked.

Remmy looked about their rag-tag group. "Not long."

A large crate toppled nearby, wood splintering, books flying out.

"Sorry," Donavon said, stooping to pick up the books, now dripping with muddy water. As soon as he bent down he started heaving, vomit splattering onto the texts he had meant to save.

Faye moved to him, resting one hand on his back as he slowly rose. His face was chalk white. "You okay?"

Donavon covered his face from her. "Couldn't be better," he lied.

"I need some help over here," Sir William said. "We need to revive him. Do you have anything that will bring him to? Epinephrine? Naloxone?"

"This isn't a hospital," Remmy said.

"And these supplies?" Faye asked.

"No, nothing."

"What about your stash?"

"I said no!" Remmy's eyes gleamed in the dull light. "Now stay quiet and pray to God for a miracle. He's the only one that can help you now."

Faye wiped her hair from her face, leaving Donavon's side to stand before the priest. "Just give me the key to your chest. You know it will bring him out."

"You've taken enough from me already." Remmy ducked back through the hole in the concrete, replacing the tapestry and leaving them in the dark.

Donavon put his back against a wall, sliding down into a sitting position. "We are so screwed."

"Where's Grey?" Kenny said. "I thought he was with you guys?"

"He's probably out there, getting help," Faye said.

"He's better off than we are," Donavon said.

Faye opened the flaps of a box that had toppled over. It was full of dusty pamphlets and cobwebs. "Check the boxes, crates – find anything we can use!"

"What, are we gonna throw bibles at them?" Kenny asked.

Faye turned toward him, a quiet rage surging through her. "We'll do whatever we have to. Search every box, every corner. As if your life depended on it."

"There's not gonna be a documentary, is there?" Kenny said.

"Focus on one thing at a time," Faye said.

Donavon didn't even bother to raise his head as he spoke. "Like making sure there's not another funeral."

Verse XXIII.

"Kendall and Chupa?" Dugan asked.

Cy waved off the smoke blowing from Dugan's cigarette. "Nothing yet. Depending on how this mountain was cut, their side could've been longer."

"Or we could have been faster," Zephyr added.

"But the cliffs are just like we thought. It goes all the way around," Cy said.

Dugan breathed in a heavy breath, letting the smoke and nicotine work its way into his lungs. The town's center was quiet except for the light fall of rain. Any stragglers from the crowd that had gathered earlier moved away from Dugan and his men, not towards them. No one wanted to be caught between him and his prey.

Across from the town square, the church waited like a whore who had already been paid. Ripe for the taking.

"Your daughter's pretty hot, Dugan." Rojo covered his smile with one hand. "That why you kept her a secret?"

Dugan didn't answer.

"She really come all this way just to kill you?"

Dugan turned to him sharply. "Don't ever mention my daughter in my presence, Rojo. You're better off not knowing she exists."

"I didn't mean anything by it, Dugan. Just good to know you're at least part human."

"Does the copter need a key?" Dugan asked.

"Maybe for the door," Zephyr said. "But there are other ways of opening those."

"It's a commercial helicopter. Probably not a combat start like ours," Cy said. "There'll be a key."

"Cy, you take Rojo and find the pilot. I want that copter ready by the time we're back out."

"What about the others? Kendall and Chupa?" Cy asked.

Dugan blew out another plume of smoke. "They can find their way."

Cy and Rojo split off in opposite directions. Dugan wanted Zephyr close, and Oso wouldn't have left if he had asked.

The native approached hesitantly, his face grim. In his hand, his notebook.

"We're going in no matter what," Dugan said. "I don't need to read it."

Oso shook his head, handing Dugan the notepad. He read:

that is not Takushkansh'kan

Dugan stared at the words, droplets of water splattering the page. "He's just a second Shaman that conjures nature at will?"

Oso snatched the small spiral pad from Dugan, quickly writing.

was but no longer Is

"Come on, Oso, stop speaking in riddles! What? What is it you want me to know?"

that is no man

"Are you afraid?"

"Why do you listen to this creep?" Zephyr asked.

Dugan ignored him. "What did he say? The Shaman, when he ... was no longer a man?"

Zephyr rolled his eyes. He held his Vektor assault rifle toward the ground, fingers thrumming against it with anticipation.

Dugan read as Oso continued writing, flipping pages with each new thought.

at the precipice

between heaven and earth

a line is raised

Oso crossed out the word "*line*" replacing it with "*prayer.*"

the old god is dead

so a new must answer

Oso tapped at a blank page with his marker.

"What?" Dugan pressed. Oso continued:

Lamielke has 2 meanings

create and destroy

to us they are the same

"That's like saying up and down are the same," Zephyr said, reading over Dugan's shoulder.

"Well what's the context? What did he say?" Dugan pressed.

he answers with Lamielke

"He answers with create or destroy?" Dugan asked.

Lamielke is an event

"An event." Dugan dropped his cigarette in the street, the water here not near as heavy as the bottlenecked road in front of the police station and school. "He thinks he's a god."

"And this tepui is his temple?" Zephyr asked.

"Wait, Oso – you said he's not a man. He's not the only one who thinks he's a god, is he?"

Oso met Dugan's stare, not needing to write to answer.

"A god couldn't be stopped. Not by tranquilizers, no matter how strong the dosage. He's a man, Oso. He may be godlike, but he's no god."

Oso wrote quickly on his pad again.

there are as many gods as stars in the sky

"If that's the case then you know they're not special," Dugan said. "And events? Events can be stopped."

"You sure you want Oso coming in with us?" Zephyr asked.

"I'm sure."

"These superstitions are going to kill us all."

Oso flicked his notepad closed and jammed it into Zephyr's considerably-sized neck. Just like Dugan had done with his own journal. The native held it there, looking the black man in the eyes. A wire coil from the spiral notebook was pressed so far into Zephyr's skin that a bead of blood ran down its circular loop, absorbed in the notebook's faded cover.

"What's wrong, Oso? If you don't like something I said, why don't you just tell me?"

As Oso's other hand gravitated toward one of his curved dark blades Dugan stepped between them, shoving Oso's arm back.

"Enough.

Zephyr shrugged his shoulders back, stepping out of reach of the mute native. Not that it would have made a difference with one of those blades.

"Are you okay with what we're about to do?" Dugan asked Oso.

Oso quickly wrote:

create or destroy

Dugan turned to face the church, anticipation now racing through his own skin. "I thought they were the same."

The door of the church crashed open, one of the hinges snapping as the plank of wood was shoved inward. Screams abated as Dugan followed Zephyr and Oso inside, the chapel full of unwavering eyes all focused on them.

"Where are they?" Dugan growled. "Donde estan?"

One of the men closest to the door holding a filthy child coughing in his arms pointed toward a curtain in the rear of the room. Mothers pulled their children back to create an open path for him and his men. Even they knew who he was, what he was capable of.

A shame his daughter had never learned.

Verse XXIV.

Faye felt her breath catch when the outer door to the church burst open, followed by the sound of men pushing through. Conversation hit like muffled gunfire from the neighboring room; though she couldn't make out the words, there was no doubt her father and his men were coming.

Water dripped from the open corner of the storage room, a light mist sprinkling down. With the exception of the rain there was a complete stillness in the room, each of those present as motionless as the jumbled decaying furniture or piles of stacked crates. Even swallowing felt too obscene an act to carry out.

Donavon's head was bowed between his legs as he sat against the wall. Faye prayed he wouldn't throw up again. They couldn't afford the noise.

She tightened her grasp on the thin coiled rebar they had found, the coolness of its touch sinking into her skin. What good it would do against men with guns – not just men, but highly trained killers – she didn't want to think about.

"Get me Shumway."

Dugan's voice, so close, he had to be just out in the hall. Faye tried to ignore the sharp intake of breath her father's presence caused.

Sir William looked up at her with concern, the frail Indian's head resting in his lap. Faye still wasn't sure what they had seen out there in the rain, or what this man was, but she knew she had to keep him away from her father.

Dugan's voice came again. "And Josue, don't make me ask again."

A gurgle broiled from Donavon's insides. He massaged his stomach with one hand. Kenny stared at the back of the tapestry covering the room's entrance as if it were a ghost. He too held a second piece of rebar, bent at its tip, his knuckles white from holding it so tight.

"Yes, what's this about?" Father Shumway said in the hall before yelping loudly, his cry like that of a high school girl.

"No games," Dugan said.

A brief moment later the heavy tapestry was pulled back. The large black man who had first shot at the old Indian stepped through. One of his hands encompassing Remmy's, which was twisted around behind the priest's back. In his other hand, the man held some kind of machine gun that looked like it belonged in a sci-fi movie.

Her father stepped through after them, followed by the thicker native with long black hair.

"So can we just skip past the part where we make threats and you act brave until we carry out those threats and people get hurt?" Dugan asked.

"We're in a church," Faye said.

"Very observant." Dugan moved his hands as if parting the Red Sea. "Everyone to the side."

Faye stepped between her father and the unconscious native on the ground. She felt a weight with each pair of eyes that fell on her. It was her show now. Hers and her father's. But the outcome was not as predetermined as he believed it to be.

She held her steel beam out like a sword, ready to use it. "Say whatever you want, do whatever you need to, but we're not letting you take this man. And by my count, we have you outnumbered."

"A drunk, a man who's too sick to stand, and my daughter. Oh, and that coward over there." Dugan looked at Kenny who seemed to wilt beneath his stare. "Hardly an army."

"You can't have him," Faye said.

Dugan sighed. "I thought we were skipping past this part. Zephyr?"

Father Shumway's face went red, his eyes shooting open wide as an audible snap broke through the room. Like a branch being stepped on. The black man – *Zephyr?* – let go of the priest who fell to his knees, his right arm trailing his movement but swinging unnaturally behind. Within his thick robe Faye couldn't make out where the bone had snapped, but by the man's cries she knew it was severe.

Zephyr raised his machine gun to Kenny who immediately threw his piece of rebar back over his shoulder, hands going up. The steel bar rattled against the cement floor behind him.

"To the corner! One hand on either wall!" Zephyr shouted.

Kenny ducked his head and moved back, tripping over a fallen box on his way. The dark skinned Indian with long hair suddenly had a knife in either hand, without Faye ever having seen him move. She had no doubt he'd be just as fast at throwing them.

"Just let them have him," Donavon said, glancing up at her from where he sat against the wall.

"Listen to your fiancé," Dugan said.

"He's not my fiancé. You know nothing about me, don't pretend to now. And don't think for an instant I will give this man up."

"Sweetheart ... you don't have a choice."

Beneath her father's mask of control she realized how tired he looked. Despite the years he was so much thinner than she remembered him.

"There's always a choice," Faye said.

"No," her father said, "there's not. You'll learn as you get older that all those little decisions you thought you were making? They were made for you. By circumstance. And need. We're just like any other animal. Reacting to what's in front of us."

"It that how you live with what you've done?"

Her father smiled back at her. The frightened sound of Remmy's pained breaths sent a chill through Faye's body.

"Time's up."

Both of the men beside Dugan acted as one, the thick native rushing in and catching her strike as if the coiled steel had been made of plastic. He ripped it from her grasp, the rebar bouncing off the ground, then struck her in the sternum with a swift thrust of his open palm.

Her breath immediately escaped.

Zephyr shoved her to the side, drawing his weapon on Sir William. Faye toppled into Donavon who did his best to catch her.

"Breathe. Breathe!" Donavon shouted.

But shouting couldn't open her airway.

The thicker native bent over the body on the ground when a shriek broke through the air, unexpected and shrill.

"Wait!"

All motion came to a fevered halt.

Faye gasped, air returning in a flood. She panted, each breath reassuring her she was okay. She was okay.

Am I okay?

In front of her the thick native crouched, both hands raised as if Sir William had a gun. Even Zephyr went still. But it wasn't a gun the Englishman had in his hand – it was the rebar Faye had dropped. Its jagged end hovered less than an inch above the old native's bare neck.

"I'll kill him," Sir William said. "If you don't back away this instant."

The slow beat of the native's heart was visible beneath his thin layer of skin, his medallions and necklaces hanging askew.

"Easy, Frederick," Dugan said.

"I mean it!"

The thick native rose to a standing position, backing a few feet away. Zephyr, Faye noticed, hadn't budged.

Neither had his gun.

"Stay in the corner!" Dugan yelled, Kenny quaking as he turned back around. "You don't know what you're doing or who this man even is.

Just drop the piece of steel and we'll leave with him, peacefully. No one needs to get hurt."

Sir William stared up at Dugan with wide, bloodshot eyes. His face was flushed, but there was a harshness to him Faye had never seen before. "I want your men to leave, and then the rest of you can go. You and I, Dugan, need to talk."

"Dugan, please," Remmy said. "No more violence."

Her father glanced between Sir William and the native on the ground. "I know why you want him. Who you think he is," Sir William said.

Dugan's face immediately changed. "What do you know?"

"That he's more dangerous than you could ever imagine."

"Who is he?" Faye said.

"Who sent you?" Dugan asked, ignoring Faye.

"It's not the first time, you know, something like this has come. Attempts have been made throughout history, but there have always been Watchers waiting for the signs. Preparing. To prevent the end."

"Who sent you?" Dugan shouted.

"I'm one of the last," Sir William said. "Most have fallen away. No longer believe."

"What is he?" Faye asked.

"A destroyer of worlds," Sir William said, looking at Faye.

She felt she barely recognized him – the drunkard had fled, replaced with a man who looked almost regal. Even Zephyr now took a step back.

Sir William returned his gaze to Dugan. "He's not what you think he is. Please, send everyone out and let's talk."

Dugan drew a black pistol from his side and in a heartbeat it was aimed at the old man. Sir William sprung, snatching at Faye and pulling her away from Donavon. She landed partly on the old native who rustled beneath her weight.

Sir William dragged her back, now holding the sharp edge of the rebar to her throat.

"Your only daughter," he said. "As a father I know I would have given anything for my own."

Faye struggled beneath the man's grip, his arm bent around her throat in a vicious headlock. She wanted to tell him, make him understand … he was wrong.

Dugan wouldn't stop to save her.

A voice suddenly shouted from behind the tapestry. "The police are on their way!"

Grey!

Faye's heart leapt at his voice; she had forgotten they had left him behind. The more frightening consideration was whether involving the police would help or make things worse.

"I only want to talk, Dugan. You *need* to hear what I have to say, but make no mistake – I will do whatever it takes to keep him from ending in your hands."

"Frederick," Faye said, her breath barely squeaking out.

"You were better off when that was pointing at the Shaman," Dugan said.

Faye's breath caught like a ratchet stuck between cogs.

"NO!" she cried.

The deafening roar of the gunshot swallowed her words.

Blood splattered against her face. The piece of steel held at her throat fell to the ground, clanking in response to the gun's echo, and then the arm around her loosened as the man it was attached to slumped backward.

He hit with a sickening thud.

Everything seemed to happen at once – Dugan's cronies rushing toward her, the beefy native lifting the man they called the Shaman; Grey slipping through the doorway behind the tapestry, eyes wide, calling her name; the Priest rushing her father in a heightened frenzy, Dugan pistol whipping him across the face, Remmy crumpling to the floor; Donavon huddled against the wall, arms wrapped over his knees like a toddler in time-out.

To Faye it was like watching a movie in slow motion – and just like a movie she was but an observer, with no ability to impact what was happening around her, only destined to watch the mistakes and failures of those she would be rooting for.

Grey raised his hands as Zephyr brought his heavy rifle to Grey's head. "Anyone moves, they die," he said.

Unbelievably he sounded calm, unconcerned. Quite the opposite of Faye's little group.

The native carrying the Shaman stepped through the doorway, tapestry falling into place behind him. Zephyr held it open for Dugan who hesitated.

"What was his name? Frederick? His last name?"

"Why?" Grey asked.

Behind her a gurgling sound emerged from the Englishman on the floor. Blood bubbled from his throat, his hands listlessly scraping against it.

"His name!" Dugan yelled.

"William," Donavon said. "Sir Frederick William. The third, I think."

Dugan nodded. "Get out of this town as soon as you're able to. If you can."

He disappeared into the hall.

"I should kill you all," Zephyr said, his gun rotating around the room. "Follow us and I will."

He let loose a round of bullets just over their heads, spraying against the brick walls and ceiling. Faye found herself ducking her head where the Shaman had lain.

By the time she looked up, the man was gone. Kenny was hiding behind crates, both Donavon and Remmy on the floor. Grey was the only one standing and to Faye's shock he appeared not frightened but angry.

Good, she thought, *I'll need someone else with me.*

"How could you?" he shouted, and Faye suddenly understood his anger was at her. "How many have to die so that you can get your way? How many?"

Donavon looked at her with the same mistrusting eyes. Was she the only sane person in the room?

Something swiped at Faye from behind and she let out a brief yelp. It was Sir William, his hand shaking uncontrollably.

His throat was torn open, the wound anything but clean. She had never seen so much blood in all her life. With only a glance it was obvious there was nothing they could do to save him.

"Bug … ger," he said, his eyes fixed on her. His head shook with the rest of him. "Stop … him."

Faye felt the power of his words course through her, giving her the strength to act once again. She rose, looking around at the miscreants all too afraid to move, to act, to do something that mattered.

She tore a heavy wooden cross from beneath a box on the table, gripping it like an axe, then darted from the room. In her hurry she missed Sir William's final words.

"The Shaman …"

Verse XXV.

The rain outside had finally ceased though the flooding in the streets would last at least until tomorrow. The clouds still hovered, heavy and vengeful, full of empty promise.

Watching the frail and lifeless body of the Shaman bounce with Oso's every step, Dugan couldn't help but smile. He had bottled his own storm. Soon that bottle would be mass produced, a little streak of lightning, touch of divinity, spreading to every man and woman in the world.

Or at least to those who could afford it.

Dugan caught sight of Rojo and Cy bounding down a side street toward them.

Rojo held a chain necklace high, small injector key dangling from it. "Found the pilot! Drunk as a skunk. Smelled as bad as one too."

Zephyr snatched the key from him. "You must be related."

"Hey, did I tell you guys what Dugan named our new tepui after?"

Oso tossed Rojo the Humvee keys in return.

"Meet back at the Facility," Dugan said. "And make sure no one follows."

"What, is this amateur night?" Rojo asked.

"You want us to look for Kendall and Chupa?" Cy asked.

"You decide," Dugan said, following Zephyr and Oso, who had already continued past.

As they approached the back of the Humvee they heard a loud crash – something striking the windshield. Zephyr swung wide, his Vektor an extension of his arm, raised without effort. Oso continued walking, undisturbed.

The crash came again, sounding this time like the windshield had been penetrated.

"Your call Doog," Zephyr called back.

Dugan's daughter stood on top of the hood of the vehicle, pulling a heavy wooden cross out of the windshield. She brought it back down like a jackhammer, slamming it against the glass which shook, the tip of the cross embedding into it, sending out a ripple of cracks.

Faye looked down at him, her face full of hatred. "You're not going anywhere. Not with him."

"Shame the cameras aren't rolling. Show the world your true side," Dugan said.

Rojo and Cy hesitated as they approached the vehicle. Oso had already moved past it with the Shaman.

"It's okay," Dugan said.

Zephyr lowered his rifle a fraction of an inch.

"She's definitely your daughter!" Rojo said, with a smile.

Faye swept the hair out of her face, blood smeared across it. "What do you want with him?"

"To save the world, what else? You and I, Faye, we're not so different."

"I am nothing like you! You killed that man in there. He was innocent. He didn't deserve to die!"

"None of us ever do," Dugan said. "One day, you'll understand." He tipped an imaginary hat in her direction as he rounded the front of the vehicle, following after Zephyr. "Thank your little green project for us, will you?"

Faye's response was lost behind the roar of the helicopter's turbines coming to life.

Verse XXVI.

Faye shielded her eyes as wet straw and drops of mud splattered up from the helicopter's rotating blades. How had she not seen what her father was doing?

The Shaman and the native who had carried him were loaded into the back of the helicopter, Zephyr at the pilot's seat. She wondered if the pilot that had brought them here was still alive.

She leapt off the hood of the armored Humvee prepared to race across the field toward the helicopter, but knew she was too late. She had failed, again. Her father always got what he wanted.

The helicopter's blades became a seamless whir, black noise filling her mind. The wind whipped at her hair and she had to turn sideways to keep it from her eyes.

The vehicle she had leapt from suddenly bucked, engine screaming. The cross she had left embedded in the windshield came hurtling down, landing with a snap of wood, one beam separating from the other. That was all it took to change a religious symbol into two ordinary planks of wood.

She glanced up in time to see the soldier with the red beard salute her before slamming the door to the vehicle. Mud spun from its tires, soaking her as it took off.

"I hate you!" she screamed, barely able to hear her own words over the helicopter.

It rose into the air, its front dipping down at first then leveling five or six feet above the ground before beginning its ascent. Her father was leaving her behind.

Not for the first time.

Faye bent down to the ground, searching for a rock or something to throw. All she felt were grainy pebbles. Even this she couldn't do right.

Just as she gave up her search, a loud whoosh sounded from behind her, accelerating over the noise of the helicopter.

She turned, surprised to find two military Jeeps stationed across from the town square. The alcalde stood in one, a grin across his grizzled face. The soldier standing next to him held an empty barrel on his shoulder, a trail of smoke blazing from it.

No.

"No!"

She turned back to see the rocket soar through the air toward the metal hull floating now thirty feet above the ground. It struck in a shrieking explosion of flame.

The blast spun the helicopter around, its metal tail severing from the body and dropping from the sky. Its frontend tipped to the side. Flames fell from its hull like shooting stars.

The soldiers shouted behind her as Faye began running toward the dying beast in the sky. The helicopter spun in a continuous circle, no rudder to direct its course, dropping lower toward the earth.

No, no, no!

Faye leapt over the fence, then saw two bodies leap from the helicopter's open door.

Her heart rose to her throat.

Images of bodies falling from the Twin Towers flashed before her eyes.

How high were they from the ground? She wasn't sure, but high enough. High enough.

The helicopter dipped in a nose dive it wouldn't recover from. Faye braced herself for the inevitable impact. It came, dwarfing any previous noise as metal scrunched, the hull burying itself into the unforgiving earth, another explosion replacing the former blast.

Faye screamed in spite of herself, heat pushing out like an invisible wave from where the copter had crashed. She ran, the jeeps leaping past her with the sudden sound of machine guns firing –

Too late, she realized, she was entering a war.

Verse XXVII.

The world pulsed, coming in and out of focus. A strobe effect, one moment full of flames and smoke and noise, the next nothing.

Darkness.

The sound of gunfire. Rat-a-tatting. Ricocheting off metal. Twangs and deep hollow thuds.

Then … Darkness.

With effort Dugan kept his eyes open. Saw Zephyr rise and tackle a Venezuelan soldier. Disarm him, then turn the same gun on the man. Blood and brain matter blew out from the side of his head.

Darkness.

Zephyr spun, firing the rifle at men Dugan couldn't see. Ghosts, maybe. Zephyr's other arm hung in ribbons of flesh, swaying like a tetherball at the end of a game. He fainted. Collapsed.

Darkness. Like coming home.

A deep-seated cough ripped itself free from Dugan's throat, the propulsion causing him to sit up. Pain exploded, flowing in constant currents from his head to his feet. The bile flying from his mouth looked the same as what had poured from the soldier's head. He felt light-headed, like at any moment he might rise and float away.

The fall had been farther than he had thought, muddy ground not cushioning the hard-packed dirt beneath. Suddenly he was back in the helicopter, landscape rotating as if he were on a tilt-a-wheel at a carnival. Ground looming. The Shaman's inert body skidding against him on the helicopter's floor. Without thinking, Dugan bent to pick him up then leapt backward, shielding the Shaman with his own body, air flurrying around them.

Darkness. Utter and complete.

Dugan glanced around dizzily.

Where was the Shaman?

Another cough forced its way out, doubling him back to his side, lying down. He was dying. His breaths coming in rasping gasps. How many did he have remaining?

A bright flicker of flames brought him back from the Darkness, its depths growing, pulling at him like a riptide.

His journal was open in his hands.

He didn't remember taking it out.

Pages curled. He couldn't read a single name. Each line was an entry into that Black Ink, an opening to the Night he might fall through. He felt himself slipping.

Who will add my name?

He had always imagined more books, entire libraries – cities of libraries – with shelves upon shelves of volumes, all filled with names. But not of victims. Not of those who had offered themselves as sacrifices.

These books were filled with the names of survivors.

People who had been cured; saved. Names of men and women who cheated death and disease all because of the names held within one small book, a sacred book, a book that would be in every drawer of every motel six, a book that mothers would read to their children at night, that preachers would praise from their pulpits, a book with a worn leather strap carrying the names of those who had given their lives so that others might live, so that Darkness might no longer ...

Boots stomped past, causing Dugan to reopen his eyes.

A soldier, kicking at wreckage, overturning debris.

Looking for what? Him?

I'm right here, Dugan thought, head spinning. But it wasn't his head on rotation; it was the world around him.

Something crashed beside him, a long scrap of titanium alloy being overturned.

"Aquí!" the Soldier shouted, standing over Dugan. But no, he stood several feet away, pointing at another body on the ground, buried beneath refuse.

The soldier pulled at the arms, raising the limp form up.

It was the Shaman.

Dugan checked his side, unsnapping the loop that had kept his Glock attached through the fall. His hand shook so he lowered his aim from the soldier's head to his torso. Two shots and the guard dropped to his knees. The Shaman slumped back to the ground, the soldier's body following suit.

Blood flew from Dugan's mouth, so Dark, so Black, he knew it was now reaching from inside to pull him down.

The gun fell from his hand.

I'm sorry, he thought, not sure who he was apologizing to.

There were so many.

He was back on the ground, breaths shallow – scrapes, really, of air that barely cycled through his lungs. The Darkness was here, no longer just at the edges but hovering above him. Encompassing him.

The Darkness moved, a snatch of light seeping past and Dugan realized it wasn't Death but a shadow standing over him. The silhouette of a man who was not a man.

The Shaman.

Death finds the Shaman. Or finding the Shaman brings death.

So it had been the latter.

The Shaman gazed at him with uncomprehending eyes. The scars on his face and chest of patterned tattoos were smeared with blood.

"I'm sorry," the Shaman said, voicing the words Dugan was unable to.

Yes.

The choked spasms in his throat kept Dugan from speaking.

The Shaman bent down toward him, his bony hands reaching out. Dugan closed his eyes and it was there to greet him –

Darkness.

He had never felt a need greater than he felt now for that emptiness of space and thought and feeling. It was fitting that his end would come from the man he had been chasing, the hunted becoming the hunter.

The world would never change.

He was no different than his daughter, believing in an idea that could never be, an ineffable hope that things could be different. Better. And that he, a mortal man, could make it that way. That his life was more than a name on a page, a page that would be forgotten.

The Shaman reached out, grasping Dugan by the head.

Searing white streaks flooded Dugan's vision, his body arching from the sudden shock. Every muscle went taut at once, every cell inside him screaming in exultation and revulsion. It was like the world was bending, his mind re-stitching, clasps that had come unlinked suddenly snapping back together. He was being frozen and burned alive at the same time, created and destroyed, baptized and drowned, the physical world slipping from beneath him.

The Darkness fled and Dugan's eyes opened to a world swimming in arcs of light.

Like streaks of lightning, they swirled in a hypnotic dance, darting then slowing, sinking and rising. They moved so quickly they appeared in streaks but Dugan knew, not knowing how he knew, that each streak was made up of millions of Glimmers, like a galaxy full of stars that from afar looked no bigger than a dot in the sky.

Glimmers …

Souls.

Spirits.

The fabric of creation.

He was seeing a part of the world he was never meant to, passing through the physical shell to another sphere, another plane, a spiritual realm.

"You see," the Shaman said. "Not all can see."

Dugan recognized that Takushkansh'kan was speaking in his native language but the words were as easy to understand as if he had been speaking English.

"He will destroy them. The Fabric. The Glimmers. I cannot stop him, but you, Inktomi …"

"The Spider," Dugan said.

"… Must play your role in the [*Creation / Destruction*]."

The word the Shaman used split into two meanings. It was as if his words began to oscillate, both *"creation"* and *"destruction"* traveling opposite peaks of a sound wave that met back together for the rest of his sentence. One word, two meanings.

They are the same, Oso had said.

Or written.

Glimmers leapt around the Shaman and Dugan realized the man was not old but young. His skin smooth, unblemished. His strong cheekbones rose to eyes that showered sparks.

"Do not let Him create Man," the Shaman continued.

"The Darkness," Dugan said.

"In His own image. He will [*destroy / create*] all."

Glimmers passed between the two men with every breath of air.

"You must stop Him." [*Stop / Trick*] *Him.*

"Stop Him." *Stop* [*Him / Me*].

"Stop Him." [*Stop / Kill*] *Me.*

The flurry of Glimmers faded behind a light green haze which swelled around the Shaman and suddenly the aura slipped.

Dugan gasped, breath flooding him with unfamiliarity. The Glimmers were gone, streaks of light lost to the world which now felt faded and colorless. The Shaman's eyes had rolled up into his head. He lay on the ground, unconscious.

Had he remained that way? Or had that conversation been real?

A military jeep tunneled over wreckage, almost trampling the both of them. Dugan picked up his Glock and rose to his feet, unable to comprehend the clarity flowing through him. The first two soldiers stepping from the jeep he put down before they knew there was even a threat. The third man fell back into the vehicle, riddled with bullet holes. The chamber on his Glock popped open, his last shell spent.

In a single sweeping motion, Dugan rolled to one of the first guards he had shot, lifting the man's rifle still attached to his shoulder and turning it on the mass of bodies leaping free from the vehicle. Men fell like the fronds of a dying tree. With his other hand, Dugan pulled free a small serrated knife attached near his boot. He hurled it at the driver. It sunk deep into the man's neck, his head falling forward into the wheel.

The jeep immediately lurched forward, its ghost driver unaware of the passengers falling out and being mowed down. It accelerated into the remaining hull of the helicopter, burying itself into its depths.

The explosion that followed was blinding but silhouetted the last remaining soldier. Without even sighting on the man Dugan sprayed the gun in an arc, the man's arms throwing back into the air as the bullets penetrated him again and again.

"Drop it!"

Dugan recognized the voice of the alcalde.

General Gutierrez.

With disgust Dugan hurled the gun down with the arm of the soldier still wrapped around it. He turned around to face the man who had betrayed him.

Gutierrez stood with one boot crushing the hand of a fallen soldier – one of his own men. He held an AK-47, its butt pressing into his considerable gut. Sweat dripped off the man's face giving him a shiny appearance. Three other men stood with him, their rifles trained on Dugan as well.

"I sorry, my friend, but jou were not de highest bidder."

"I didn't know there were other offers," Dugan said.

"Dere are always other offers." Gutierrez's face split into a smile, his thick mustache like two eyebrows rising.

Behind the General two men dragged the body of the Shaman toward a third jeep.

"This isn't over," Dugan said. "It doesn't matter where you go or where you hide him, I will find –"

A Glimmer sparked from near the General's waist, something slamming against Dugan so hard it swept him from his feet. He landed, leaning against a hunk of twisted metal.

"I think, no, jou won't," Gutierrez said.

Another Glimmer flashed against the dark backdrop of night. Not a Glimmer, a spark, igniting as a second and third bullet travelled down the corroded short barrel of the rifle. They hit Dugan in the gut, lower than the previous slug which radiated heat from his right pectoral.

So this is what it's like to die twice in one day, Dugan thought. His only consolation was that he no longer felt a need to cough.

"Help – Let go of me!"

Dugan watched as three soldiers carried Faye, her limbs flailing with every step. One of them pulled free a machete, setting it against her neck. Her body finally stilled.

In that moment she locked eyes with him, tears spilling down her face. "Dad?"

"Jour daddy is dying, princesa," Gutierrez said, adding something in Spanish so quickly Dugan couldn't understand him. Or maybe it was the world losing its focus once again.

They carried her the rest of the way to the Jeep, her screams on an endless loop, a hurt child calling for her father.

"Dad? Dad!"

She hadn't called him that since her ninth birthday.

Gutierrez raised one hand in farewell as he climbed onto the back of the remaining vehicle. The jeep slowly grew smaller, rocking back and forth on the muddied and uneven field.

More gunfire ripped through the night but it seemed far away, someone else's concern.

First the Shaman, then his daughter.

Everything he loved. Everything he had fought for.

A tall soldier suddenly stood before him, his face so young he didn't need to shave. His dark eyes calloused of emotion.

So young. So young to feel nothing.

Dugan watched as the man raised a nine millimeter toward him, the Darkness staring back at him from that tiny round hole. And then those eyes bulged with surprise, the boy's mouth drawing open.

Oso stepped out from behind him, letting the boy fall as he pulled his black blade from the back of the soldier's neck.

He removed Dugan's vest, guiding it gently over his arms, raising him just enough to pull it free. Dugan counted three holes in its front, only two on the back, though it was hard to trust anything he was seeing anymore.

"The book ..." he said, forcing the words out.

Oso nodded. Reverently he removed the notebook from the inner pocket of the vest. Dugan couldn't remember putting it back there.

It was safe. Unmarked.

Those names would be remembered.

In some ways Dugan had always known his name would end up in that book. He had no home to return to – not in the States and certainly not here or anywhere else the hunt might have taken him. On a blank line in that notebook, it was the only place in the world he really belonged. It would be a homecoming of sorts, welcome faces and names greeting him as he joined their ranks.

Instead of leaving with the book, Oso pushed it back into Dugan's hands. His eyes, imploring.

Rojo suddenly appeared beside him. "Oh shit."

Oso pointed with his lips at something in the distance.

"Yeah, yeah, I'll bring it. Hold tight, Dugan, we'll get you home!"

How to tell them he already was?

As soon as Rojo left, Oso slid his black plated knife from its sheath. He placed one finger against his thick lips.

Shh.

Before Dugan could make the connection that Zephyr had been right about the native all along, he felt the tip of the blade plunge into his side. The pain quickly exceeded that which Dugan was capable of, and the world, with a quiet finality, slipped to black, replete in

Darkness.

End of Chapter Two

THE CREATION Continues
with Chapter Three in the full length novel

THE CREATION:
LET THERE BE DEATH

God spoke, and the world was created. But the Bible only revealed a part of what occurred. For in order to Create, one must first Destroy ...

As a new dawn awakens, Faye Moanna finds herself a prisoner in one of the darkest dungeons created for man. To escape with her life, she may have to sacrifice a part of herself that can never be reclaimed.

Her soul.

Meanwhile, new allegiances are formed between Dugan and his men, but betrayals come from unexpected corners. And the power they seek, in the form of the Shaman, may yet prove to save the world. If they can learn to control it.

For as the second day in The Creation begins, the world continues to be transformed. Day has arrived, but this is no ordinary light. And it is but the precursor for something far worse.

And God said, Let there be Death.
And He saw that it was Good.

A NOTE FROM THE AUTHOR

The Creation Series was an idea I had a few years ago that, like most good ideas, grabbed onto me with hooks. While what you have read is just the beginning, this series goes deep, exploring pseudo-Christian beliefs in a very non-religious yet deeply frightening way. Part fantasy, part horror, part thriller & sci-fi, it's a series that is difficult to pin beneath a single umbrella.

Having had the opportunity to live in Venezuela for two years I thought I might include a note regarding the differences between my creative work and my experiences within the country. This novel truly does not do justice to the kindness I received, nor the respect which I hold for the amazing people I met. The Venezuelan culture is truly one in which people would literally give the shirt off their backs to help another in need. My characters were not created from people I met but rather the dark corners of my imagination.

As to the country itself, the Gran Sabana is one of the most breathtaking places I have ever visited. Words come up wanting when attempting to portray such beauty. The tepuis, cenotes, and hundreds of waterfalls, the Rainforest and sheer magnitude of nature … it all leads me to look upward, marveling at the Great Creator who could devise such a world. How tiny and insignificant we are, and yet how important in His eyes.

I hope you've enjoyed the start to The Creation Series. If you have, I would be honored if you would consider leaving a review on Amazon, Goodreads, or another media outlet. Reviews make such a difference in the algorithms of a book's discoverability, and are the best "virtual tip" an author can receive.

I'm excited to continue this journey with you through the seven day period of The Creation, although a slightly more deranged version than you may be familiar with. What's coming is more frightening than you could ever predict. Thank you again for reading my work and embarking on this journey with me. I promise there will be many more to come!

ABOUT THE AUTHOR

The Behrg is the author of dark literary works ranging from screenplays to 'to-do' lists. His debut novel, Housebroken, was a first-round Kindle Scout selection and semi-finalist in the Kindle Book Awards. He has had numerous short stories published both online and in print anthologies. His 'to-do' list should be finished by 2017 (though his wife is hoping for a little sooner).

A former child actor turned wanna-be rockstar, The Behrg served a mission for his church in Venezuela where his newest series, The Creation, takes place. He lives in Southern California with his four children, pet Shih-Tzu, and the many voices in his head.

Stalk him at TheBehrg.com.

www.ingramcontent.com/pod-product-compliance
Lightning Source LLC
Chambersburg PA
CBHW070825120626
46556CB00002B/655